IT'S A NERD! WITCH IS SLAIN!

WITCHY EXPO SERVICES MYSTERIES BOOK 2

AMY MCNULTY

Crimson Fox
PUBLISHING

"Y*ou may win this battle, but I, my one-time friend, shall triumph. Nothing—nothing—can overcome the power of justice. The people of this planet believe in me!*"

Nimue Toothaker sat on the edge of her bed, her legs crossed over the purple comforter. She popped another handful of popcorn into her mouth, not noticing she'd spilled a kernel over one of the rose designs embroidered into the material over her bed.

"*Justice only prevails in fairy tales,*" sneered the man who'd turned into a big-headed yellow alien after he'd been invaded by an alien parasite.

Gowdie, Nimue's familiar dragon about the size of a household cat, stuck out his taloned foot over the top of the turret-shaped platform on his castle-style, floor-to-ceiling cat tree. Licking the blue scales in the style of a feline, he kept one eye on the projected screen from Nimue's perma-charm TV replicant crystal.

In Cauldron Cove, it was far more common to have human TV shows and movies beamed into one's perma-charm TV replicant, then projected onto the wall, ceiling, or wherever else they wanted to watch something. Since the crystal could fit in one's hand, it was far more convenient than attempting to lug around a giant collection of plastic electronics.

"Humans watch entertainment on their small electronic phones and tablets, too," said Gowdie in Nimue's head. He could pick up on her thoughts, even when they innocently strayed to how much more convenient life was as a witch living in a town full of witches and warlocks.

"Still more convenient to have a perma-charm crystal do the job." Nimue popped another handful of popcorn from the bowl on the tray on her bed into her mouth and nodded at the glowing, shiny crystal currently on her dresser. Skilled witches concocted the devices by intricately brewing potions that solidified into shatter-proof, glass-like objects.

Well, *nearly* shatter-proof. There'd been the whole murder-of-a-visiting-author incident last month that had proven perma-charm crystals were breakable with the right intent.

But that had been one very determined warlock at work.

Nimue was more confident that the new History Charm "security camera" perma-charm crystals the floor crew of Witchy Expo Services had been installing throughout the Bessa, Cauldron Cove's spacious convention center, would be more resistant. No human would notice and be able to reach the crystals throughout the place, at least.

That had been quite a special order Nimue had had to

give her grandmother extra time to complete. Bernadette Toothaker, former Head Witch General Manager of Witchy Expo Services for over a hundred years, was a genius when it came to perma-charm crystal creation, but she still needed time to work. In fact, she was *still* working on some of the order, so History Charm perma-charm crystals weren't in place everywhere in the Bessa yet.

On the screen, Superstellar-Man held a sword and smirked, his dark brow arched and a coif of curly, dark hair falling over one of his bright-blue eyes. Then he blinked and his eyes turned emerald, shooting laser beams at the sword, which in turn glowed neon-green.

"The Sword of Stellar Planet," Gowdie said reverently. *"We're finally going to see it in action."*

Nimue refrained from reminding her familiar that she knew. She'd paid attention to the movie so far. The sword had been a superpowered item from the hero's home world that would enhance the superhero's already impressive repertoire of powers.

The beams from Superstellar-Man's eyes stopped, though the sword stayed green, and the superhero charged the alien who'd once been his best friend.

Well, Colton Carter's best friend. Nimue was proud of herself for following along with the story. This was usually totally Greg and Willow's thing, and she hadn't watched a Stellar Comics Extended Universe movie since Willow had been a little kid—before she and Greg had gotten divorced and Nimue had moved back to her witchy hometown, Cauldon Cove.

Superstellar-Man started floating to avoid a mind-beam attack from the alien. His white cape with red trim spun around, the camera lingering on every sculpted angle of the man's almost-inhuman physique. Then he spun and discharged those eye beams again, this time directly at his enemy.

"Bet you wish witches could use a charm more than once in a day like that," Gowdie said. He flapped his thin, membrane-covered wings and floated down onto the bed beside his witch. *"Look how convenient that is!"* He punched a little fist in the air, then followed with a kick of his foot. *"Wham! Pow!"*

"That's what perma-charm crystals are for." Nimue took a sip of the iced tea she'd put in a tumbler with a straw, the hollow echo of her having reached the bottom of the cup almost as loud as the heart-pounding sound-track of the superhero fight on screen. "And that's why witches and warlocks live in such big communities for the most part. If you need to repeat a charm, you can just ask a friend."

Every witch or warlock could perform any charm they knew once a day, at any time from one sunrise to the next. Then the magic in their bones reset and they could perform it once again. Inconvenient, maybe, but a creative witch could think of different charms to achieve the same result, too. Some witches, like her own parents, didn't rely on living in large witch communities, after all. Her parents traveled the world selling their charms for a good price to the right people—or even for free if circumstances required it.

Gowdie kicked the errant kernel of popcorn on the comforter clear across the room with a mighty, *"Hi-ya!"*

It bounced through the projection of the latest install-ment in the SCEU and hit the wall with an overhyped little dud of a *thud*.

"Hey," said Nimue, putting her cup down on the tray with her popcorn bowl. "You've got to go fish that out or we'll get bugs."

Gowdie pulled back his lips to reveal a row of tiny, white teeth, and a little burst of flame popped out from his maw. *"Any bugs in our room will be met with fire and fury."*

"Settle down, Comic Hero." Nimue chuckled and pet his scaly head. She sometimes wondered why her soul had shaped her formless familiar into a little dragon at birth. Did that mean she was fantastical, like Gowdie was? Most witches—though not all—shaped their famil-iars into animals that existed in the real world. Though usually in fanciful colors and sometimes in smaller—or larger—sizes than one would find in the real world. Her parents had both created bats. Her grandmas had created lovebirds—as if their souls had known, deep down, somehow they'd wind up together someday. Not every married couple had matching familiars, sure. She was pretty sure that was mostly a Toothaker thing, and besides, her grandma had been happily married to Nimue's grandfather first long ago, though he'd died before Nimue's birth. But there was no way Nimue was coming across a warlock with a dragon, so she wasn't about to follow family tradition.

Gowdie was one of a kind.

Gowdie soared through the image of Superstellar-Man landing his final blow on the alien parasite with the

Sword of Stellar Planet, the dragon disappearing behind the dresser and popping back up with the popcorn kernel in his mouth.

He flapped over to the tray and spit the kernel back down on the hard surface. His expression soured. *"Salty."*

Nimue chuckled. He'd probably never tasted popcorn before. He didn't need to eat. He just liked playing with food on occasion.

"It's good," Nimue assured him.

Gowdie rolled his sapphire-blue eyes. *"If you say so."*

The sword cluttered to the ground on the screen and Superstellar-Man held the alien enemy in his arms now, a tear escaping from his eye as he ranted about the injustice of losing his best friend. *"I shall triumph,"* he said again, repeating his catch phrase. *"But that won't mean I'll feel good about it."*

Gowdie curled up on Nimue's lap, his eyes riveted to the screen. *"That guy's a good actor. I know some people find these movies and comics a little silly, but I always thought they tell some really good stories. And those effects! This series has the most witch-crafted special effects in all of movie history."*

Though Gowdie couldn't go too far from Nimue as her familiar, he had often watched the movies with Willow when she'd been here, before she'd moved off to human college for at least the current school year. It was late October, so there was still so much of the school year to go. And she was visiting her dad for most of Thanksgiving break, but at least he was just the next human town over. Willow would spend some time in Cauldron Cove, too.

"Witch-crafted special effects?" Nimue asked. "Like

witches and warlocks are responsible for the effects on screen?"

"Yup! Cheaper and much faster than relying on humans' computer effects. And I don't just mean Illusion Charms for complete immersion, which can be hard to capture on film. This company uses a lot of practical effects on set, driven by charms."

"I think I did hear about that. I'm glad humans are hiring more and more witches for that kind of thing." She stared at the screen. "Maverick Vanedestine *is* a good actor," Nimue agreed.

She'd never seen him in anything else. He'd become a superstar after being cast as Superstellar-Man, and sure, he'd done a few other projects, but nothing Nimue had seen. She thought, perhaps, she should correct that, though, as not only was Maverick Vanedestine quite *something* to look at—she knew those muscles were real because his shirt had been off more than a few times throughout this film—but Gowdie was right. He made a world in which no witches existed but a chunk of humans were just *born* with magic powers, powers that didn't require rationing like a witch's, seem real. Full of real emotion.

Superstellar-Man's superhero friends came to support him in his grief, offering pats on the shoulder. His love interest, Megastellar-Woman, offered him a hug and a kiss on the cheek.

For a brief moment, Nimue pictured herself in Megastellar-Woman's skintight, purple supersuit with cape and skirt and knee-high boots. They both had a snow-white complexion and long, black hair. True, the actor on the screen probably—definitely—had a finer physique, all lean muscle and slight curves, and Nimue had at least a decade on her since she'd just turned forty, but surely, she wouldn't look *that* bad in that outfit.

"You should cosplay," Gowdie told her in her head as the credits rolled. That witch-crafted special effects company he'd mentioned, Crimson Fern Special Effects, got a prominent position in the credits. *"A lot of con-goers will. It's Comic Hero Con."* He spoke as if it were obvious, as if you couldn't have a comic book convention without cosplayers, con-goers dressed up in costume as their favorite characters.

He wasn't wrong. Willow had loved to participate. But Nimue had never even thought to wear a costume herself.

"Willow's going to be so upset she can't come this year. She'll miss Maverick Vanedestine," Nimue said, stroking Gowdie's back.

Yes, *the* hottest star of *the* hottest comic book movie franchise was coming to Cauldron Cove this week for Comic Hero Con. Comic Hero Con was an annual show for Witchy Expo Services, though there were a lot of firsts this year.

There was a new head of the Comic Enthusiast Society, the group responsible for booking and managing the con—well, mostly, they relied on Witchy ExS's guidance. The CES was one of Witchy ExS's more hands-on clients, though, and especially with this new head, Mia Estrada. She took her new position *very* seriously. Perhaps a bit too seriously.

But Nimue could empathize. It was just last month that she and Soren Southern had become co-Head Witch

General Managers of Witchy ExS. With great responsibility came...

Well, Nimue was sure she was messing that comic quote up, but she knew her ex-husband and daughter certainly loved it.

"Maverick does so much charity work, and he's always so nice to his fans. I can't believe he's finally coming to a witchy convention! To our con!" Gowdie got up from Nimue's lap and dramatically swooned across the comforter, one wing smacking the almost-empty popcorn bowl. It teetered over the edge, and Nimue grabbed her cherrywood wand from its holster at her hip and waved it in the bowl's direction. "Hover Charm."

The bowl and the few kernels left that had been about to spill out over the floor all floated in midair.

Gowdie laughed sheepishly, his blue cheeks darkening.

Nimue directed her wand so the bowl and the kernels all floated back over the tray on her bed. "Undo Hover Charm."

The bowl clattered back to the tray, the kernels plinking one by one into the bowl.

It was time for bed, anyway. Nimue hadn't used those charms yet today, and she was unlikely to need them before sunrise.

"Busy day tomorrow," she told Gowdie. "All the VIPs are arriving, and a number of guests come in the day before the con starts, too, just to register and pick up their badges and grab bags."

"And so they can skip the registration line and head straight to the showroom floor on the morning of con opening to

buy a con-exclusive six-inch, poseable, deluxe Superstellar-Man figurine." Gowdie was frothing at the mouth.

Laughing, Nimue picked up her tray, tapping the perma-charm crystal with her wand as she passed by to shut off the human-made film. "I really wish Willow could have traveled back home for the con. If only she hadn't picked a human college hundreds of miles away."

"She could have flown home on her broom," Gowdie pointed out. *"Even if Reoch is a bit scared of heights."*

"She's too young to fly that long," Nimue said. Reoch, her daughter's familiar, a little, white puppy, would have trembled the whole way home, too. "We'll just have to tell her all about it. And she can watch some panels on the human internet, too." Mia Estrada had been particularly *insistent* on that. Previous Comic Hero Cons hadn't bothered since there was so much at a witchy convention that couldn't be experienced over human internet video regardless, but Mia was insistent that all the human comic conventions did this now, and it was something they needed to do, too.

She was the boss. Or client, more accurately. The CES funded the con, and the happier the con-goers were, the better the energy to feed the giant cauldron under the Bessa that kept Cauldron Cove safe.

"I guess we'll have to be sure to get her one of those figurines," Nimue said, at the door to her bedroom. "But only if there's enough to get two." She winked at her familiar.

He thrashed his long, scaly tail around on the bed and beamed back at her.

Nimue's second major convention as Witchy ExS co-

Head Witch General Manager—not including a few small trade shows over the past few weeks—was bound to go much better than her debut.

Considering the murder that had taken place at Bookshop Con, there was no way Comic Hero Con wouldn't go amazingly well in comparison.

Nimue was quite certain of that.

CHAPTER TWO

Nimue had plenty of time before she'd be expected at the Bessa. Guiding her broomstick to a lazy, circular stop below on the sidewalk, she landed in front of Sylvie's Sweets Bakery and laid her broomstick in the corral beside the outdoor tables and chairs already half-full with witches and warlocks enjoying some baked goods and coffee before the start of their day. There was only room for one or two broomsticks left, but Nimue managed to slide hers in, brush upright, at the very edge.

Gowdie flapped his wings and landed on her shoulder as they approached the front door. In addition to parts of the giant tree that poked its branches and roots all over town, willow trees forever green marked the façade of the front of the shop, framing a large, glass window and a wooden door fastened with a perma-charm crystal that opened on one's approach.

Gowdie made a show of sniffing the air as they stepped inside. *"I wish I could eat,"* he grumbled in his witch's mind.

"She doesn't sell hotcakes," Nimue reminded him. Those were Gowdie's favorites, as he liked to bounce on their springy surface.

"Pity." Gowdie slumped a little but brightened as soon as Nimue joined the end of the line—at least a dozen people long—and most of the heads turned their way.

Gowdie was used to the spotlight among human guests. They couldn't get enough of a dragon familiar.

"Is that a dragon?" someone whispered.

The man in front of Nimue—a human man, no doubt, as he wasn't wearing the long robes a warlock typically put on each morning, just as a witch tended to wear a puffy-sleeved dress similar to her own red one—did a double-take as he looked at Gowdie on Nimue's shoulder.

She smiled up at him. He had close-cropped dark hair that almost blended in with his dark complexion. And he was big—tall and muscular—and wearing a sleek, navy suit over a white shirt and red tie that strained to contain his muscles. A pair of sunglasses dangled from his front suit pocket by the temple.

He looked tough enough to be a linebacker. Which made it all the more surprising when he cracked a smile and pointed at Gowdie. "You have… a dragon."

Nimue laughed and ran a finger under Gowdie's chin. His foot tapped on her puffy, red sleeve like a rabbit's. "He's my familiar. Gowdie."

The man looked around at the crowded bakery. The tables inside were full—no wonder so many people had decided to eat outside despite the slight chill in the

October Midwestern air. "I've seen a number of familiars but never a dragon."

Gowdie puffed up his chest and spread his wings, the usual effect of most of the room gasping or clapping in delight inevitably following. As well as the typical whack of one of his thin membranes across Nimue's nose.

She craned her head around him, gently encouraging the troublesome wing back down with her hand. "Gowdie's one of a kind."

"Fascinating." The man nodded. "This is my first time in Cauldron Cove. I've never seen so many witches and warlocks in one place."

His gaze landed on Sylvie Palmer herself, busy as a bee behind her counter wrapping bakery treats up to go. She usually scheduled more help for when a convention was in operation, but since Comic Hero Con didn't start until tomorrow, and even then, it would be a weekday, not as crowded as it would be during the weekend, it was awfully strange that there were so many tourists here already. Nimue had had the idea on the way over to grab some bakery goods for the employee break room at the Bessa. She should have just asked Herne, Sylvie's husband and a member of the Witchy ExS team in charge of showroom floor placement and operation, if he could have grabbed some before the bakery opened. They lived right above this place, in an apartment extending up into the boughs of the willow trees.

A pygmy goat let out a little cry as it bucked across the crowded bakery toward a table of customers about to leave. The humans jumped in place as Temperance the rainbow-colored goat started eating what they'd left on the table, paper plates and all.

"Temperance!" Gowdie shouted mentally. The goat looked up, still chewing, her jaw moving sideways as the human customers giggled and headed toward the exit. She let out a *baa*, but Nimue wouldn't know what she was saying to Gowdie. Gowdie flew over and landed on the table in front of her, starting a conversation.

"You are busy today!"

A familiar could always speak in their own witch's or warlock's mind. And they could speak to one another. But because no witch could hear another witch's familiar in her mind, conversations between them always seemed almost one-sided. A witch had to count on her familiar to translate anything of importance.

"They *are* awfully busy today," Nimue said to the man in front of her, even if he hadn't heard Gowdie start a conversation with Sylvie's goat familiar.

The man grunted and looked ahead of him. Sylvie was doing her best—and Nimue saw wands waving behind her by the industrial ovens as her staff tried to keep up with an unexpected burst in demand—but the line was only just dwindling down by one more person.

Nimue recognized the witch who'd just finished her order, beaming that perfect customer-service smile at Sylvie as the pink-haired bakery owner wiped the back of her arm against her brow. Glinda Redferne, newly appointed Director of Guest Services, had worked for Witchy ExS since before Nimue had been born. She would have been promoted long ago, except that the previous head of the department, Linden Varlett, had done such an impeccable job.

Or so everyone had thought. He'd been a bit of a difficult boss to his underlings. And a one-time wicked warlock spy. And a murderer.

The human-lover had hated his own kind.

"Nimue!" said Glinda as she reached the end of the line, a cardboard tray with two coffee cups and a bag between the cups in her hand. Her familiar, a giant, kitten-sized Titan beetle, white with pink stripes, shook its antennae from atop the curly, blond-and-silver hair on Glinda's head. Nutter got quite a few double-takes as well, especially since he was often hidden beneath Glinda's lilac witch's hat. Like most Witchy ExS employees, though, she kept her hat in her locker at the Bessa between shifts. It was more part of the uniform—the look the human tourists expected—than something witches wore in everyday life.

"Good morning, Glinda. You had the same idea that I did, I see." She pointed to the tray.

"Oh, just something for Humphrey and me." Humphrey was a young member of Guest Services who'd been bumped up to Glinda's old job, second-in-charge of the department. The nervous young lad had sort of been overwhelmed by the job, but it was nice to see that, unlike his last boss, Glinda was doing all she could to make him feel welcome.

"Is that a cruller?" Nimue asked, gazing into her bag. There certainly seemed to be enough pastries in there, more than enough for two. "Looks delicious."

"Why, yes, it is." Glinda shoved it down into the bag and folded the top closed. "A favorite of Humphrey's."

The man in front of Nimue in line couldn't stop staring at Glinda's giant beetle familiar, but he didn't say anything. In fact, his jaw twitched just slightly, his arms folded in front of him and his muscles stiffening, as he tried to look ahead of him. His gaze kept getting drawn to the beetle.

"Any idea why the bakery's so packed?" Nimue whispered. Nutter took to the air, flipping his thin wings and causing the hulk of a man in front of Nimue to cry out a little and lean away as the insect flew over to Gowdie and Temperance. Temperance had moved on to another table as guests sat in the first one she'd cleaned, and Gowdie kept up his chatter, beaming with delight as Nutter joined them.

Glinda smiled at the human man, the movement of her face highlighting the spiderweb-like wrinkles around her eyes. "No need to fear Nutter. He's my familiar."

"I figured," said the man, chuckling nervously. "I apologize if I was insensitive. I just don't… like bugs."

"I love them." Glinda's eyes crinkled. Nimue knew those steely blue eyes could get severe during any con-goer crisis. Which was just what Witchy ExS needed—cutting off any crisis early before it messed with the aura of the convention. "They're such hard workers." Her peachy-tan complexion was starting to sag—she was, Nimue thought, around a hundred, like her own parents, but witches aged so much slower than humans.

The whole reason why Bookshop Con had continued

even after the VIP author's murder was because the entirety of Cauldron Cove depended on it. If the Bessa had been flooded with negative energy from unhappy con-goers—or none at all—Nimue shuddered to think of what would have happened to the giant cauldron beneath the town. It would have exploded and taken the whole town with it.

The man smiled politely.

Glinda lowered her voice. "You're with Mr. Vanedestine, aren't you, sir? I was provided with photos of our VIP's staff for purposes of issuing VIP access."

Nimue's mouth opened slightly. She should have pegged the man for a bodyguard or something. But the VIP guests weren't due quite this early in the day.

The man nodded. "Jaxson Blevins."

"Glinda Redferne." Glinda shifted her tray to extend her hand to him. "Director of Guest Services for Witchy ExS."

Glinda seemed to notice Nimue's confusion as she watched the two shake. She looked around and lowered her voice. "*He* got in last night, a little early. Clarke sent me a message over the witch network." Her gaze darted to the perma-charm crystal she wore over her wrist, which Nimue wore over hers, too. It was how the Witchy ExS staff communicated with one another since they all only had one Communication Charm to use per day. It was similar to the humans' internet in some respects, but one could either dictate or just *think* a message to it. And it only worked for witches and warlocks.

"Clarke" had to be Clarke Southern, co-owner of the Southern Hotel, and Soren Southern's father. Nimue assumed that meant Soren, who lived at the hotel, would have been aware of the guest's early arrival, too. She wondered why *she* wasn't aware yet. She'd thought she and Soren—or Ren, more accurately, the personality inside Soren's body who disliked Nimue—had been working together better since Bookshop Con.

"His fans seem to know—or expect him to show today—and there are a lot more checking in at Southern Hotel than we usually get the day before a con starts," Glinda continued.

"Ah. That explains the crowd." Nimue smoothed her red skirt over her gray-and-white-striped tights and tried to let go of the rise of irritation. She'd message Ren about his lack of communication later.

"Did you even check for a message from him?" Gowdie pointed out.

This morning, Nimue thought back. She glanced at her perma-charm witch network crystal and saw a blinking message from Cassie, her and Soren's assistant. It was timestamped about twenty minutes before, after Nimue had last checked.

VIP Maverick Vanedestine arrived at hotel last night, it stated.

So Nimue wasn't being left out of the loop, after all. Maybe Soren had already been asleep when Maverick had arrived.

She really needed to stop jumping to the worst conclusions when it came to her co-manager.

Jaxson seemed to pick up on what Glinda had whispered. He lowered his voice and spoke to the two witches. "Maverick fans can get a little… obsessed. There are those who seem to follow him everywhere he goes, so word about his movements gets leaked early. I have no idea how they're even supporting themselves because they certainly don't seem to have jobs." His eyes scanned the bakery, as if looking for one of those obsessed fans right now. But despite the fact that the crowd may have been due to Maverick's presence, Jaxson didn't seem to find any of them a threat.

"Let me introduce myself, too." Nimue extended her hand to him. "Nimue Toothaker, co-Head Witch General Manager of Witchy ExS."

Jaxson's light-brown eyes lit up as he took her hand. "Oh! Thank you for having us."

"We're honored to have you." She lowered her voice. "And him."

Jaxson let go of her hand; he'd had a firm grip. "I'm surprised he wanted to come, actually. The boss is… well…" He swallowed. "I thought he didn't do well around witches."

Nimue cocked her head. The Hollywood superstar of the hottest comic book franchise didn't "do well" around witches? Weren't there a number of witches and warlocks who worked in special effects for humans' films and TV shows, as Gowdie had pointed out? They'd be all over the average set.

"Well, we'll do our best to make sure he has nothing to worry about," Glinda said smoothly, her customer-service smile back on. Nutter flew over, the buzzing of his wing's thin membranes reaching their ears before he showed back up to land on his witch's shoulder. He landed next to a golden chain pin that was looped around the collar of Glinda's dress. Jaxson let out a little yelp again and leaned back, though Nutter had been in no danger of hitting him.

Glinda kept speaking, unfazed. It was true that her familiar caused more negative reactions than most. "Zelena Varlett, our Director of Security, should be at the hotel momentarily."

Jaxson nodded. "I just have to pick up an order for the team and I'm heading back."

The door leading outside flew open and a professional-looking, petite human tourist shot inside, her face a bit harried-looking as she tripped over her open-toed sandal wedge heels and bumped into Temperance's butt.

"Whoa! Watch out!" shouted Gowdie in Nimue's mind, though only she could hear his words and it came out as a sort of grumbling croak to all other ears. The blue dragon swooped in and grabbed the woman's teal cardigan by the shoulder, leaning her upright.

Her bright-green eyes widened as she stared at Gowdie flapping his wings above her. Her strawberry-blonde hair was fastened into a French braid, her porcelain skin splattered with freckles across almost every spare inch.

"A dragon," she said reverently. Gowdie let go of her sweater and kept flapping above her head.

"Esther?" Jaxson said.

That snapped her back into the moment. "Jaxson!"

"You haven't been checking your texts." She clomped forward, perhaps not quite used to those shoes, though they gave her pantyhose-covered legs a sophisticated look. "Forget the donuts! Code red! Code red!"

Without waiting for a reply, she turned around and

clomped right back out, drawing the attention of every single being within the place. Even Sylvie stopped scrambling to watch the clomping woman—no taller than five-foot-three—exiting the bakery.

Only Jaxson moved at all for those first few seconds, whipping a phone out of his suitcoat pocket and barreling after the woman he'd called "Esther" out the door.

Glinda and Nimue exchanged a look, Gowdie flapping back over to land on his witch's shoulder.

"Celebrities," Glinda said softly—without judgment, but as if that explained everything. "See you soon." She headed for the door, too, and the crowd in the bakery went back to their business, Sylvie doing her best to get the line moving quickly.

CHAPTER THREE

"*I take it we're headed to Southern Hotel?*"

Nimue and Gowdie had passed the seven-story building—among Cauldron Cove's tallest—on the way to the Bessa, her arms stuffed with a giant bag full of Sylvie's pastries. But after dropping off the goodies in the employee break room, picking up her witch's hat and employee badge, and heading to her office to find both Ren and Cassie absent, Nimue sent her assistant a message.

They were both at the Southern Hotel.

Handling a VIP crisis, Cassie had written.

That meant the "Code Red" Jaxson had been summoned to deal with was something that needed to involve Witchy ExS, apparently.

"We're not having another narcissistic VIP on our hands," Nimue told her familiar as her boots echoed out against the floor of the employees-only corridor. "We know how that went last time."

"*No one wants Maverick Vanedestine dead, surely,*"

Gowdie pointed out. *"He's Colton Perfect-Cheekbones Carter!"*

"A fictional character," Nimue pointed out. "That doesn't mean he doesn't have a few enemies—"

"Uh-oh. Who has enemies?" Tituba Jonesdochter skipped off her broomstick as she came in for a landing on the second-story balcony entrance for employee witches and warlocks. Tituba's familiar, a neon-green frog, croaked from atop her puffy, yellow sleeve over her shoulder. The yellow really complemented Tituba's dark-brown complexion.

Nimue sighed. "No one. As far as we know. I'm just checking in with the others at the hotel because Cassie mentioned a VIP crisis."

Tituba put a hand on her hip, holding her oaken broomstick upright beside her like a walking stick. "Another diva?" Her dark brows narrowed, the braids of her brown-and-golden hair waving across her face as she shook her head. The gullet on Graves, her familiar, expanded as he croaked again, likely filling his witch with some commentary about last month's diva author.

"I don't know." Nimue pinched her lips and pointed over her shoulder. "I brought some baked goods for everyone."

Tituba smirked. "You remember I'm in charge of Food Services, right?"

As if she could forget that about her lifelong best friend. "Even the best chef needs to be fed food prepared by someone else on occasion."

"Touché." She wrinkled her nose. "And I have to admit, I'm a fool for Sylvie's Danish."

"Hold down the fort," Nimue told her, sliding onto her broomstick. She fastened her red conical hat tighter atop her head.

"Will do. I've got to check in with my staff about those Superstellar muffins."

Right. The head of the Comic Enthusiast Society had asked—just a week ago—that they include some comics-themed items among the food offerings.

Gowdie flapped his wings, floating up and down in front of Graves. *"I'll get you an autograph."* Nimue caught just the end of his conversation with the frog, who let out another croak.

Nimue *tsked*, but she couldn't help but smile.

There was a skywalk between the hotel and the convention center, but it was typically turned off when a convention wasn't in progress. Besides, Nimue had just a few moments before she was technically supposed to start work. She hadn't gotten to enjoy the ride here with her free arm full with the bag of baked goods. Trusting her co-workers to handle the crisis for a bit longer, she decided to take the long route around a couple of blocks, over the park nearby.

She soared off into the sky, putting a little speed into her flight, remembering how much faster she'd soared through these streets in her youth. She spared a glance behind her as the Bessa grew more distant, and the whole building came into view.

It was vast, four stories of steel and glass and giant tree branches all woven together and glittering in the morning sun. Inside were thousands of glittering candles offering light—when the sun itself wouldn't do the trick

—and mostly ambiance. Con-goers stepped inside and immediately knew this convention center was unlike any other.

There was the giant tree, for one thing. It wove its way through the convention center and most of town, through and around and up and over buildings, its branches and roots vast.

Beyond the center was Lake Salem, the large body of freshwater that served to make the convention center even more picturesque and played a secondary role whenever the Bessa hosted water sports enthusiasts. Witchy ExS usually let Mother Nature do her thing, but for the right price, they could make sure autumn or winter temperatures were closer to summer for the duration of a convention.

Weather was one thing, it seemed, Mia Estrada was *not* concerned about micromanaging.

"Do you ever wonder if the giant cauldron can bubble over with good energy?" Gowdie asked as they flew over Iron Cast Park. A large statue of the giant cauldron currently beneath the soil was positioned at one end of the park.

"What?" Nimue laughed into the wind.

Gowdie flapped his wings harder to keep up. *"Well, it's, like, we know to avoid overrunning it with bad energy, which could bubble up and destroy the town."*

"Yes…"

"So why not the opposite?"

"Every convention we hold is full of good energy," Nimue pointed out. "It keeps the cauldron happy. But it never bubbles over with good energy." They'd reached the other end of the park, the statue on the opposite side of all of the trees coming into view. Bessa Toothaker, for whom the convention center had been named, Nimue's great-grandmother.

Founder of the town. Over four hundred years ago. "If it did bubble over with good energy, well... I wonder if the town's witches would just have to harness it."

"Hmm, so like a power boost? I wonder how many witches it would take to harness it?" He cocked his head as they turned a corner and the Southern Hotel appeared at the end of the route. *"Can you imagine that much power going into just* one *witch? They'd be, like, as strong as Superstellar-Man!"*

On the outside, the hotel seemed all clean-lined and modern, though the plant life that grew throughout the building poked its boughs and leaves out here and there.

"Are you trying to tell me something?" Nimue asked. "I think you've been watching too many superhero movies." She jumped off the last foot or so to the ground from her broomstick as she descended in front of the lobby.

Resting her broomstick in the corral, Nimue waited for Gowdie to land back on her shoulder and they stepped inside.

The lobby was grand, half gold-and-white and half indoor forest. Soren's parents clashed when it came to hotel décor, but the end result worked well with the Bessa and most of Cauldron Cove's architecture. The whole town tended to feel like it had sprouted out from the ground and melded into a forest.

People milled about the lobby. Nimue spotted Soren's mother speaking to a man by the bar to the side of the front desk. Clarke Southern, the debonair, tall warlock with close-cropped blond hair and a rosy complexion, was off by himself in a chair in a corner, taking small bites of what looked to be a cruller and sipping from a paper cup of coffee as he checked his projected witch network screen. His familiar, a blue red panda, had curled up on his lap. Nimue headed right for the front desk, passing Clarke as she did so. He didn't notice her, but as he reached to put his coffee cup on the table with a lamp beside him, a golden chain connected to a set of cufflinks dangled from his dark-navy suitcoat sleeve.

At the front desk, Fidelity, a strapping young man with a pale-brown complexion and voluminous, shoulder-length black hair wore the hotel's dark-blue uniform. His familiar, Rhutwine, a white lizard, scurried about on the desk.

He was facing the teleportation pad and didn't seem to notice Nimue sneaking up on him. She opened her mouth to say something and Fidelity jumped.

"Yes, Mrs. Southern!" he said quickly. "Right away, Mrs. South..." He turned around, pasting on a smile. "Miss Toothaker. It's you."

Nimue didn't bother to correct him and ask that he call her by her first name. It was his job to be formal, and Nimue was starting to get that a lot of the witches and warlocks her daughter's age didn't quite feel like peers around her yet, even if she tried to be open around them. Besides, she didn't work with him directly.

Even if his girlfriend was Nimue and Soren's assistant.

"You were expecting Esmerelda Southern?" she asked.

"Not *expecting*, but..." He leaned forward a bit. "She

has a tendency to sneak up on me when I'm sort of spacing out. She's right behind me before I notice she's even nearby, and I usually get chewed out."

"You always seem to be on top of things when I see you."

He chuckled. "Well, I try to meditate before a big crowd is due. Makes it look like I'm not working, though." He winked.

"I know better," Nimue said. "You're a hard worker."

Gowdie landed on the desk besides Rhutwine, giving the lizard a little foot-to-foot high-five. Familiars, at least, didn't seem to have issues befriending each other, even when there was an age difference.

"I'm looking for Ren and Cassie," Nimue said.

Fidelity winced visibly, though his charming smile never fell from his face. "They're on the fourth floor, but I don't know if another witch will help matters…"

Nimue cocked her head. "What do you mean?"

Fidelity looked over Nimue's shoulder, his gaze flicking to the bar. Then he lowered his voice and leaned closer. "Rumor is Maverick Vanedestine is… terrified of witches."

Nimue did a double-take. "But he knew what Cauldron Cove was when he agreed to come—"

Fidelity leaned back and shrugged. "The staff is talking. That's all I know."

Nimue tapped a finger to her lip, thinking. "And Ren and Cassie have it in hand?"

"Cass can do anything." He tossed his head back, clearly proud of his girlfriend. "Zelena headed up there, too, to coordinate security with Mr. Vanedestine's team."

Zelena had thrown herself into work since getting back from questioning by the Council of Witches and Warlocks of the Greater Midwest. Not that the Director of Security had ever been lax at her job.

"Nimue!"

Nimue checked over her shoulder. Esmerelda Southern waved at her from over at the bar, the human man still with her. Esmerelda's husband, Clarke, appeared to be gone from the lobby. Nimue thanked Fidelity for the information and backed up from the front desk, Gowdie trailing in the air behind her.

Nimue approached Soren's mother. The Southern Hotel and Witchy ExS worked in tandem to make each convention a success, but Nimue had never been particularly close to either of Soren's parents, nor had she been the one to coordinate much between the two businesses. Not when their own son worked for Witchy ExS.

Still, she remembered the cheery, rosy-cheeked Mrs. Southern from her days as a student. For a brief period, Soren had been her first boyfriend—in that "let's say we're boyfriend and girlfriend and just hold hands" little-kid way.

"I was just telling Dr. Choi about you." Esmerelda beamed, threading her fingers together. With wavy, blonde hair and a full figure, Esmerelda looked amazing in her clingy white dress, a cheerful sort of lounge singer who'd melt hearts with her kindness rather than her sultriness. Her familiar, Faulkner, was a gold-spotted white snake who draped herself over Esmerelda's shoulders like a boa, slithering around a golden chain on which hung a golden pendant hidden partially behind the snake's body.

"Dr. Choi!" Nimue brightened. "Delighted to meet you."

The human doctor had salt-and-pepper hair swept back into a sort of perpetual wave, though it was a bit thinning at the temple. He had on thin, wire-frame glasses, and his tawny complexion had more than a few wrinkles, but he held himself straight and tall with all the energy of a much younger human man. He was fairly thin but broad-shouldered, with long limbs. He probably wasn't that much older than Nimue, but humans aged so much faster than witches.

"Charmed." The man held his hand out and then burst into a fit of giggles as they shook. Nimue was taken aback. "Charmed... So many charms at work in this city!"

Ah. Nimue laughed as well.

"Nice to know he doesn't take himself too seriously," Gowdie said in Nimue's head as he landed on her shoulder.

"I do say, these familiars are quite intriguing." He leaned over and looked at Esmerelda's snake. "Oh, what a beautiful jewel that is."

"This little old thing?" Esmerelda brought her golden pendant out from behind her snake, who hissed.

"That's actually a perma-charm crystal," said Nimue, having gotten a better look.

"Why, yes, yes it is. An Awake Charm, you know?" She blinked hard. "I try not to overuse it, but I need to stay on my feet so much on this job. Best to be able to stay alert."

"Hmm," both Dr. Choi and Nimue said at once.

Nimue wondered if Dr. Choi knew what she did—that it wasn't recommended witches rely on Awake Charms too often, let alone walk around with a perma-charm crystal allowing multiple uses in one day. There was no way she'd gone to Bernadette for such a charm. Her grandmother wouldn't have allowed it. Too much artificial energy boosts and the body was sure to crash. Nimue wondered if she should mention something to Soren about it.

Dr. Choi's eyes grew wider as he looked at Nimue. "Fascinating," he said, adjusting his glasses and leaning toward Nimue's shoulder to get a closer look. "I thought it was a bat at first. A *dragon*?"

Cue Gowdie's preening.

Esmerelda laughed as well, petting her snake's scales. "Yes, Nimue has the strangest choice for a familiar!"

Gowdie deflated a bit.

Nimue patted his back and kept talking to the human doctor. "We're so thankful you decided to give our convention center a trial run of sorts."

"Well," the doctor said as he leaned back, "I've been looking for a new practice, and when your Soren Southern contacted me about working with your medic witches to add some human-doctor insight to any medical emergencies—I leaped at the chance!"

"His room is ready for the next few weeks. One of our best suites." Esmerelda put a hand on Dr. Choi's elbow. "My son always comes up with the best ideas, doesn't he, Nimmy?"

Gowdie snickered. Nimue had almost forgotten Mrs.

Southern's strange nickname for her back when she'd "dated" her "little Soreny."

"Um, yes," she said quickly, focusing on the human doctor. "And if you find the work intriguing, I hope you'll consider signing that long-term contract. Then we can get our real estate office on top of finding you more permanent housing. Do you have family to bring with?"

"Oh, no, I'm a life-long bachelor." Dr. Choi's dark eye twinkled, a devious smile on his face, and Nimue stiffened. Was the doctor hitting on her?

She hadn't been hit on… well, since she'd divorced Greg. She hadn't had time for a love life since diving head-first into her job at Witchy ExS.

"Hmm," Gowdie said in her head. *"It's unlike you to even notice. I have to wonder if you've become… a little more aware of the potential for romance these days."*

What does that mean? she thought back to him.

"Oh, if it's just you, we can talk long-term rental rates, too. You'll be *fully* pampered as our resident guest." Esmerelda slipped her arm through Dr. Choi's. Wearing a simple navy suit, he didn't have a white lab coat on like the medic witches, and he leaned down to pick up a black briefcase, rather than the medical bag Nimue realized she'd been expecting from a human doctor.

Nimue figured she must have been imagining the doctor's flirtation. She couldn't compete with the gorgeous Esmerelda.

"Hey, you're cute," said Gowdie in her head. He puffed up again. *"And you have a gorgeous familiar to draw all the guys' attention to you."*

Nimue shook her head but patted him anyway.

Dr. Choi was here on a trial basis—a trial for the doctor himself, and for Witchy ExS. They'd never needed a human medical professional before, but it was an idea Ren had had, and Nimue was open to it. They were working on improving Witchy ExS together.

Dr. Choi likely wouldn't have been able to help last month during the disastrous murder at Bookshop Con. But better to have too much help when it came to con-goer health and safety than not enough.

Nimue headed back out toward the lobby, glancing at the elevators off to the side of the front desk.

"Are we going to see what's up with Maverick?" Gowdie asked.

"You just want his autograph," she pointed out.

Gowdie whapped his spiky tail, bouncing it off her back. *"I just thought you'd want to see what's going on with him! Fan adulation can come later."*

"Mm-hmm," said Nimue skeptically.

The elevator door popped open and out scurried a human woman, probably around thirty, with a light-brown complexion and shoulder-length black hair pulled back into a very small ponytail at the base of her neck. Her glasses were thick, and her frame rather skinny, the T-shirt with a drawing of Superstellar-Man far too baggy over her black jeans and white sneakers.

Her sneakers came to a halting, screeching stop on the shiny, laminate flooring in the echoing lobby.

"You!" The woman pointed directly at Nimue.

Nimue looked around and pointed at herself when she found no one else around her. "Me?"

The woman squeaked her loud sneakers straight over

to Nimue. "I've seen your picture! You're Nimue Toothaker."

For a second there, Nimue felt what it must have been like to be Gowdie. Her back straightened as she smoothed down the skirt of her dress, a little taken aback to be identified by a mysterious "picture" like some kind of celebrity. "I am. Can I help you?"

The woman took hold of Nimue's hand and shook it— far too enthusiastically and while squeezing the life out of her fingers. "Mia Estrada. We spoke on the phone."

Oh. That was an understatement. Mia had called Cassie about seven times a day for the past month.

So this was the new head of the Comic Enthusiast Society, the client behind Comic Hero Con.

And boy, did she have a powerful grip for such a small frame.

CHAPTER FOUR

"**M**s. Estrada," Nimue said, trying not to wince as she extricated herself from the small woman's powerful grip. "It's a pleasure to meet you."

"'Mia' is fine, please," she said, dropping the handshake and pushing her glasses up her nose. She didn't look happy to see Nimue. In fact, not even the blatant peek she stole at Gowdie on Nimue's shoulders could brighten the woman's suddenly dour expression.

"Someone woke up on the wrong side of the bed this morning," Gowdie quipped.

"May I be blunt?" said Mia, gesturing toward a set of couches and chairs to the side of the Southern Hotel lobby.

"Of-Of course," said Nimue, not completely following along. She walked with Mia toward the couches, waiting for the woman to sit back in the nearest chair and— Nimue winced—kick her feet up on the glass coffee table in front of her.

"It's not going to work." Mia sighed, threading her hands together and resting them over her abdomen.

"What…" Nimue cleared her throat. "What's not going to work?" She pasted on her widest smile, her thoughts running through the countless times she or Ren had run interference on this woman's calls to complain or change something for Comic Hero Con. She'd thought surely, now that the con was just one day away and guests had begun to arrive, there was nothing more to be done.

"Think again," Gowdie murmured in his witch's mind, whapping his tail back and forth.

"The Interactive Comic Scene Booth?" Mia said. She waved her hand in the air dismissively. "Your assistant gave me a walk-through almost as soon as I arrived."

"On her insistence, no doubt," muttered Gowdie. Cassie certainly would have been busy the day before a con. Tours of showroom floor exhibits for clients were more often left to Morpheus Fowler and Herne Palmer and their showroom team.

Nimue straightened her back. "She didn't make me aware of any issue. The Book Scene Booth was a hit at last month's Bookshop Con—"

"I know, I know. That's why I wanted a version of it for Comic Hero Con. But now that I've experienced it— it's just… too stale."

Nimue blinked. "Stale?"

"I mean, it was the talk of the internet last month. What's so special about it now?"

"But it's…" Nimue swallowed. "This time, it allows

people to think of scenes from their favorite comic book movies or from the comic books themselves."

"I know, but it felt weird. Like I was a cartoon myself." She pursed her lips and cocked her head, not looking at Nimue at all. "I mean, that seems to break the illusion. Making everything around me into art instead of a scene I could *actually* be stepping into."

Nimue ground the heel of her boot against the shiny, hotel lobby floor. "You specifically asked that we make the comic book scenes resemble the art. The movie scenes are closer to real life, if that's what a con-goer is looking for—"

"Yes, but what if I want to be in a scene that hasn't made it into the movies yet? Or a scene that *has* but was better in the comics?" She waved her hands around as she spoke, letting out a great sigh. "We all know that *Superstellar-Man: Return of the Stellar* was an *approximation* of issues 491-512 of the original run of the comics, but because the arc was condensed into such a short running time and moved much earlier in the hero's story, so much was left on the cutting room floor. The scene where he and Megastellar-Woman confess their love for one another just doesn't have the same impact in the movie, nor does the scene where he evolves his powers to defeat —" She kept talking and Nimue blinked, not really able to follow along.

"*Let me try to distract her.*" Gowdie flapped his wings and dropped down onto the coffee table in front of Mia's sneakers. He stretched, not-so-casually, preening and posing and displaying his full wingspan, almost as if in a dance in front of the client.

Mia kept talking, oblivious to the little blue dragon trying to gently direct her shoes off the table.

"So," said Nimue, raising her voice to be heard. Gowdie let out a little snort of smoke and settled down next to Mia's sneakers, just staring at the client, who still hadn't reacted at all to him. "What you're saying is you want us to remove the illustration feature? It's probably too late for that. The perma-charm crystal has already been crafted, and it takes many hours of work to formulate such a thing. And ingredients that cost—"

"Yes, yes, I know." Mia finally removed her shoes off the table and sat straighter in the chair. She rolled her eyes up at Nimue. "Every time I ask for something, one of you witches has to explain *the cost, the cost,* as if I'm not unaware."

"Well, like I said, it's also a matter of time at this point. Besides, we had begun to craft an all-realistic version of the perma-charm crystal, and you then said that the illustrations option *would* be the thing that made the experience unique for this con."

"Yes, yes, and the Comic Enthusiast Society was hit with another bill for that change, I know." Mia sighed and got to her feet, finally looking Nimue in the eye once more. Gowdie sulked on the table, as he continued to be fully ignored.

Nobody ignored a miniature dragon. Nobody except Mia Estrada, apparently.

"Look. I'm the first woman head of the CES. I worked hard to get elected. It wasn't a unanimous vote. I *have to* get this right, don't you see?" Mia rubbed at the skin at her neck, and Nimue softened a bit as Gowdie flew back and landed on her shoulder. "They could easily vote me out."

"Witchy ExS always does its best." Nimue tried to sound soothing. "Are any other members of the CES here yet? Have they tried the Comic Book Scene Booth?"

"They're coming tonight," she said softly, her breath hitching, almost as if the thought terrified her. "It'll be too late to make any changes if they don't like it—or will it?" Her eyes widened hopefully.

"Yes, tonight will definitely be too late. I think it's too late now, frankly. There's only one witch in Cauldron Cove even up to the task of crafting perma-charm crystals of that caliber—"

"Good," said Mia, taking Nimue's hand again and shaking it. "Then contact her."

Nimue dropped the second painful handshake, wiping her hand down the black bodice of her dress. "Unfortunately, she's unavailable." Nimue didn't actually know what her grandmother was up to today, if she planned to finish crafting more of the History Charm perma-charms she'd ordered, but her grandmother was retired, and Nimue certainly wasn't in the mood to deal with this anyway. "Look. The bottom line is: I think you're underestimating the appeal of *your* idea." She emphasized "your."

Mia cocked her head. "What do you mean?"

"Well, it was *you* who wanted those illustrated scenes to be how the con-goer experienced a scene from the comic book. And you were right. It's bold. It's unique. It'll be the talk of the con."

"*After Maverick Vanedestine,*" Gowdie added.

But Mia couldn't hear that. She was tapping her finger to her mouth, pacing back and forth. Then she smiled. "You know, I think you're right." She nodded, almost more to herself than to Nimue. "I'm going to go try it again and see."

"Oh, well, the staff is still setting up the showroom floor—" Nimue started.

"Nimue, just let her go," Gowdie said. "She's clearly too focused on this Comic Book Scene Booth to even take note of the dazzling dragon in front of her face. It's not something she's going to let go."

"Let me message Morpheus for you," Nimue said, gesturing toward the teleportation pad that would take guests straight to the Bessa—the ones who were unable to or didn't want to take the scenic route of the invisible skywalk. "Do you have your badge yet?" she asked.

Mia fished beneath her Superstellar-Man T-shirt and drew out a badge that hung from a green lanyard around her neck. She fidgeted with it, almost petting it beneath her fingers. "I've kept it on since I got it."

"Okay, that'll get you to the convention center lobby early since you're a VIP," Nimue said. "I'll have Morpheus come meet you and he can take you back." Nimue lifted her wrist and thought at the perma-charm crystal to bring up the witch network projection screen.

"Oop. And she's gone already." Gowdie scratched his cheek with a back foot, staring at the teleportation pad as it flashed brown to indicate transportation to the Bessa's lobby.

"Well, she's Morpheus's problem for now," Nimue said, wincing and sending a silent apology to her staff.

She mentally dictated the message and marked it as high priority, then sent it off to Morpheus before scrolling through her inbox.

"Clever maneuvering there, to get her to stop wanting that perma-charm crystal recrafted."

"I don't think she'd be happy even if we managed to scramble to get it done in time," Nimue muttered. "If dealing with her the past few weeks has taught me anything, it's that she doesn't know *what* she wants. Other than for the con to be a success. She just won't sit back and trust us to make it one."

"Bernadette didn't have such trouble with the previous heads of the Comic Enthusiast Society when she ran Witchy ExS," Gowdie pointed out.

"Well, Mia and I are both new in our positions. I suppose I should cut her some slack. Witch knows I've made a few missteps."

Gowdie grunted.

Nimue found a message from Cassie, sent just a few minutes before, when Nimue had been talking to Mia. It explained that Ren had been attempting to deal with a crisis with Maverick Vanedestine, but that his presence was only making the situation worse, so he was headed back to their office. "Since—and I quote," Nimue read aloud from the message, "'Nimue was married to a human for several years and lived among them, perhaps she'll be better suited to the task of assuring our VIP he has everything he needs,'" Nimue said to Gowdie. "Why do I get the feeling Ren didn't mean that as a compliment?"

She frowned, her eyes darting over the rest of the

message. "They think he has strogaphobia. Really?" She thought back to Fidelity's explanation that Maverick was uncomfortable around witches. But to have a clinical fear of them?

Why in the cauldron had he agreed to come to a convention hosted in a town of witches and warlocks?

Gowdie read the rest of the projected message. *"They want you to head up to his hotel room?"* He started dancing in place. *"Let's go!"*

"All right, all right." Nimue headed back to the elevator and, once inside, pushed the button for the fourth floor.

The hotel was quiet, despite the fact that con-goers were showing up in town early. The door opened and Nimue found no one waiting for the elevator on the other side, so she stepped out without delay.

"Which room was it?" she asked Gowdie.

A blood-curdling shriek whipped her head to the left.

"That's not good." Gowdie took to the air.

The screams didn't stop. It sounded as if someone were being attacked. Flashes of the dead author's final screech last month shot through Nimue's mind as she whipped her wand out and headed in that direction.

CHAPTER FIVE

The screams didn't abate as Nimue and Gowdie turned the corner of the hotel's fourth floor.

"Someone is being attacked!" Gowdie flapped his wings harder.

A group came into sight at the end of the hallway as they made one last turn.

"Sir, sir, please, calm down." Zelena Varlett's gruff, harsh tones echoed down the hall to Nimue. Zelena was *anything* but a reassuring presence when someone needed to calm themselves down.

Messenger, Zelena's all-black sloth, turned her head slowly toward the approaching witch and dragon and extended an arm in their direction.

Zelena turned, and her already dour expression became even more dour, if that were possible. The witch —somewhere around one hundred years old, Nimue had learned, even older than she'd guessed at first—didn't look to be out of her fifties compared to a human. She was tall, broad-shouldered, with brown and gray hair pulled tightly into a bun behind her back. She was back to work now, but she'd taken a few weeks off to deal with her husband's arrest, and, as one would expect, the time off had not improved her temperament.

"Toothaker," she said, which drew Nimue to a stop. The woman had never shown her much respect—and always sided with Ren—but she'd at least been on a first-name basis with Nimue. Until Nimue had gotten her husband arrested, Nimue supposed. As if that were her fault—he'd tried to kill all of them. Zelena stepped aside and gestured behind her. "We have a problem."

Nimue saw Jaxson and Esther behind Zelena, Esther chewing her nails and Jaxson furtively checking both directions of the hallway. There were a couple of other men as large and imposing as Jaxson—at least, he was now suddenly quite imposing, compared to how he'd been at Sylvie's Bakery—both tanned and dark-haired and difficult to tell apart, down to the identical golden watches on their right wrists and the black briefcases they held in their hands as they stared downward through dark sunglasses.

"*Oh, my,*" said Gowdie, flapping to sit atop a bough sticking out of the hallway wall. The large tree woven into the Southern Hotel's structure often poked out at odd places.

Nimue followed his line of sight.

Curled up on the floor, in front of a hotel room door, was Maverick Vanedestine.

As Gowdie approached, one of the almost-identical

men looked up and lifted his briefcase as if about to open it, but Jaxson placed a hand on his arm, and the man lowered it. A gleam of light bounced off the back of the imposing, unknown man's sunglasses as he turned his head back again to look at his charge.

"Oh, Mr. Vanedestine! Mr. Vanedestine!" Esther bounced on her feet, her heels flopping out of her shoes with every upward movement.

Maverick's thick arms covered his head as he shook and whimpered, and at the sound of Esther's voice, he lowered one arm just enough so that his wide, azure eye peered through.

Right at Nimue.

He shrieked again, his scream surprisingly high-pitched. "Another one! They're everywhere!"

Nimue tugged on the brim of her witch's hat subconsciously as all eyes turned her way. Then she remembered Cassie's message, and their theory about Maverick's strogaphobia. She pulled the hat off her head and hung it from the bough on which Gowdie rested.

"Mr. Vanedestine," Nimue said as softly as she dared. "Please allow me to address your needs. I'm co-Head Witch General Manager of Witchy—"

He shrieked again.

Esther's eyes widened. "Don't say that word right now!"

"Which word?" Nimue asked.

Maverick's wail grew higher in tone.

"*Wrong 'which,'*" Gowdie observed. But they sounded the same anyway.

Two doors down, the hallway popped open and Nimue nodded at Zelena to take care of the onlookers.

"Nothing to see here, folks." Zelena's voice carried down the hall.

Nimue cleared her throat. "Yes, all right, then. Can we, maybe, get Mr. Vanedestine to his room?"

Maverick was hyperventilating now.

Jaxson nodded and pulled a hotel keycard out of his pocket, tapping its perma-charm crystal against the handle of the door in front of which Maverick was curled up on the floor. He reached over the celebrity to push it open behind him. "Sir, just roll inside."

Maverick whimpered.

"Boss, there are fans down the hall—"

That was enough to get the man to curl up like a pill bug and roll like a ball back into his room.

It was a suite. One of the largest Southern Hotel had to offer. The door opened up into a large seating area, complete with a dining table in one corner behind a miniature kitchen and a circular couch around a large, human-style TV on the other. A closed door led off into the grand bedroom, the ensuite luxury bathroom another door beyond that.

One of the almost-identical bodyguards passed his briefcase to his would-be twin, and then he and Jaxson swooped down and whispered to their charge, who, still breathing hard, managed to crawl up to his knees. The men each took an arm and dragged him to his feet—he was a few inches taller than either of them. The man's dark, curly hair drooped like oily rags limply over his haggard face, and his feet dragged across the plush, red carpet. His eyes darted up to the large piece of tree trunk affixed in the corner of the room, but it was minimalistic in this suite design, no branches or leaves dangling out in any direction.

The men seated him on the couch, facing out toward the door, before the sunglass-bodyguard grabbed his briefcase again. Behind Nimue, Esther stepped in softly and went to shut the door just as Gowdie flew inside, the brim of Nimue's hat in his grip. A witch and her familiar could only be parted across a short distance.

Esther's jaw dropped as she watched Gowdie in flight. He passed Nimue—who sent him a mental thought to maybe not be so showy, considering the state of Maverick —but he ignored her and flew straight to the coffee table in front of the hyperventilating star, dropping the hat on the TV stand as he passed it.

Gowdie did what he'd done to Mia, making a great show of spreading his wings and coming in for a gentle landing. His head held high, his shoulders thrust back, he let Maverick get a good look at him.

Maverick's shallow breaths grew deeper, softer. "A-A dragon." His voice was deep—as deep and commanding as the one he used in the movies as Colton Carter—so the hesitance in his speech seemed extra unnerving.

Still, a smile cracked on his face as he leaned over and held out his index finger to Gowdie like one might with a cat to sniff.

"He likes the dragon!" Esther whispered, clutching Nimue by the arm rather tightly despite the fact that they'd never been formally introduced. She was giddy, though, her eyes lighting up as she watched the star with

Nimue's familiar, so she couldn't bring herself to shirk away.

"That's my familiar, Gowdie," Nimue said.

Esther's brow furrowed and she shuffled across the carpeted floor toward Maverick.

She cleared her throat, the sound almost as diminutive as she was. "Mr. Vanedestine, that dragon's name is Gowdie." She gestured to Gowdie, who rubbed his scaly scalp under Maverick's extended finger without bothering to sniff it.

The man laughed and pet Gowdie all over his head, tickling him under his chin.

"Now this is more like it," Gowdie said to Nimue.

Play it up, Nimue mentally told him.

"Permission to butter up my own ego for once? Yes, please!" Gowdie flapped his wings and though one of the bodyguards ominously seemed about to open his briefcase again, Jaxson extended a hand out to stop him and Gowdie curled up on Maverick's lap, practically drowning amidst the man's thick thighs.

Gowdie let out a little grumbly purr and lazily flicked his tail as Maverick kept petting him with one finger.

"Gowdie," he said. "What a strange name for a dragon."

Gowdie's eyes snapped open at that, his little nose stuck in the air as she closed them haughtily. *"Oh, like 'Maverick' is any less strange of a name. 'Gowdie' is a witch's surname, I'll have you know. Most familiars have witches' surnames."*

"He understands you," Nimue said, taking slow, careful steps toward the group. "He can speak, too—but only to me, in my head. He's my familiar." Maverick frowned a bit as he stared at Nimue, but since he didn't cry out, she hurried on. "He explained his name is a wi-a, uh, an old surname. Most familiars have surnames. He's very proud of it." She left out the bit about "Maverick" being an odd name, too.

Maverick stared at Nimue, as if just taking her in. Then he looked back at Gowdie and laughed, continuing to pet him gently. The movement seemed to be calming him and Gowdie eventually broke, dropping his haughty look and curling back up into the pets.

"He, uh, he'd like your autograph, too," Nimue said. "And one for his friend, Graves. Graves is a frog familiar."

Maverick blinked rapidly, his mouth slightly agape. Then he laughed again.

"You sure you don't just want one, lady?" one of the unknown bodyguards asked.

Nimue arched a brow. "Do you doubt familiars can want things for themselves?"

"I have a hard time believing them things *speak*," he said, shaking his head.

Jaxson sent him a sharp look. "Sorry about that, miss," he said to Nimue. "Some of us"—his eyes darted to the other bodyguard who'd spoken, as well as Maverick—"just aren't used to being around witches."

Esther gasped, her hand flying to her mouth. "You said the word." She swung her head to Maverick.

But he was focused on Gowdie, and he didn't have a panic attack this time. "Are you my little fan, baby Dee-Dee?" he said in a sweet voice, giving Gowdie a baby-ish nickname. Nimue could sense Gowdie's slight irritation, but he didn't have a comment this time. Instead, he played it up, as Nimue had asked, and put a gentle foot on top of Maverick's hand, batting his eyelids demurely.

Maverick drew him to his chest to give him a hug, and Esther giggled.

Nimue let out a deep breath, the stiffness in her limbs leaving her. "Everyone, feel free to call me 'Nimue.' I want to make sure your experience here is as pleasant as possible. I'm-I work with Ren. We head up the convention center." She still didn't want to push using the "w-word" too much until she was sure Maverick would take it well.

Jaxson nodded, clutching his hands together in front of his waist. "We appreciate that. We're Mr. Vanedestine's team. Security: me, Jaxson Blevins, we've met briefly before. This is Kovac and Davies." Those were probably last names. Davies was the one who'd doubted Gowdie could even talk. "This is Mr. Vanedestine's personal assistant, Esther McQuaid."

She smiled broadly at Nimue and did a little curtsey of sorts.

"And you know—or know of—Mr. Maverick Vanedestine." Jaxson gestured at the celebrity, who was laughing as Gowdie flew up and settled on his shoulder.

Despite asking him to play it up for the celebrity, Nimue had to admit she was a bit jealous. Gowdie only landed on *her* shoulder.

Gowdie sent her a wink.

Maverick let out a loud sigh and stared at Nimue, as if challenging himself not to break away. She'd left her witch's hat—normally a piece of attire the humans found charming in Cauldron Cove—sitting on that TV stand, so if you didn't know she was a witch, there was a chance you wouldn't suspect it.

If you could ignore the wand in the holster at her hip. She took note of Kovac and Davies. Davies was all tension, his back stiff and his head looking every which way throughout the room, as if expecting a threat from anywhere. Neither of them carried any weapons, and neither did Jaxson, but Kovac had brought his briefcase up all full of tension several times since she'd observed them, so she wondered what, exactly, was inside those.

She stared at him. He looked away. There was that glint behind his sunglasses again.

Did you see that sparkle? she thought to Gowdie.

"Huh?" Gowdie looked up, a bit bleary-eyed from all the petting.

Never mind. But she focused on Davies for a second. There wasn't a sparkle emitting from behind his sunglasses as his head moved every which way, so she thought it must have just been a trick of the light.

"I apologize," said Maverick, his deep voice commanding the room.

"Sir?" Nimue said.

He smiled awkwardly at her. "Did anyone ever tell you you look like Aria Grant?"

Nimue cocked her head. "The actress who plays Megastellar-Woman?"

He nodded.

"No, I—" She felt herself blush as she swept a piece of hair that had fallen out of her bun behind her ear. "I can't say they have. Maybe my daughter could get confused for her. I'm much older than that."

Maverick arched a brow. "You have a daughter?"

She nodded. "At college. She's… Um, my daughter's father is a human."

Maverick relaxed even more into the chair. "You're married to one of us?"

Nimue chewed her lip. She didn't particularly like the "us" versus "them" mentality of humans versus witches, but she wasn't about to poke the bear now. "I was. We co-parented our child together, though. We're still friends."

Maverick frowned. "I wonder if witch-human relationships ever work out." He'd said the forbidden word himself.

"Sure, they do," Nimue said, though she didn't personally know of any of them. She didn't really know anyone from Cauldron Cove who'd married a human besides herself. She'd been a bit of a rebel back then. But there were witches and warlocks all around the world. "They have their challenges, sure, just like any relationships do."

"Well," said Maverick, staring hard at Nimue as he absentmindedly stroked Gowdie on his shoulder, "I can see why a human married you. You *can't* have a kid in college."

Nimue blinked rapidly. She certainly hadn't expected to be hit on by a celebrity—an incredibly handsome one, and also one who'd just been screaming curled up on the hotel hallway floor just moments before. She smoothed the front of her dress.

"Thank you. Witches do age slower than humans."

"Don't I know it," Maverick muttered. "Gets hard to compete for parts when warlock actors who were handsome in the 1950s are still sticking around trying out." He chuckled to himself. As if there were *tons* of well-known warlock actors, or as if Maverick Vanedestine, star of the hottest comic book movie franchise, had anything to worry about when it came to securing acting parts.

"I thought—well, I have a therapist," he said, dropping his strange flirtation and focusing on the wall straight ahead. He stopped petting Gowdie and folded his hands between his spread knees. "I don't really like talking about things, even with her, but she's great at what she does. I thought I'd made progress. I thought I was ready for this."

"A convention in Cauldron Cove?" Nimue asked. "A town of witches?"

He winced but nodded. "Yeah. Comic Hero Con is one of the biggest comic book conventions in the country. I was tired of missing out. I thought I was ready. Now… I'm not so sure."

"We won't hurt you," Nimue promised softly.

He arched a brow and looked her way. "Didn't a warlock kill a guest here last month? That was *after* I'd decided to come. It almost made me change my mind, frankly. Nightmares come true and all that."

Nimue stepped closer and sighed, biting her lip. "I'm sorry. He-He really was the only witch or warlock I've ever known to hurt someone. Really." She reached her arm out and Gowdie took his cue, flapping over and landing on her wrist like a trained bird of prey. "And it was personal for him. He worked here for decades and nothing happened."

"I know. I know. My therapist and I studied the news, everything about the case." He chuckled. "She even suggested I try out for the movie they're talking about making, about Sherman Abbott and the whole tawdry Rona Brynhild affair. But my agent didn't think I was right for any part in it."

Nimue tried to paste on a smile. Witchy ExS had fielded inquiries about shooting such a movie here, but they'd declined. Whatever they came up to represent the Bessa would have to be a set or digital effects. She hoped the project never went anywhere.

"We hired a human doctor," Nimue said, the idea striking her. "Would you like me to send him in? We have witch nurses, too—"

"No, the human doctor should do. Sorry. I just… need a minute to compose myself before I try with a witch again." Maverick directed a crooked smile at Nimue, and she found her knees wobbling at how utterly charming it was. Despite the fact that she'd just seen him shrieking on the floor. But he couldn't help his fears, could he? It sounded like he was taking steps toward overcoming them. And Nimue admired that.

Nimue extended her hand out for a handshake. "Well, you're 'trying with a witch' right now and I think you're doing just fine." As if to make a point, she grabbed her hat off the TV stand and put it on her head before extending her hand once more.

Chuckling, Maverick shook her hand.

"Thatta girl," Gowdie said in her head. *"We can't have him cancel. I don't think the con-goers would take it well—"*

And the negativity might overload the cauldron, Nimue thought back to him.

She'd make sure this neurotic celebrity was comfortable enough to make it to all of his appearances. He'd made it this far—he had to see it through.

Or all of Cauldron Cove would pay.

CHAPTER SIX

The day before Comic Hero Con had been jam-packed, though Nimue's days often were. The staff had worked a bit overtime, and the booths were set—and fortunately, Morpheus had done a good job at convincing Mia not to insist on last-minute changes to the Comics Scene Booth, he'd reported via message. Moonlight and candlelight were the only things lighting up the Bessa's showroom floor now, as Nimue did one more sweep of the finished floor.

"In just twelve hours, exhibitors will start to arrive on the Bessa floor and finish adding in any extra items they want on display." Gowdie flew in surveying circles in front of Nimue. Nimue had already used a charm to transform her witch dress into something a bit more appropriate for an evening soiree, as tonight was the VIP dinner in the Southern Hotel. Though it was entirely a Southern Hotel affair, it was a tradition the night before a convention started, as most of the con's VIPs made it into town by the evening.

At least no one had changed the time of the dinner this time. As far as Nimue knew.

She checked her witch network projection screen to make sure they still had time to finish this sweep of the floor. A few more minutes.

"Who else is coming?" Gowdie asked excitedly. As if he hadn't gone over the guest list for the convention along with Nimue. But that didn't mean all of the VIPs would show for dinner. Dr. Choi had messaged that Maverick was unlikely to show—that he'd improved somewhat and had taken some anxiety medications humans in his situation sometimes relied on, but he still wasn't up for a larger social gathering with witches present.

Nimue certainly hoped he would be by con's start tomorrow.

"There are comic book writers, artists, and editors; other actors from TV shows and movies; voice actors for animated versions of popular comics; and maybe some kind of comic book scholar? I lost track of all their job descriptions," Nimue said. "Fidelity has reported most of them have checked in, and I imagine they all have their invitations to the dinner."

Gowdie only just barely missed flying into an illustration of Superstellar-Man scrawled across a massive banner hanging overhead. Even though there was only dim light in the place, she could see the sparkle in Gowdie's wide eyes as he imagined the crowd of celebrities. Nimue wished again with a pang that Willow had been able to come. She and Gowdie and Reoch, Willow's familiar, had always had a blast discussing comics and comic movies together.

"I never did get Maverick's autograph —" Gowdie started. Then he shrieked, his little throat producing audible growl-like sounds as well as the squeal in Nimue's head.

Her high heel clomped hard against the thin, red carpet as she whipped her wand out. Even with her dress transformed into a sleek, auburn evening gown with puffy sleeves, she'd kept her wand in a holster at her hip.

Gowdie didn't seem to notice her readiness for a fight. He swooped down and around and up over a booth ahead, continuing to squeal.

"Gowdie!" shouted Nimue, running over to him.

He was fine.

What had caught his attention was the giant image of the Comic Hero Con-exclusive collectible that flickered to life above the largely white booth. The image showed the golden Superstellar-Man toy flying, punching, and shooting beams from his eyes. Words flashed in the bottom of the image that read: *Actual figurine is not magic-enhanced. Does not move.*

Nimue supposed *that* would have been an idea. Manufacturing perma-charm crystals to put in every limited edition toy to make them move. But the Comic Enthusiast Society had been in charge of arranging the production of their exclusive merchandise, and that was one thing Mia hadn't thought to involve Witchy ExS in.

Gowdie soared all around the booth, which had been empty for most of the day. The boxes containing the exclusive deluxe figurines were on display now, stacked up in a pyramid with more boxes full of the additional figurines behind a table.

"They each weigh four pounds," Gowdie said, reciting a

list of facts about the figurines again. *"Made of real metal and spray-painted with genuine gold."*

Nimue chewed her lip and put her wand away. "Seems awful heavy for a toy."

Gowdie kept on unabated, zipping up and around the pyramid of figurine boxes. *"They're not meant for kids,"* he explained further. *"Each comes with a genuine 1:36 replica of the Sword of Stellar Planet. With an actual sharp-tipped blade."*

Nimue smirked and crossed her arms just as the perma-charm banner showed the toy figurine holding a gleaming, golden sword high above its head. "An 'actual replica,' huh? Isn't that an oxymoron?"

Gowdie was unfazed. "Only one thousand units were produced, and there are *tens of thousands* of guests expected—"

"I don't know how you're going to get one, let alone *two,*" Nimue pointed out. "You can't wait in line without me, and I'll have too much to do tomorrow—"

"But they're right here! Right now! Can't we evoke executive privilege and leave some money behind to buy them?" Gowdie coughed out a little spurt of fire and then landed —right on the top of the pyramid of figurine boxes.

A giant wail screeched out across the wide, empty Bessa showroom floor.

Red lights flashed, the siren growing louder.

Gowdie screamed and Nimue whipped out her wand. "Get over here!" she shouted over the noise.

Gowdie did as bidden, landing on her shoulder, as Nimue waved her wand. "Undo Protection Charm!" she shouted, waving it over the length of the booth.

The red lights stopped flashing, the wailing sound

cutting itself short.

Gowdie was breathing heavily, his hot breath glancing Nimue's cheek. She arched a brow at him and turned to look at him as best she could. "Your exclusive, super rare genuine replica is so valued, the Comic Enthusiast Society requested an alarm system on this booth, remember? Only the approved members of the CES are able to touch the items after Herne and Morpheus set up the Protection Charm. Well, until payment is exchanged and the CES recognizes ownership transfer of the individual product." She frowned. "Now I have to set the Protection Charm back up again, since I just undid it…"

Gowdie was still breathing hard, his eyes caught on the stack of figurines, as if it had shocked him somehow. It wouldn't have caused him pain, though—just alerted the entire convention center there was an issue.

Of course, this being long after hours and just before the VIP dinner was to start, Nimue doubted anyone else—

A feline's hiss drew her attention.

Balfour trotted out in front of Nimue's feet. The black-and-orange spotted cat familiar leaped up onto the table separating the pyramid of figurine boxes from the rest of the figurines still in shipping boxes and sat up rigidly, staring them down.

Gowdie hadn't warned Nimue they were nearby. He must have still been panicked.

"It was just an accident," Gowdie said in Nimue's head, though she figured he was talking to Balfour. His talons dug into Nimue's shoulder and she winced. *"I was not stealing!"*

Balfour whapped her tail on the table, arching her back and letting out a rumbly, laughing purr.

Gowdie stomped his foot. *"She said I must have been drawn here because dragons steal shiny things. She asked if I confused it for my hoard of gold! I don't have a hoard of gold! What a stereotype!"*

"I know, I know." Nimue patted his head and looked over her shoulder for Balfour's warlock.

Her chest tensed for a moment as he stepped out of the shadows. If it was Soren, they might laugh it off. If it was Ren, she was in for a lecture, even if it had been her familiar and not she who had set off the alarm. Of course, even if it was Soren, it would eventually get back to Ren, so…

"Testing our alarm systems, I see?"

Ren. Broomsticks.

Ren Southern was the personality that had inhibited Soren Southern's body after he and his wife, Lydia, had had an accident brewing a potion twenty years ago. The same incident that had claimed Lydia's life had led this second spirit to inhibit Soren's body.

"It was an accident," Nimue said bluntly. "Gowdie got a *little* excited about these rare figurines—"

Balfour meowed as her warlock neared her, looking around at the booth.

"That does not mean I was hypnotized by the gold!" Gowdie shouted in Nimue's mind.

She flinched.

Ren wouldn't have heard Gowdie's words, but he would have heard whatever Balfour had said. And they both knew their familiars rarely got along.

Ren whispered to his cat and she stuck her little nose in the air, jumping into his arms. Ren's slicked-black blond hair paired especially well with the tuxedo he had on, the dark color highlighting the sharp cheekbones on his pale-white face. The warlock was tall, and on the thin side, though from what Nimue could tell, he was fairly toned.

Not that she was often analyzing how toned he was or anything.

"It's a wonder such special care has to be taken for these… toys," Ren said, his deep voice taking on a snobbish tone.

Gowdie crossed his front legs over his chest like arms and folded a bit, sullenly. *"They're collectibles, not toys."*

Balfour let out another rumbly, laughing purr as Ren pet her head.

"Yes, well, not everyone's tastes are as *refined* as yours, Ren Southern." Nimue put a hand on her hip. "And it's comic book fans who drive the profits for this convention, so I wouldn't look down on any nerds—"

"We're not nerds!" Gowdie shook his head. *"Honestly, Nimue. You watched one of the Superstellar-Man movies last night!"*

Balfour looked up at her warlock, likely relaying Gowdie's half of the conversation.

Nimue felt her cheeks flush. "I didn't mean 'nerd' as an insult," she said honestly. "Geeks, fans, enthusiasts—what have you."

"A paying customer is a paying customer, nerd or not," said Ren simply. He stared up at the moving promotion for the figurine.

"Great. Now that word's going to stick. Thanks, Nim." Gowdie *tsked*.

Nimue's voice grew hushed. "You know Greg's a nerd! Willow's a nerd! I love nerds! I'm a book nerd!"

"A 'nerd' is more someone who's really smart. Of course, there are comic book fans who are nerds, but their love for a single topic doesn't make them nerds—" Gowdie was starting off on a rant that Nimue was tuning out. At least until he said, "Did you hear that?"

Hear what? she thought back to him.

He perked his head up. "Nothing, I guess. I thought I heard a fizzling sound."

Balfour meowed.

Ren arched a brow in her direction. "You heard *what*, too?" he asked aloud. He looked to Nimue. "I thought your familiar was talking about nerds versus geeks and fans or something."

"He was." Nimue laughed nervously.

"Did you put the Protection Charm back in place?" Ren asked, thankfully not pursuing the "nerd" topic any further.

"Not yet," she confirmed.

Ren pulled his wand out. "Shall I?" he asked over his shoulder. "I was here when Herne set it the first time."

Nimue shrugged. "Have at it."

"Protection Charm." Ren waved his dark-colored wand, his eyes narrowed as he focused all of the right magic into the charm. Nothing visibly changed about the booth, but Nimue was sure that if anyone unauthorized touched those boxes again, the alarm would go off.

"Thanks," Nimue muttered to Ren, petting Gowdie's

head. He'd stopped ranting, instead letting out a sigh as they started moving in the direction of the nearest teleportation pad, away from the limited-edition figurines she hadn't let him buy in advance of the con's opening.

"Of course. Good to test such things sometimes, I suppose." Ren smirked as he started walking beside her and Gowdie, his familiar in his arms, but it was clear he was trying to bite the grin down as he looked around at the other booths along the way.

Nimue refrained from firing back. He'd known it hadn't been a test.

"What are you still doing here?" Nimue asked. "Isn't the VIP dinner about to start?"

"I could ask you the same thing."

"I just wanted to do one more sweep of the showroom floor," she said.

"I as well."

Their eyes met for a moment, and Nimue was surprised to find she didn't want to shout and run in the opposite direction.

Soren was a sweetheart. Ren was good at their job—but he was a royal pain to be around.

"And so is that cat," mumbled Gowdie.

Balfour perked up in Ren's arms and stared at him, but at least she wouldn't be able to read Nimue's thoughts.

They passed one booth with floating comic books, which opened themselves and flipped through pages every few moments. It made for a sort of gentle, waterfall-like sound. It was meant to draw the eye to the booth, which looked to be ready to sell rare issues of old comics.

"I hope they didn't use expensive comics for those displays," Gowdie said, tapping a talon to his jaw. *"That'd destroy the value if they get any bends or tears—"*

Nimue bopped his little forehead. "Spoken like a nerd," she teased.

They turned the corner to another aisle. Balfour grumble-purred again at Nimue's remark and Ren studied Nimue... almost softly. She caught her breath and felt *weird* around him all of a sudden, here in the darkened showroom floor of the Bessa, after-hours. Both of them were here, checking to make sure everything was set for the convention to begin. Both were committed to making sure they did their combined job to the best of their abilities, that Comic Hero Con was a convention that fed the cauldron beneath the Bessa only the very best energy. They actually—sort of—made a good team.

Balfour let out a yowl, her back arching in Ren's arms, and her fur puffing up.

Nimue whipped her head forward, reaching for her wand, as Gowdie took to the air and flew on ahead.

Something fairly large was lying there in the middle of the aisle, a tripping hazard if left there until the next day.

Nimue drew closer and her breath caught.

Ren gasped.

The "something" in the middle of the floor wasn't some errant item the showroom team had left in the way.

It was a person. A witch.

Glinda Redferne, recently named Director of Guest Services.

And she was dead.

CHAPTER SEVEN

R en scrambled forward, his face drained of color. "Glinda? Glinda!" Balfour jumped out of his arms and started sniffing Glinda's hand.

Ren rolled the Director of Guest Services's sprawled body over and grimaced. It was an unsettling sight. All Nimue could focus on was the lifelessness of her eyes, the pallor of her skin. And the long, red line across her neck.

She whirled around, waving her wand. "Communication Charm!"

"Who are you calling?" Ren asked, his voice cracking.

"Florence," she told both him and the charm at once, picturing the Head Medical Witch in her mind's eye.

She'd be off-duty right now, but she was the finest medical professional Cauldron Cove had.

"Nimue, she's dead," he said, reaffirming exactly what Nimue had also thought the moment they'd come across her. "Though she's still warm," he added, checking her pulse at her wrist.

Gowdie patted his witch's head gently with one wing,

then screwed up his face in determination and took off to the showroom ceiling, as high as he could go, fluttering up past a floating banner.

In Nimue's field of vision, a portal revealing Florence Thornton appeared, the silver-haired witch with a pixie cut. She was at her desk at her clinic downtown, where she was open some hours when conventions weren't currently in operation. She startled as she looked up, cutting something she'd been saying to someone short; she'd probably been trying to catch up with some last-minute work before closing the clinic entirely until Comic Hero Con was over.

Comic Hero Con… Another convention Witchy ExS would have to hold after a body had been found.

And this, clearly, had been no accident.

"Nimue? What's—"

Nimue cut her off. "We need you at the Bessa show-room floor. Emergency."

Florence's mouth narrowed into a grim line and she grabbed her rainbow-colored witch's hat from where it hung on a coatrack beside her desk. "I'll assemble the team."

"No need." Ren stood up, now visible in the Communication Charm's window as well. "We'll keep this quiet —for now."

"We will?" Nimue looked over her shoulder at him.

He gave a curt nod.

Nimue ended the Communication Charm and whirled on him, wondering what he could mean. Yes, they couldn't risk canceling the convention—or the entire town might explode—but he couldn't expect to keep *another* murder under wraps until convention's end, could he?

Didn't the public need to know?

Especially if… Nimue glanced at Glinda again. There was no "if" about it. Glinda hadn't done that to herself.

As Gowdie's wings swept up above them, Nimue bent down beside Balfour to take a closer look at their poor, departed friend. She swallowed as she stared at her wide-open eyes. Glinda was a happily single witch, and she'd never had kids—but she had friends and a brother who'd moved to the human world some decades back.

They owed him the truth of what had happened.

The staff… To lose one of their own so close after one of their own had turned out to be a murderer.

Nimue gently leaned over and shut Glinda's eyes with a delicate touch.

"Communication Charm." Ren waved his wand, using his single use of the charm for the day. Until now, the little issues coming up before the start of the con hadn't warranted the use of the charm, really. But Communication Charms got more attention than a message over the witch network.

The image of Zelena popped into view. She was still in her Witchy ExS uniform.

It made sense he'd call her. She was the closest thing to law enforcement the entire town of Cauldron Cove had, since the whole town was built upon the Bessa's foundation. Nimue left them to their conversation and turned back to Glinda.

"Glow Charm," she said to her wand. Its tip lit up. Since she couldn't cast the "Undo Charm" again until the next sunrise, she was going to be stuck with a lit-up wand all evening. Unless another witch undid it for her.

She ran it over Glinda, trying to take in the full picture of her. The line across her neck had been hard to see at first, thanks to the mess of red, but at a closer look, Nimue noted it was long and thin—but deep. A clean cut, like someone had taken her by surprise and she hadn't fought back at all.

There were no other blemishes to her body. She was still in her witch outfit, complete with hat—though a fair few witches often wore their witch dresses everywhere around town and merely transformed the dresses to other outfits when they felt like it. Like Nimue herself was currently doing. Glinda's work badge hung around her neck on a lanyard—those, Witchy ExS staff usually kept in their lockers at work when not at the Bessa, for security purposes.

Without it, Glinda wouldn't have had access to the showroom floor, especially after hours. The entrances and teleportation pads relied on perma-charm crystals that could read a badge and determine the level of access the wearer had. A regular con-goer could not have been on the showroom floor outside of con hours.

Only the staff and the VIP guests were given access outside of hours, the latter so they could get special tours and access parts of the Bessa without always being intercepted by a crowd.

That left only a small number of people who would have had access to this spot. Ren was right. It was fading, but Glinda was still warm.

Had she been here when Nimue and Ren had been

making their final sweeps and they'd never run into her? Had she been doing a last sweep of the floor as well?

Balfour let out a little mew and nudged at Glinda's right hand with her nose. It was in a tight fist even now, but her wand wasn't sticking out of it.

Nimue found that still in the holster at Glinda's hip. Further confirming Nimue's burgeoning "taken by surprise" theory.

Nimue set her own glowing wand down and sent a silent apology to Glinda—pushing aside an image of her smiling this morning at Sylvie's Bakery—and opened her hand.

In her palm rested a pin. Just an unassuming pin in the shape of four gold bars arranged crisscross over one another. Nimue had seen a lot of those in the descriptions of Willow's pictures on the human internet.

"Hashtag!" shouted Gowdie in Nimue's mind, reading her thoughts and offering his more youth-savvy opinion. But he was still flying around, looking for…

A culprit, Nimue realized. If Glinda's body was still warm—

"History Charm," said Ren without preamble. She hadn't even noticed him finish his Communication Charm with Zelena and come up behind Nimue.

The scene shifted, as Nimue, Ren, and Balfour as they currently were grew invisible, replaced by shadowy figures of the three of them stumbling on the body— joined by Gowdie, who seemingly flew backward to the scene as a record of time unwound.

Lighting was awful here, only a sliver of moonlight and a halo of the candlelight high up above flickering down below. Nimue watched as they all moved backward, going from panicked to relaxed as they turned the corner, then shifting out of sight.

Glinda lay there a little while, alone and unmoving.

And then, her body stood up.

Not really, of course. But it was unnerving nonetheless.

She went from crumpled up, as they'd found her, to standing, the red at her neck pooling up and inside her.

Her hand remained clenched the whole time.

"Wait!" Nimue said. Their voices could be heard over the illusion, though no sounds from the history shown in the illusion itself would be audible through the charm.

Ren must have heeded her advice and paused the charm. This was the moment where Glinda's neck changed from clean to bloody.

And there was *no one* else around.

Nimue stood and squinted, checking the illusion of Glinda from all angles, wincing as she felt her foot bump into Glinda's current prone form. She stopped.

"What cut her?" Nimue asked.

Ren controlled the charm forward and backward, and Nimue focused.

Glinda's eyes widened. She fell.

That was it. No words passed Glinda's lips as far as Nimue could tell.

Only *something* had to have moved in front of Glinda's neck, from her right side to her left, leaving a trail of red across her skin.

Nimue looked around in the History Charm for sight of anyone, but she saw nothing.

"Let's keep rewinding," Ren said grimly.

Unnervingly, illusion Glinda popped up again, dead to alive before their eyes.

"There!" Gowdie shouted from somewhere.

Ren paused the History Charm. Nimue looked around. A few feet away from Glinda, something small and gold in color—she was sure of that because of the yellow glint when it caught some of the candlelight—flashed into existence, then flashed right out of it again.

"What *is* that?" Ren asked.

"I don't..." Nimue tried to examine it closer. It *did* seem familiar, but...

"I'll keep going," Ren said.

Then the illusion of Glinda started walking backward, nothing particularly of note happening. Glinda bent over, effectively putting the object in her hand on the ground. Then, bending back up, she walked backward.

So she'd just picked up this golden hashtag pin mere moments before she'd been attacked.

She walked backward and down another aisle and outside of the charm.

"Keep going," Nimue encouraged, looking for sign of anyone else.

"What was Glinda doing here?" Ren asked. "Was this just her final sweep of the showroom? It was"—his breath hitched—"it *is* almost time for the VIP dinner. She should have been headed to the hotel." The Director of Guest Services generally attended the dinner, to better acquaint themselves with the VIPs.

"Her being here isn't too strange," Nimue said. "She may have been headed to the dinner afterward. Linden always did a final sweep of the showroom the night before the con opened." As Bernadette's former assistant, Nimue had been more familiar than Ren with a lot of the movements of the staff. "The Director of Guest Services doesn't spend much time on the showroom floor during the convention, but they want to be familiar with the layout for any guest questions. Sure, there's a map, but Linden always said firsthand knowledge was best."

"So she wasn't meeting anyone?"

"Didn't look that way to me."

Ren grunted and kept the History Charm up, and the showroom continued to be empty. Sunset reversed and more light streamed into the place, and then more witches and warlocks walked backward into the scene, adding finishing touches on booths in reverse. Nothing too suspicious. At one point, Zelena walked by with two of Maverick's bodyguards, the two nearly identical ones with sunglasses. Were they doing a security sweep of the area in preparation for tomorrow? They didn't so much as stop in the aisle, though, as the History Charm moved quickly through their movements. Then there was more of the showroom floor team setting things up.

"Wait!" Nimue said, and Ren paused the charm. She bent down to approximately where she'd seen Glinda pick up that hashtag pin.

There was no pin in sight.

"When did someone drop that pin?" Nimue asked.

"What pin?" Ren paused and Nimue could hear Balfour purring as she caught him up to speed. "Oh. That's what she was picking up there, then?"

"Yes, but we never saw anyone drop it." Nimue

frowned, though she knew no one could see it. "It was dark for a lot of the visuals, but—"

"Hello?"

Nimue recognized Florence's voice, followed by Zelena's.

"Ren. Nimue?"

They'd have walked in on the History Charm. Ren ended it and the fake light disappeared from the aisle. Glinda's prone form reappeared and Nimue's heart sunk.

Florence—standing just a few feet to Nimue's right, seemingly out of nowhere, thanks to the History Charm masking reality for a bit—gasped and flung herself to her knees in front of Glinda, checking her all over and waving her wand, casting charm after charm.

Nimue knew it was too late.

Zelena's jaw dropped and she petted Messenger at her neck as she began to pace.

"Who did this?" Her eyes narrowed on Nimue.

Nimue shook her head rapidly, feeling the sting of Zelena's accusation. Perhaps not of the *murder*, but of letting it happen. "We-We don't know."

Zelena turned to Ren. "We need to do a sweep of the Bessa. Now."

Ren nodded solemnly, looking down at Glinda.

Florence was casting a Create Charm now, weaving a blanket out of thin air and settling it over Glinda's body. But as she came to Glinda's head, she removed the dead witch's hat.

Balfour trotted over as Nutter, Glinda's familiar Titan beetle, slipped out of the hat.

The cat poked her nose at him, nudging it. But its legs

were curled up, the insect lifeless. A familiar died when their witch did.

Balfour sat up straight and let out a little yowl. Zippel, Florence's neon-orange leech familiar, made a rare appearance and slipped out from the collar of her dress to start flailing about. As did Messenger, who grunted an unsettling cry, her little sloth mouth curled into an "o."

Up above them, Gowdie let out a roar, the largest fireball he'd ever spurt to date soaring through the air, catching one of the banners on fire.

Without saying another word, Ren waved his wand above him. "Extinguish Charm."

The banner—or the ash left from it—stopped kindling, no danger of the fire spreading.

Gowdie… Nimue thought up to him.

She could feel his pain. It was like hers with Glinda's, but it was somehow deeper, too. Something that felt more like the magical energy beneath their feet, rumbling up from the cauldron.

The cauldron was starting to catch on to the negativity above it. Nimue could sense its unease.

"Do your sweep, but keep it quiet," Nimue said. She locked eyes with Ren. She knew he felt the cauldron, too. "Comic Hero Con needs to go on." He nodded.

Zelena frowned but brought up her witch network crystal and started thinking orders at it, the perma-charm flashing different colors.

"The pin," Nimue said to Ren, who'd picked up Balfour and was stroking her softly. "We have to see who dropped it and when. Have Zelena do another History Charm—" The realization dawned on her. "The perma-charm History Charm crystals! Our new surveillance system."

Ren nodded. "We'll check every angle of them. But you really think the pin is relevant?" His gaze was unfocused, like his thoughts were elsewhere.

"I don't know," Nimue admitted. "I just don't like that we can't see when it appeared—and who else was around to hurt her. It's worth—"

Gowdie roared a mighty baby dragon roar above their heads, drawing everyone's attention, though only Nimue and the other familiars could hear his words. *"Nimue! There's someone up here! Come quickly! They're—They're running!"*

Nimue didn't stop to explain or to wait for the other familiars to catch everyone else up.

Her broomstick would have been a boon here, but a little ingenuity would just have to do.

Nimue snatched her glowing wand off the ground and waved it over herself. "Hover Charm!"

And she flew. Weightlessness gnawed at her stomach —flight was far less controllable when she was just floating in the sky instead of gripping a broomstick and being in command of the movements—but she kicked her arms and legs as if swimming through air and made her way toward where Gowdie flapped his wings near the balcony of the third floor overlooking the showroom floor. At the end of a darkened hallway, a figure loomed, shadowed in bright light. A man, Nimue thought, holding a briefcase.

"What? Whoa!" someone shouted as Nimue swam through over the landing and into the hallway.

The figure at the end of the hall vanished around the corner and instead of swimming after him—she couldn't use her Undo Charm to lower herself to the ground—Nimue tumbled in midair, head over feet, losing all control of her hover, her body hurling toward a window overlooking Lake Salem.

And in front of that window, right in Nimue's path, was Megastellar-Woman.

CHAPTER EIGHT

Megastellar-Woman, complete with cape and purple bodysuit, shrieked as Nimue soared right at her. Fortunately, she was short enough—too short for Megastellar-Woman, come to think of it—that Nimue simply slammed into the glass above her head.

The superheroine—or more accurately, Nimue saw, as she tumbled head over foot against the glass, Mia Estrada, without glasses, in a Megastellar-Woman costume—looked up and met Nimue's eyes before scrambling off into the dark.

"Undo Hover Charm!" Ren's voice carried out down the hallway. His footfalls grew louder, echoing out over the linoleum.

Nimue tumbled to the floor.

Only Ren caught her in his arms with an "oomph."

"I'll get the lights," said Zelena from the end of the hallway. Her silhouette framed in bright light from behind her reminded Nimue of the man she'd seen moments before. Zelena tapped her wand to the perma-charm crystal beside her, and the hallway glowed with soft, magic light.

Nimue shouted down at Zelena. "There was a man where you're standing! He had a briefcase and he ran. That way." She pointed to Zelena's left. That direction could have led to any number of places. The showroom floor, the convention center lobby, the hotel, and the rest of Cauldron Cove outside via door or teleportation pad. Of course, only staff members and VIP guests would have had badges that allowed them to use the teleportation pads at this hour.

Zelena didn't need to be told twice. She turned on her heel, her wand at the ready.

Nimue let out a deep sigh, the evening's events slowly catching up to her, as Mia blinked and stared at her, hard, and Gowdie flew up above.

"That was quite a tumble," he told her. *"Maybe I need to give you some flying lessons."*

"I'll stick to my broomstick most of the time, thanks," she told him aloud.

Balfour purred and rubbed at Ren's ankles, sending a yellow-eyed glance up at Nimue.

Up at Nimue.

Still in Ren's arms.

She looked up at him. He looked down at her.

She thought she caught the tips of his ears reddening.

And then, just as he was about to open his mouth, his hair lost its shine and fell forward, his narrowed eyes growing wider, brighter.

He blinked. "Hey, Nimue." He looked around, still not letting her go. "Um, where are we...?"

Balfour tapped at his ankle with her paw.

"She's getting him up to date," Gowdie explained, still flapping his wings above them.

A shadow fell across the usually cheerful face of Soren Southern—the true, original personality of the warlock, even if he appeared less often than Ren these days—as Balfour explained. Still, he didn't set Nimue down, and she was surprised she didn't ask him to. In fact, his grip on her calves and her lower back grew tenser with each passing moment, as if looking to her for succor.

"Um, excuse me?" Mia's voice broke the silence. "What's going on?"

Soren jostled in place and set Nimue down, bending to gently let her high heels hit the floor. Gowdie settled on Nimue's puffy-sleeved shoulder as Balfour hopped up into Soren's arms to take Nimue's place.

Nimue looked to Soren, who smiled softly at her.

"Thanks," she said quietly.

"I'll be sure Ren knows you thanked him." He looked at Balfour, who, as both personalities' familiar, was the one to catch the other up on what he had missed. "He's the one who saved you." His chest hitched.

Nimue reached over and took Soren's hand, squeezing it. The loss of Glinda was hitting her, too, and they still needed to focus on uncovering the truth of the situation.

Nimue dropped Soren's hand and stared down Mia. The cosplaying head of the CES shirked back under Nimue's all-business glare.

"What are *you* doing here?" Nimue asked. There'd be time to explain the crisis to the client representative later. Once she was cleared of suspicion.

If she was cleared of suspicion.

Mia's hands flew up, shaking in front of her. "I didn't know I wasn't supposed to be here—"

"Glin—" Nimue's tongue tied on the name. Gowdie patted the back of her head with a thin wing. "Glinda would have told you when VIP members were allowed in the Bessa. You're due for the VIP dinner over in the Southern Hotel right now."

"I know, but… Oh, no. I'm in trouble." Mia started hyperventilating, pacing back and forth, moving away from the co-Head Witch General Managers of Witchy ExS.

Soren brought up his witch network perma-charm crystal on his wrist, which flashed red. "We're late," he said quietly. He probably hadn't expected to show up at all, since Ren was so take-charge about their work with Witchy ExS. "Cassie's been messaging."

Nimue let out a deep breath. "Update her. And check in with Zelena."

Soren eyed both ends of the hallway, as if looking for a place to escape. Usually, he escaped inside himself.

"You can do it," Nimue said softly.

"I don't know why he left me in charge," he whispered. Then his breath caught as he took in Nimue in all her fine-dining glamor. "No, I do, but now's not the time to let his crush on you stop him from—"

"Did he just say 'crush' on you?" Gowdie asked, cocking his head.

Balfour grumble-purred and Gowdie just cocked his head back and forth, not translating whatever she'd said.

Nimue's jaw dropped. She blinked again. Then she shook her head. He had to be mistaken. It wasn't like

Soren and Ren ever communicated directly. And Nimue knew Ren had bailed the last time a woman had been in his arms—and that woman hadn't been Nimue. Intimate contact and Ren just didn't mix.

"Um, never mind that," said Nimue, shelving that topic for later. She wouldn't forget it, despite everything. "Please, Soren. You're here now. Help me handle this."

He took a deep breath, his bangs fluttering over his eyes. "Right." He nodded at Mia. "You got her?"

Nimue nodded back.

Soren jumped into action, jogging down the hallway as his witch network crystal blinked on and off, his messages being sent out to everyone who needed to know.

Nimue swirled back on Mia, who was pacing so far away, she was almost at the other end of the hallway now.

Gowdie took to the air and reached Mia before Nimue did, flying in front of her and letting out a tiny, mighty roar.

Mia shrieked and put both of her hands on her head, stopping.

"It's okay, Gowdie," Nimue said, drawing to a stop beside Mia.

Gowdie lifted his head in the air. *"She's not ignoring me now."* Then he flapped his wings and settled on the top branch of a plant near the end of the hallway, as if standing guard like a gargoyle to prevent Mia from slipping away.

Why would she want to slip away? It wasn't like Nimue would never be able to find her.

"Mia, please, take deep breaths." Nimue gestured for Mia to calm down. "There's-There's been an incident, and I need to know everything you know."

"Incident?" Mia grabbed two fistfuls of her hair. "What kind of 'incident'? I can't let the first Comic Hero Con under my tenure be a disaster—" She gasped. "Is it canceled? Is Comic Hero Con canceled? It *can't* be!"

"No, it's not canceled," Nimue said firmly. "You're actually right about that. It *can't* be. Once a convention is this far along, there's no going back. The magic under the town of Cauldron Cove demands an exciting convention."

Mia's brows scrunched together as she stared Nimue down. "That's right. That Bookshop Con last month. It was still held, despite the fact that an author was murdered—"

"Um, yes." Nimue swallowed. That was all public knowledge now. And the public had seemed to dismiss it by and large. Would they, with a second murder?

Was that something they had to tell people, considering the victim was one of their own? The Council of Witches and Warlocks of the Greater Midwest would have to be told, of course.

But the humans…?

Well, Mia, as their client representative, would have to know. And if she told anyone, then it would behoove Witchy ExS to get on top of it. But not until they knew the full story.

"Mia, what I'm about to tell you must stay quiet," Nimue said. "But just now—about thirty minutes ago—

one of Witchy ExS's staff members was killed. On the Bessa showroom floor."

Mia froze, her look of utter fear so ill-placed on the brave Megastellar-Woman's face.

"Hmm," Gowdie observed to Nimue alone. *"She's either an amazing actor, or this is truly news to her."*

That was good. Nimue would have hated to suspect their own client.

"Glinda Redferne," Nimue continued. "Our Director of Guest Services."

"Beginning to think that position is cursed," Gowdie muttered, shaking his head. *"Kill or be killed if in charge of guests."*

Nimue didn't respond to his quip, though it cut her sharply. He wasn't wrong—at least not since her grandmother had stepped down.

"So please," Nimue said. "I need to know why you're here."

Mia's limbs shook as she headed over toward the wall, leaning against it and slumping down to the floor. She sat on the edge of her cape awkwardly, hugging her knees to her chest. Nimue kneeled down beside her, carefully maneuvering her legs to accommodate her tight dress.

"I just… I wanted to get one more look before tomorrow and the con opening." Mia's voice shook and she fidgeted with the con badge around her neck, stroking it as if to calm herself. "The other top members of the CES are arriving tonight, and I wanted to give them my report. I didn't know—or if I did, I forgot—that I wasn't supposed to be here after a certain time." She leaned back and held her VIP badge up. It dangled around her neck, over her costume, breaking more of the illusion of the character. "It let me step through the hotel's teleportation pad. I just wanted to do a quick sweep and then go back to the hotel for the dinner."

"But the lights are mostly off," Nimue said. "That didn't seem like a sign to you that we'd closed down for the evening?"

Mia shrugged. "I didn't expect to meet anyone else here. I just thought, since I was your client paying for the whole thing, that I could come and inspect whenever I liked."

Mia's "inspections" had been never-ending, her ever-changing requests difficult to accommodate. Nimue supposed Mia's explanation tracked.

"But *did* you see anybody?" she asked.

"No!" Mia's eyes widened in terror. "I definitely didn't see a witch. I remember Linda—"

"Glinda," Nimue corrected.

Mia nodded, a bead of sweat on her brow. "I'd recognize her. I didn't see her. I didn't meet anyone until…" She frowned.

"I came tumbling down the hall in the air after you?" Nimue supplied.

A faltering smile appeared on Mia's face. "That scared the life out of me." Then her face fell. "Sorry. Inappropriate."

"It's all right," Nimue said. "But then, did you see that man I was after? I saw him before I noticed you, since he was standing in the light at the end of the hall." She pointed that way.

"I *did* see him," Mia said, "but only after you showed.

He didn't rush past me or anything. I know it was dark, but I think I would have seen someone running by." She pointed to the end of the hallway. "He just came from one side to the other. He froze in the entrance to the hallway when you shouted, but he didn't pass this way."

Nimue looked up at her dragon. "Gowdie? You're the one who said you saw someone. Was it Mia or the other person?"

"He can talk?" Mia asked, her jaw dropping.

"Just to me," Nimue said quickly. She wondered how Mia could have been so focused on the convention before that she hadn't even *noticed* the little dragon.

"*It was Mia, I think.*" Gowdie told Nimue. "*Someone looking out the window. Didn't notice that other guy at all, despite the sweep I was doing of the area.*"

Nimue nodded. At least that confirmed Mia's story. "How long have you been here?"

"I'm not sure." Mia smoothed out her cape and adjusted her legs beneath her. "I got dressed for the dinner"—Nimue didn't comment on the fact that she'd planned to wear a superheroine costume to it, apparently —"and was about to head to the banquet hall in the hotel, but I just wanted to do one more check. Make sure everything was ready for tomorrow." She bit her lip. "You really want the convention to go on as planned?"

"It has to," Nimue said again. "So would you say you've been here half an hour? Longer? Less time?"

"Half an hour sounds right." Mia looked around her. "I *did* walk the showroom floor, but I ran into nobody. I swear. Then I wanted to get a look at it from above." She nodded down the hallway toward the landing that would overlook the showroom floor. "I got distracted by the pretty view of the lake at night for a bit, but that's what I was doing up here."

Nimue looked across them to the wide windows. Lake Salem sparkled in the moonlight, she knew, an even prettier sight when the hallway wasn't flooded with light like it currently was. "Did you see anything? Hear anything?"

Mia nodded eagerly. "Oh, yes. Some sort of alarm went off down in the showroom floor. Just for a few seconds. That happened when I was making my way upstairs. I went back down to see what it was, but it had stopped already. Do you think that had to do with the murder?" She sat up straighter, on her calves, as if hoping they'd solved the mystery already and could put it all behind them.

"That was... me," Nimue said sheepishly. Gowdie flapped over toward them, seemingly satisfied Mia wasn't going to bolt, and started doing a swoop over the hallway.

"*Thanks for covering for me,*" he shouted mentally to her.

Nimue didn't totally let him off the hook, though. "My familiar was excited about the limited edition Super-stellar-Man golden figurines—"

"Dragons and gold, huh?" Mia said, letting out a light chuckle.

Gowdie slapped his talons across his face. "*The stereotypes.*"

"Yes, well, he landed on the pyramid of boxes. That set off the Charm we put up, the one where only members of your organization can touch the boxes until a sale is made."

"Morpheus walked me through that earlier today. I stacked that pyramid." Mia shot a look upward at the dragon, who was flying up and under over superhero banners hanging from above. "I got them settled just right. I hope you didn't mess it up."

"*Well, so-rry,*" Gowdie muttered, though Mia wouldn't hear his sarcastic tone.

"He's sorry," Nimue relayed. "And no, it's all fine."

Mia nodded, her eyes glazing over a bit as she kept nodding. Nimue wondered what, particularly, she was thinking about.

"So nothing else drew your attention?" Nimue asked.

Mia shook her head. "I didn't know what had set off the alarm—though I was going to ask the next member of Witchy ExS I ran into—but I went back to my plan of looking over the showroom floor from above. If anything was off, I thought I'd notice it then. I can't believe I didn't think of the alarm on the figures, after Morpheus told me about it. But we'd never tested it or anything, so I hadn't heard it before."

"But you never made it to the balcony?" Nimue asked.

Mia shook her head. "No. I sort of… I stared out the window. I don't know how long, sorry." She winced. "Sometimes I just get lost in thought like that. Especially when I'm stressed."

"*Hey!*" Gowdie shouted into Nimue's mind. "*I found something!*"

He swooped in for a landing at the end of the hallway,

where the figure had been backlit, and where both Zelena and Soren had gone to handle the search.

But both had missed something Gowdie had found.

"How's that for feeding into my own stereotypes?" Gowdie muttered. He was on the floor now, his foot tapping the ground and the talon clacking as he pointed something out. Both Nimue and Mia approached, the latter cradling one arm to her side and walking almost dejectedly a few steps behind Nimue.

This was the direction of the balcony, which Mia had claimed not to have reached before now.

On the floor, where the unknown man had briefly stood, was another glittering, golden object.

Nimue bent down to examine it.

"What is that?" she asked. "It looks like—"

"The Sword of Stellar Planet," Mia said, hovering overhead. "The limited edition sword packaged with the golden Superstellar-Man figurine. The one sharp enough to actually cut."

Nimue stared back at the toy sword, no larger than her palm. It wasn't entirely glittering gold. It was speckled here and there with a reddish-brown splatter.

"That looks like blood," Gowdie practically whispered.

CHAPTER NINE

Nimue thought starkly of Glinda bending down to pick up that golden hashtag pin in the History Charm moments before her death.

What was gold doing sprinkled throughout the convention center flooring?

"You should perform a History Charm right here while the others are busy. Or maybe an Origin Charm on the Sword of Stellar Planet." Gowdie came in for a landing beside the toy sword.

"Zelena and her team are more adept at Origin Charms," Nimue said aloud.

"You said that last month. And look what happened." He grunted.

Last month, Zelena had used an Origin Charm and pinpointed her own husband as the source of a threatening letter—a letter meant to be a distraction to throw everyone off the scent. And she hadn't shared that with Nimue or even Ren, whom she respected more. Later, she'd admitted it was because she'd wanted to confront

Linden about it first. And because she couldn't let herself believe her husband of over half a century could have been responsible for a murder.

How little she'd known him.

"Someone else on her team, then," Nimue pointed out.

"Um, excuse me?" In the stillness of this hallway, the theme of the Superstellar-Man movies rung out, though it was muffled and a touch tinny. Mia lifted her human smartphone into the air after digging it out of a pocket hidden in her cape. "The rest of the Comic Enthusiast Society Board must have arrived by now. One's calling. Can I take this?"

Sighing, Nimue looked from Mia to the toy sword on the ground and back. "Take your call, but don't go into details about what's wrong just yet. I'll get someone to escort you."

Mia gulped and touched her phone, putting it to her ear. Nimue tuned out their conversation as she brought her wrist up to focus on her witch network crystal.

Cary, she thought to it. *Charity. I need someone from the security team on the third-floor hallway, near the overlook. Is Zelena still tracking that suspect?*

It took a moment, but Charity wrote back. *No luck. Security team is spread out, hasn't found anyone. Zelena is about to call us back for a series of History Charms. We can swing by you first.*

Appreciated. Nimue's gaze tilted upward, and she took note of the gleam of one of her new perma-charm History Charm crystals.

She directed her next message to Zelena. *I'm borrowing Cary and Charity. Recommend visiting Security Office and examining the perma-charm History Charm recordings for an overall look at the scene.*

Nimue stood up and turned both directions, waiting for another witch to show. Mia was still on her phone, covering her lips with one hand as she whispered. Nimue grimaced. She wondered how much her client was sharing, and if what they were discussing would impact Witchy ExS. And the convention.

She was certain she could feel a quiet rumbling far beneath her feet.

After a moment, Zelena wrote back. *Roger. History Charms of the scene would be easier, though.*

Gowdie flapped his wings and landed on Nimue's shoulder, reading the message. *"Would it be, though? Seems like Zelena just wants to do things her way."*

It's always best to have someone on the ground, Zelena added.

Nimue messaged back. *Perform the traditional History Charms after the perma-charm check. If it's still necessary.*

Then she dismissed the witch network.

At the end of the hall, Cary Staten and Charity McAllister walked side by side, a warlock and a witch on the security team. Both were tall, their faces pinched, still wearing their witch and warlock hats above their security uniform tracksuits. Security team usually did go off-shift later than the rest of Witchy ExS.

"You summoned us?" Charity asked. She was thin, so her brown tracksuit hung oversized over her limbs. Her dirty-blonde hair was pulled back into a tight bun under her brown, conical hat, and her ruddy cheeks stood out against her orangish, tanned skin. Beside her, her pink chimp familiar, Lucas, was gazing in all directions, giving him the appearance of being shifty-eyed.

Nimue swallowed. "I have a potential murder weapon." She almost didn't realize she thought that until she'd said it aloud. It didn't completely make sense, but *something* sharp and small had cut Glinda, and this was suspiciously where that man had been. And there were the stains on it. She gestured down to the tiny sword on the ground. "I need an Origin Charm, a History Charm of this area…" She looked in the direction the man had run. "This is where I first spotted the suspect Zelena went after. I told her to head to the Security Office and examine the perma-charm History Charm footage, but it can't hurt to have someone on the ground here."

Gowdie let out a rumbly laugh. *"Isn't that what Zelena said?"*

Nimue patted his head as Miller, Cary's mint-green hare, raised her muzzle and twitched her nose rapidly. Everyone seemed to know about the tension between Zelena and Nimue. Nimue would argue perhaps it had to do with bad blood between the two since Zelena's grandmother was Gala Varlett, town founder Bessa Toothaker's best friend slash nemesis. Bessa being Nimue's own great-grandmother. But Zelena had respected Bernadette, Bessa's only daughter, just fine.

Still, the comments and asides had nearly dried up from Zelena since her own husband had been arrested. Perhaps she realized that put her on shaky ground.

"I need someone to escort Ms. Estrada back to her hotel room, too," Nimue added, looking over her shoulder. Mia pulled the phone away from her head and touched the screen, her shoulders rolling forward and her head drooping.

Charity stepped up and Nimue leaned in closer to her ear. "She's not a primary suspect, but everyone with access to the building at this time of night is a suspect until they're entirely cleared. She probably wants to meet with the other members of the Comic Enthusiast Society who just arrived, but make sure they stay where you can see them."

Charity nodded curtly and brushed past Nimue, introducing herself to Mia. Mia looked over her shoulder at Nimue one more time, but she hung her head and followed Charity and Lucas dutifully down the direction the mysterious figure had disappeared, to the nearest teleportation pad.

A fast runner could have been there and gone to *anywhere* before Zelena had even started the chase.

"Soren," Nimue said aloud to her witch network crystal, speaking for Cary's benefit, "anyone with VIP access needs to be questioned. Those at the dinner?"

"And anyone with staff access," Cary muttered. Most of the Witchy ExS staff was still sore about Linden. And now to lose Linden's replacement in an even more gruesome way… "And the hotel's staff."

"The hotel?" Nimue asked.

Cary shrugged. "Southern Hotel staff has all-access to the teleportation pads in the Bessa, too, with the perma-charms on their master keycards. Just in case they need to attend to a guest at the convention center."

Hmm. Nimue wasn't sure she'd known about the

Southern Hotel staff having after-hours access to the Bessa before.

Soren wrote back. *I'm on it. Been updating Cassie at the dinner. Dad is helping out as well. Every VIP member is here, other than Mia.*

"She's on her way with Charity," Nimue wrote, again speaking aloud. "The rest of the Comic Enthusiast Society is supposed to have arrived as well."

They came too late to have possibly been involved? Soren wrote back.

"We think, anyway," Nimue dictated. "Just check into them to be sure."

She lowered her witch network crystal and turned her attention to Cary, who was waving his wand over the toy sword without touching the suspicious item. The broad-shouldered security warlock looked a bit comical crouched on the ground, his hair completely hidden by his blue warlock hat.

"What have you got for me?" said Nimue, determined to catch the culprit as soon as possible.

"I doubt we're getting any sleep tonight." Gowdie sighed. The first day of a con, especially one as large as Comic Hero Con, was always stressful. They'd need all the rest they could get.

But no matter what... The loss of Glinda wouldn't allow for easy sleep.

Cary gave a frustrated shake of his head. "I can see it came from... a box? With a golden man?"

"The limited edition Superstellar-Man figurine." Nimue and Gowdie exchanged a look. Without even saying a word, Nimue knew. But who could touch the box… other than Mia herself? Unless another member of the Comic Enthusiast Society had arrived early. *Someone* would have noticed the alarm going off otherwise.

Though a witch could have performed an Undo Charm and a Protection Charm again to put the charm back in place, if they knew to expect the Protection Charm on the items.

Broomsticks. *The alarm system wasn't foolproof after all,* Nimue thought to Gowdie.

"It was only there for keeping human con-goer thieves away, really. And for upsetting blameless fanboy dragons."

Miller thumped over to Nimue's feet. Gowdie landed beside her, put a taloned foot on the hare's back and said, *"Let me catch you up to speed while your warlock is doing that."*

"After that box, though…" Cary shook his head and cut off the charm with a flourish of his wand. "Everything's unclear."

Nimue crossed her arms over the bodice of her dress. "Like a witch used an Obscure Charm or something?"

Cary produced a little bag from the pouch at his belt and gently nudged the sword inside it with the tip of his wand. "Probably not. Origin Charms are tricky to begin with. They're focused more on the item's moment of creation than anything else. In my vision, I saw what appeared to be a factory." He stood, tying the bag closed with a drawstring, and Miller hopped over to him, her nose twitching, and Cary appeared to be listening. "Yes, that makes sense. Part of one of those limited edition toys downstairs. I could pinpoint its moment of being crafted and slid into a box, but other than that, its journey from then to now—it was less important to the essence of the thing." He grimaced. "Even if it wound up being used for nefarious purposes."

Nimue let out a deep sigh. "Then try to track who might have grabbed it with a History Charm."

Cary nodded and tucked the bag back into his pouch. Then he waved his wand, his mouth opening.

"Wait!" said Nimue, a sudden thought striking her. "Where's Glinda now?"

"I understood Florence hovered her to her clinic. She confirmed the cause of death to be the wound to the neck." Cary swallowed. "She cleaned up any trace of the crime, too, though for now, it's still being hidden away behind a Concealment Charm so we can investigate the area."

"Glinda was holding a pin," Nimue explained. "It looked like a hash brown." The word felt foreign in her mouth. "An internet hash brown," she clarified.

Miller's head cocked.

Gowdie laughed. *"Not a hash brown. A hashtag."*

Nimue grimaced. "In the History Charm Ren did, we saw her bend over and pick it up just a few moments before she d-died." She stumbled over the acknowledgement that her work friend was gone. "We need an Origin Charm on that. It was still in her fist, last I knew."

Cary nodded. "I'll confer with Zelena and get in touch with the clinic to let them know. Assuming they didn't already pass it over to the security team." He looked at her. "Want to stay for the History Charm?"

Nimue nodded.

Cary cast the charm and the two of them and their

familiars moved in reverse in the illusion as Cary worked his way quickly backward through the scene. Charity and Mia left one way, then Soren, then Zelena, who'd appeared on the scene just as quickly. And before that, there was the figure with the briefcase.

"Hold it," Nimue said.

Cary did. Though she couldn't see herself as she currently was, she walked around, feeling Gowdie hop onto her leg and grip her ankle as she passed him.

"You nearly kicked me," he protested.

Sorry, she sent back. But she was focused on the man.

The lighting here—bright against the darkness of the hallway in this moment of time—pretty much obscured him entirely. There could be no enhancing the visual or swapping out the light. This was a record of this moment in time.

"Broomsticks," Gowdie muttered. *"Wonder if those human cameras would have allowed for more light editing."*

No one would have known how to operate a human camera system at the Bessa. They would have said it was unnecessary, considering their magic.

Maybe magic wasn't infallible after all.

"Keep going back," Nimue said.

She watched as the History Charm rolled back, focusing on any sign of the figure dropping that toy sword, but there was no glint of light, no subtle movement from the man's hand or briefcase to the floor as he walked backward—into the shadow. Into further obscurity. And down the stairs.

"Not very easy to identify him," Cary said, his deep voice gruff.

"Agreed." Nimue sighed. "Hopefully, Zelena can catch sight of him from another angle with the perma-charm crystals."

"Should I dismiss this, then?" Cary asked.

"Sure—Wait." Nimue held her hand up, though she knew Cary wouldn't have been able to see it. She crouched down to the ground, Gowdie shifting off her ankle as she did so.

It was hard to see, but that was what she'd been looking for. A golden glint on the carpet.

"This is *before* that man heads this way?" Nimue asked.

"Yes. Why?"

Despite knowing she wouldn't feel it, Nimue reached out to touch the toy sword. It was just as she'd found it later, with blood stained on the metal.

"The murder weapon was already here," she said. "That man who ran by wasn't the one who'd dropped it."

CHAPTER TEN

"**W**hat *next?*" Gowdie asked as Nimue headed toward the nearest teleportation pad, clutching the staff member badge over her neck embedded with a perma-charm crystal that would give her all-access.

"Cary's off to confer with Zelena on our findings and go over the perma-charm History Charm security footage," Nimue reminded him, "so that means we'll join Soren and Cassie at the VIP dinner."

"Do you still have an appetite after all this?" Gowdie cocked his head.

Nimue put a hand on her abdomen. She *was* feeling light-headed, but no, she didn't have much of an appetite. "We're not going for dinner." They reached the teleportation pad, and Nimue took a deep breath, stepping through. The white glow blinked black as she made it to the Southern Hotel.

The lobby was more crowded than she'd figured it'd be at this time of night, early arrivals for the con's opening day milling about the space—a number of whom were in costume already. Fidelity looked focused behind the front counter, helping the front of a long line of guests alongside another witch on the hotel staff.

Esmerelda was talking to two men in identical Super-stellar-Man T-shirts—a design Nimue had seen Mia wearing earlier that evening. She looked up as Nimue crossed by the lobby and excused herself, making her way over to join Nimue as the latter headed for the hallway leading to the banquet hall.

"Nimmy!" she cried, though she kept her voice hushed.

Nimue stopped and allowed Esmerelda to take her by the arm and guide her into the darkened hallway. Gowdie and Faulkner bobbed their heads at one another.

Esmerelda glanced down at Nimue's hip, where her wand was glowing in its holster. "Were you not able to Undo that glow?" she asked, blinking. It *was* particularly bright in the dark.

"Used it up today," Nimue said.

"May I?" Esmerelda reached across her torso to get her own wand out from the holster at her right hip.

Nimue took her wand out and nodded. "Thanks."

"Undo Glow Charm," Esmerelda said, waving her wand in the air in front of Nimue's.

The glow stopped, and both witches holstered their wands once more.

Esmerelda's face fell. "Soren filled me in. Poor Glinda." The older witch cradled her arm, looking down. "Glinda was a loner, true, but she was my friend. We grew up together—her, her brother, Clarke, and I."

Clarke was her husband, Soren's father.

"I didn't know that," said Nimue. It was hard to tell witches' ages most of the time. Her own parents were slightly over a hundred, which would have made them a bit older than Soren's parents. "I'm sorry for your loss."

"Why, you could find Glinda here a lot of mornings, dropping by to say *hello*." Esmerelda brushed a lock of hair behind her ear and Faulkner the snake stuck her tongue out from around her witch's neck. "It was all cordial these days, mind you. Age makes people grow apart. But still… This kind of thing hits you, you know? You wish you'd taken the time to stay closer. I mean, we lived in the same town and yet, I barely made the time to reach out to her…"

Nimue swallowed. "We'll find who did this." It was all she could offer.

Esmerelda let out a deep sigh. "I wondered if I might be the one to contact her brother? We were close… once." Her eyes flittered.

"Yes, of course. But perhaps not yet," Nimue told her. "Not until we have some answers for him."

She nodded glumly, then gestured down the hall. "Soren and Cassie are at the VIP dinner. We're still serving it—no sense in anyone going hungry—but Zelena has some of the security team posted outside to make sure everyone stays put until their alibis are clear." Nimue's stomach grumbled and Esmerelda smiled. "Perhaps you should get something to eat, too." She stepped back and took a look at her. "You look stunning."

Nimue felt her cheeks blush. "Thank you."

Esmerelda *tsked*. "Shame this evening took such a terrible turn. Speaking of, do *you* know why my son is present at the moment? Don't get me wrong, I do love to see Soren, but—"

"Ren usually has a better handle on crises," Nimue agreed.

"He just handles heroically catching his co-Head Witch General Manager crushes a whole lot worse than sensitive Soren," Gowdie added, nudging the side of her head with his elbow.

Faulkner perked up at that, looking toward her witch. Nimue wondered if she was relaying Gowdie's comment.

Thanks for that, Nimue muttered as Esmerelda put her left hand over her mouth, taking another look at Nimue as if seeing her for the first time.

"Soren's gotten braver," Nimue said, straightening. "And I think he's ready to step up."

"Hmm." Esmerelda tapped a long finger over her lips. "You know, I never imagined my son working for Witchy ExS. We always thought he'd take over the hotel—and even then, that would be only reluctantly."

Clearing her throat, Nimue looked to the ground. She wasn't sure now was the best time to talk about this, but she didn't want to be rude. "He… He's very creative," she said. "Whimsical."

"Airheaded," Esmerelda snapped. But then she laughed at herself. "Don't get me wrong—I love all of that about him. Lydia certainly did, too. She was perfect for him." She sighed. Lydia had died so young. "At first, Clarke and I thought 'Ren' was Soren's way of coping."

"He kind of is," Nimue pointed out.

"Yes, I know, but he's also *another person.*"

Everyone knew that now. Bernadette and Nimue's

other grandma, Prue, had studied him extensively. Nimue had been married to Greg and living in a human town at the time, but she'd heard it all later.

"A wandering warlock spirit," Nimue said. "Ripped from the energy of the cauldron and trapped inside Soren during the backfire."

Esmerelda leaned closer. "It was Lydia's fault, you know. She was the potions brewer. And she was always *pushing* things. Trying to create new magic."

Nimue bit her bottom lip. She hadn't been especially close to Lydia, but she'd liked her. She didn't want to disparage the poor, dead witch. "Well, she *did* do something no one ever had before."

"Yes, but I don't think her intentions were to die and stick a wandering warlock spirit into my son." Esmerelda shook her head. "You know, you're good for him."

Nimue's eyes snapped back up. "Sorry?"

"I always thought you and he would make a good couple, long after your little childhood sweethearts fling was over. Why *did* that end anyway?"

Gowdie snickered, and Nimue knew she had to admit the truth before it got through the familiars' grape vine anyway.

"I was jealous because he kept talking to other girls," Nimue said. "He was always so friendly to *everyone*, not just me. But keep in mind I was *ten*—"

Esmerelda laughed. "I won't judge you. But I hoped you'd make it work out when you were older. You'd ground him. Then you left and he turned to Lydia. What's done is done."

Nimue opened her mouth to speak, her mind a mess

of far more important things at the moment. Still, she wanted to clarify a few things. "My marriage to Greg had nothing to do with Soren choosing to marry Lydia—"

"It had *everything* to do with it!" Esmerelda's voice grew just slightly louder. "He nursed a broken heart when you went away. He'd wanted to ask you out again as an adult, and he just hadn't screwed up the courage." Faulkner's tongue darted out and Esmerelda ran a hand through her hair, brushing it out of her face like her son often did, a lock getting caught on her wedding ring for a moment. "Though perhaps it's none of my business."

"Soren doesn't—He didn't..." Nimue took a deep breath.

"He didn't seem embarrassed at all about revealing Ren's crush on you. You'd think he would have if he felt the same way," Gowdie pointed out.

Faulkner stuck her tongue out again and Gowdie nodded, taking in her half of the conversation.

"Balfour has told her that Soren's always had a crush on you. That's part of why Ren finds you so irritating, only lately, Ren himself has started feeling—"

"Okay!" shouted Nimue aloud, her skin on fire. "Esmerelda, I appreciate the help, but I really need to go."

Esmerelda nodded but smiled, sending a wink her familiar's way. "If my son is going to take so long to tell you himself, he can't blame his mother for trying."

"Now's not a good time," Nimue said, walking away. That was true enough.

She headed away from Esmerelda, her mind unable to push aside all of the interactions she'd had with Soren and Ren over the years, despite the gravity of the situation. Charity and her pink chimp familiar, Lucas, flanked the doors to the banquet hall up ahead and she tried to focus on them.

But Soren... had always been a friend to her. But surely, just a friend, right?

She remembered how jealous she'd been thinking Soren and Nicola, Lydia's human friend, might have had a romantic attachment last month—but Nicola had been seeing another man entirely.

And in all these years since Nimue had been back in Cauldron Cove, she'd never seen Soren—or Ren, but that had never been as surprising to her, considering his dour personality—interested in dating anyone.

She'd chalked it up to grief over the loss of his wife.

Now she wondered... if she'd been missing something else.

Gowdie snickered. *"Who'd have thunk Nimue Toothaker would be interested in romance once again."*

"Quiet," Nimue hissed at him. Lucas's ears perked up as they approached. She hoped he was just taking a survey of the potential security risk and not picking up on Gowdie's quip about her love life.

Lucas winked up at Nimue as she stood in front of Charity.

Gowdie giggled again.

She sighed and focused on the security witch. "Anything to report?"

Charity shook her head. "No. I escorted Mia inside. Two of the four members of the Comic Enthusiast Society Board were already there. The other two should arrive shortly, she said."

"I might have seen them in the lobby," Nimue said, wondering if they all had those matching Superstellar-Man T-shirts.

Charity nodded. "I'll let them in if they approach. Esmerelda was going to make sure they got their VIP badges."

"All right, thank you." Nimue was about to step inside, when she noticed Soren at the end of the hallway. She walked away from Charity and Lucas and headed toward him, but she froze when she saw Soren put his hand on someone's back and turn around the corner. Nimue headed to the end of the hallway and peeked around the corner for a better look, not wanting Soren to know she was spying on him.

"*Is that Clarke?*" Gowdie asked, referring to Soren's father. The blond warlock was hunched over, a bit more disheveled than his usual debonair self.

"Is he crying?" Nimue asked. His face looked red, anyway, and he seemed about to fall over. His blue red panda familiar jumped harrowingly around his ankles, as if panicked. Soren had to stumble to catch his father and Clarke waved him off, a faint smile on his face. Did that mean... Did Clarke know about Glinda? Had Soren just told him? Would that have caused him such distress? Clarke had been helping with the dinner until now, according to Soren's message.

Gowdie flapped his wings and flew closer to them, just as Soren and Clarke went their separate ways, Soren turning left toward the back entrance to the banquet hall, Balfour staying back just a moment and looking up at Gowdie as Clarke left in the direction of the elevators.

Gowdie flew back. *"Checked in with Balfour real quick. She said Soren did tell Clarke about Glinda earlier, but he stuck around to help with dinner before he bolted. He didn't want to talk about whatever was upsetting him. He said he just wasn't feeling well and wanted to go to bed. But Frone, Clarke's familiar, was clearly worried about him. Kept groaning and saying, 'Nuts, nuts, nuts.'"*

"'Nuts'?"

He shrugged as he settled on Nimue's shoulder. *"They messed something up, maybe?"*

Nimue frowned. Maybe his distress hadn't had to do with Glinda's death after all. She headed back through the entryway Charity and Lucas were guarding, knowing she didn't have clearance to unlock back doors in the hotel like Soren did.

The banquet hall was full with about forty people at a glance. All the comic book writers, artists, and editors were seated together at a few tables, and most had a family member or two alongside them—more than the authors and booksellers had had last month during a similar VIP dinner.

There was a head table where Nimue would have been due to sit, and that was where she found Soren and Cassie, Soren just sitting down again. Beside Cassie was a surprisingly meek Mia, who picked at the steak on her plate, two talkative men in those Superstellar-Man T-shirts discussing something beside her.

Nimue let the room soak her in—or more accurately, her dragon, as he always caused a few tongues to wag—and approached the head table. Gowdie took to the air, taking the stares and a few whispers along with him.

She stood on the opposite side of the table, in front of Soren and Cassie. Cassie Cabot, their shared assistant, looked a bit tired beneath her wide, green witch's hat, her wavy, blond hair hanging limply down and just skirting her shoulders. She had on a green evening gown that complemented her sepia-tone skin and brought out the bright green of her eyes. She looked almost as sullen as Mia beside her, but she instantly snapped to attention as Nimue approached.

"There've been a few updates," Nimue told them, her eyes darting to the members of the Comic Enthusiast Society beside Mia, then back to Soren, but if he knew about Balfour and Gowdie's little tête-à-tête, he didn't say anything. Maybe he figured it was a private, family matter.

"Only Ms. Estrada knows," Cassie said, her softly feminine voice at odds with her take-charge personality. "We decided not to let the news get out until after the convention."

"Or until we know the truth of what happened," Soren added quietly. He stood again and gestured toward an unoccupied corner of the room.

Cassie and Nimue headed in that direction, the plates in front of where Soren and Cassie had been sitting still untouched.

Nimue cradled her own stomach, which almost took her off her feet with a sharp pain of hunger and distress, and leaned up against the wall as they met in the corner. Balfour, who must have slipped under the table, settled across Soren's feet, and Laveau, Cassie's forest-green ferret, jumped up into his witch's arms.

Gowdie let out a little roar of fire and the room burst into applause.

"Looks like Gowdie's got the room distracted for us," Cassie said.

Nimue's dragon winked at her as he flew overhead.

Nimue gave him a thumbs-up and updated Soren and Cassie about her finds with Cary. She blinked hard the first time she found herself looking into Soren's dark-brown eyes but had to look away.

The pain in her stomach had softened somewhat at the sight of his face. Even the scar that ran across it from the accident with his wife made him seem… gentle, somehow.

Cassie snapped her back to the moment. "So that was the murder weapon. And the suspicious man might not have dropped it?"

"Not unless he'd already run that way before," Nimue said. "But I kept having Cary take us backward in time. We couldn't figure out who'd dropped it. People passed by earlier in the afternoon, sure, but we never pinpointed who might have dropped that sword. Besides, that was long before Glinda… died."

"Are we sure it's Glinda's blood on there?" Soren looked a bit green. Balfour meowed from the ground and he winced. "Ren just won't come back," he whispered. "Sorry. I know he can handle things like this better than I can."

"You're doing great." Nimue took his hand in hers and squeezed. Then her eyes widened as she realized what she was doing and let go. Soren rubbed at the back of his neck and looked at the floor. "Thanks."

Cassie didn't seem to notice the oddness of the exchange between them. "Mr. Southern tells me the time of death was about 5:50?"

"Yes. That much, we could determine anyway. Zelena's supposed to be checking out the perma-charm History Charm footage so we can see what Glinda was up to before she wandered the showroom floor."

"Well, I was here at that time," said Cassie, though Nimue knew she didn't mean it to establish her own alibi. "And so were a number of these guests. People tend to arrive early when there's food involved. We had some hors d'oeuvres ready. Soren's dad kept running back and forth between the kitchen and the dining room to make sure we had enough."

Nimue looked around at the crowded room. Gowdie had landed on the table in front by Mia and was doing a little dance now, to the delight of much of the crowd.

"All of those people were here," Cassie said, gesturing to the tables of comic book artists, illustrators, and editors. "And them. And them." She nodded at each one in turn. Laveau twitched his nose and climbed up to her shoulder.

"Oh, right, the two members of the CES were late—and Mia came much later, as you know."

Nimue studied the men beside Mia. They'd stopped talking long enough to observe Gowdie dancing across the table right in front of them. One reached beside his empty plate to grab a briefcase off the table to make room for Gowdie to dance.

A briefcase.

"We'll need to talk to them," Nimue said. The man at

the end of the hallway had been carrying a briefcase—
and only members of the CES could touch those figurines
without setting off an alarm. Well, or a careful witch or
warlock.

"Don't forget the movie star," Soren said.

Nimue blinked. Could Maverick have come here?
Hadn't he requested his dinner be in his room?

She gazed over the room. Sure enough, there he was—
his table full with his three bodyguards and his assistant.
Maverick looked more like Colton Carter at the moment
—a wide smile on his face, a friendly, approachable
demeanor. His dinner was only half-eaten, though, and
he held his fork to it as his focus was exclusively on
Gowdie a few tables away.

"When did they get here?" Nimue asked.

"Not until after I did," said Soren.

So none of them had Cassie for an alibi.

And two of Maverick's men had carried a briefcase,
too.

Esther took a sip of water and then her focus zeroed in
on Nimue, Soren, and Cassie in the corner. She leaned
over to Maverick and whispered something to him. He
nodded, and she stood.

Maverick's eyes moved from Gowdie—who was just
wrapping up his dance, his wings spread wide—straight
to Nimue.

Nimue blinked hard and looked away, but she noticed
Esther approaching them.

"All right," Nimue said. "We need to establish the
whereabouts of Maverick's team and those members of
the CES at the time of the incident."

"Shouldn't Ms. Varlett and her team do the asking?" Cassie proposed.

"Zelena needs to focus on the perma-charm History Charm crystals. And current surveillance. A killer is still out there."

Soren and Cassie nodded grimly.

"Perhaps you should handle Mr. Vanedestine," Cassie suggested. "We heard you made good headway with him—"

"Did I hear my boss's name?"

Everyone turned around. Esther had headed straight for them.

Nimue smiled as Gowdie flapped across the room and landed on her shoulder, his breathing shallow.

"Distracted them as long as I could," he told her.

Excellent work, Nimue thought directly to him. *You've got some wicked dance moves.*

He chuckled.

"Esther," she said aloud. "Yes, we were… concerned about Maverick's appearances tomorrow. We want to make sure he's entirely comfortable and that all of his panels and signing sessions go off without a hitch."

"He'll be there." Esther cradled one arm by the elbow. "That's actually why I came over here. He wondered if you might… be there to walk the floor with him?"

Nimue blinked, then looked over her shoulder. But Cassie and Soren tilted their heads at her.

"Me?" she asked, whipping back around.

Esther laughed. "Yes, you. Because he hasn't felt as comfortable around a witch as he did with you in… a long time." Esther nodded. "The security team and I thought, well, if he had you with him during the con… I know you must be busy, but—"

"She'll do it," Cassie said, jumping up to stand closer to Nimue. "Mr. Southern and I can take care of everything else. A VIP's comfort is of the highest importance. As is their *schedule*." She gripped Nimue's arm and squeezed it, as if to signal her.

Nimue jumped. Right. Someone needed to figure out where Maverick and his team had been before coming to the dinner—though she doubted they'd had anything to do with Glinda's murder. Why would they?

"I'd be happy to." Nimue smiled.

Esther beamed, her freckles flexing as the smile worked its way across her face. "Thank you! Thank you!" She took Nimue by both hands. "You don't know how relieved this makes me." She looked over her shoulder and then back to Nimue, leaning in and lowering her voice. "Though fair warning—I think my boss has a bit of a crush on you."

Nimue's jaw dropped.

Gowdie guffawed. *"Looks like Nimue's in her second bloom."*

CHAPTER ELEVEN

Tituba would have chastised her for having a very quick and meager meal of bread and the fish left on Soren's plate, which he'd offered to her so she wouldn't have to wait for the hotel staff to bring her own dish. But Tituba wasn't here. Most of the Witchy ExS staff was off-duty and still needed to be informed about the murder—something Nimue wasn't quite ready to face. Not until they knew who had done this. After eating, Nimue was about to break off from Cassie and Soren, as the three planned to go their separate ways as the VIP room dispersed for the evening. Soren was going to touch base with Zelena and the rest of the security team, Cassie was going to ascertain the alibi of the new arrivals from the CES under the guise of welcoming the client, and Nimue was to escort Maverick to his room to get his team's alibi as well.

Several of the other VIP members were gathered in a corner of the banquet hall as Nimue headed toward Maverick's table. Everyone there was standing, likely not expecting Nimue to join them until the next morning. But she would come up with an excuse to touch base with them earlier.

She practically tripped over something soft at her ankles before she managed to get there, though.

Balfour rammed into her shins over and over, like a normal housecat rubbing her scent over one of her humans.

"She's probably marking you on behalf of Ren and Soren, heh." Gowdie flapped his wings and took to the air. Balfour stuck her little snooty nose up at him. He cackled. *"I'll stall 'em."* Then he flew over to Maverick's group and the celebrity's nervous, clipped smile broadened into a wide look of excitement that took over his expression.

Soren appeared behind Nimue, taking hold of her elbow and speaking in a hushed tone. He'd been conferring with Cassie before heading out last Nimue had known.

He looked tired, the skin under his eyes darkening. That was how Nimue felt, too.

"I just wanted to tell you… to be careful," he said softly.

Balfour was weaving between all of their legs now.

Nimue smiled gently, feeling the tension in her body ease slightly. "You, too."

"Thanks. But I mean…" His gaze darted over her shoulder to Maverick, who held his hand out as if awaiting a bird of prey and chuckled deeply when Gowdie landed on it. "Celebrities are fickle." Soren seemed to just notice he had Nimue by the arm and dropped it as suddenly as if it burned him.

Nimue felt a tingling in her chest she didn't have the brain space to address just then. "He's certainly… something," she added. But as she stared over at Maverick, she found herself softening. He sure was a handsome man, Maverick Vanedestine.

Balfour nipped at her foot through her shoe and Nimue let out a yelp.

"Balfour!" Soren chastised. The cat familiar jumped up into Soren's arms. She purred loudly as Nimue glared at her. It had hurt for a second, but she didn't think the bite would leave a mark or anything.

"I know," Soren whispered, leaning down to his familiar. "But you never *bite* anyone, for cauldron's sake."

"Unless it's the culprit we're looking for," Nimue said, giving Balfour her due for helping take down Linden's familiar last month.

Balfour purred and closed her eyes, her nose going even higher as her warlock pet her.

"I just want you to be on your guard. Against any… flirtation." Soren cleared his throat. "Balfour said you were drooling after him. Maverick."

"I was *not*." Nimue flapped a hand over her face as if to cool it. "And I've *seen* the man curled up on the floor in fright. Bit of an awkward first impression. Made me feel sorry for him, though. I think that'll cross my mind every time I interact with him. Besides, Esther was probably just teasing me." She narrowed her eyes on Soren and he shirked back a bit. "*And* I think we have more important things to worry about right now." She turned to go, but she hesitated, clenching her hand into a fist. "But thank you. For your concern."

She didn't wait to see how he might respond.

As she approached Maverick's group, Jaxson, Kovac, and Davies all gave her a onceover, though Jaxson's was somehow friendlier than the other two's, both of whom clenched his own briefcase in his hand. Esther waved and walked up to her. "Did you need something before tomorrow?" She glanced at Gowdie, preening himself like a bird on Maverick's arm. "Or are you just here to pick up your dragon?"

Nimue held her own arm out and Gowdie took his cue, flapping his wings and coming over. "I was wondering if we might talk?" She grew quiet as a group of VIPs walked by, deep in discussion. Nimue picked up the words "underwater castle" and "issue 781" before they passed out into the hall. "Somewhere quiet?"

Esther arched a brow and stepped aside, as if to give Maverick a better view of the witch.

Nimue's breath caught. "I mean—I need to talk to *all of you*. About tomorrow."

"Mm-hmm," said Esther, though she seemed to be suppressing a smile. "Well, Mr. Vanedestine?"

"Let's head back to my room," Maverick said, running a hand through his luscious, dark locks. Nimue flinched as she realized she'd even thought that. "All of us," he added. Then he winked.

"Guess he's not afraid of witches anymore," Gowdie said, mirth in his voice.

They filed past the security witch and warlock outside the banquet hall door, and Nimue nodded at Charity as Soren seemed to be filling the security team in.

Maverick's group headed for the elevator, faint classical music echoing out from the hotel lobby, as well as the murmur of conversations as yet more guests arrived. Check-in times went late to accommodate travelers who wanted to sleep on site the night before a convention began, and Comic Hero Con was one of their busiest annual conventions.

Esther pushed the button and the group waited. Nimue took note of the fact that Jaxson, Kovac, and Davies formed a triangle behind and to the sides of Maverick, Davies placing himself just slightly between the elevator and his celebrity charge. People lingered nearby, a few whispering in hushed tones, but some of the other VIP guests formed a cloister around Maverick between him and any meandering hotel guests. Even they couldn't stop themselves from looking over at the movie star every few moments.

Maverick clenched his hands together in front of his abdomen, standing with his legs apart, very much in imitation of Superstellar-Man himself.

"Mr. Vanedestine needs to be in bed by midnight," Esther said, not dropping a beat as the elevator door opened and a group of several women and a couple of men stepped out. Davies pressed backward to allow them space, and Kovac and Jaxson closed in on Maverick as well.

"It's Maverick Vanedestine!" said one of the women, a rather tall woman in a Megastellar-Woman baby tee that hugged her curves tightly.

Esther reached out to stop the elevator door from closing. "Tomorrow, ladies. Sorry. Mr. Vanedestine has to go."

Maverick offered a quick wave as he stepped inside

the elevator, moving as a unit with his three security guards. Nimue watched with a strange fascination until she noticed Esther's eyes widening, her head nodding toward the elevator.

Nimue scrambled inside just as Esther stepped in front of her to stop another of the VIPs from joining them. Despite her small stature, she carried herself taller. "If you don't mind catching the next one. Thank you." Her smile seemed pasted on.

Nimue had to admit she'd briefly wondered, earlier today, how the flustered young woman had gotten her job in the first place. But she seemed to be doing a good job of crowd control.

"Who's that woman with Maverick?" the baby-tee woman asked the man beside her. "His girlfriend?"

"A *witch*?" he said back, as if the prospect were unbelievable.

It really was. For so many reasons.

The elevator door slid closed and Esther hit a button before turning around to look up at Nimue, who was adjusting her witch's hat awkwardly.

"If we stopped to talk to every fan at the convention, he'd never get anywhere. We have a schedule to keep." She glanced at a digital watch on her wrist. "And Mr. Vanedestine has exactly four hours before he needs his beauty sleep. That includes time for grooming, a bath—"

"Thank you, Esther." Maverick's jaw clenched through his tight smile. "Our guest doesn't need to know everything about my routine, down to when I shave."

Esther's freckled complexion flushed red as she faced forward and the door opened.

Jaxson stepped out first, looking both ways, then nodded, this the apparent signal for the group to head out.

Nimue couldn't help but remember the sight of the strapping celebrity on the ground as they approached the man's hotel suite. Esther pulled the keycard out of her pocket and waved the perma-charm crystal embedded in the device over the door handle. The door opened.

Nimue stepped through after Jaxson and Esther as Maverick gestured she should.

Gowdie grew lax on her arm, as if about to melt. *"He really can be a gentleman, can't he?"*

Don't forget we're here for a reason, Nimue thought to him. *And it's not to get his autograph, either.*

Maverick shut the door behind him, but Davies and Kovac hadn't stepped through.

"Oh!" said Nimue, for they were among her top suspects for the shadowy figure at the end of the convention center hallway. "I need to speak with them, too."

Maverick cocked his head as he took a load off on the couch in the center of the suite.

Jaxson stood behind and to the side of Maverick. "Anything you want them to know about the con, I can relay to them. They're doing a sweep and then getting some rest before their next shifts. We work in shifts overnight."

Broomsticks, thought Nimue. They could be off to any number of dastardly deeds, and Soren had been counting on *her* keeping an eye on them. But she wasn't sure she wanted to let this group in on the murder just yet. Maverick certainly didn't need another reason to freak out and not show up to his scheduled appearances. That would devastate the crowd of con-goers, which would in turn send bad energy to the giant cauldron, endangering the lives of everyone here.

"I'm not even sure you should hint at a security issue." Gowdie took off from her arm and settled on the back of the couch, letting Maverick call him a "good Dee-Dee" and pet him under his chin. *"Not until you feel you have no choice. I'm turning out to be his emotional support dragon, but even I might not be able to stop him from having another anxiety attack if he has reason to fear a witch again."*

The killer might not be a witch, she thought back quickly. She smoothed down the front of her evening gown and took a step forward.

Though she didn't see how magic couldn't have been involved in some capacity.

Esther had seated herself in the armchair kitty-corner to Maverick and was tapping at her human phone screen.

"Well, um, I wanted to check Mr. Vanedestine's schedule for tomorrow—"

Maverick stopped petting Gowdie long enough to lean his elbow on the top of the couch and wink at Nimue. "'Maverick.' Please."

Nimue's voice caught just a bit, but she kept plowing on. "I, unfortunately, have a lot of tasks that will keep me busy tomorrow, but assuring that Mr.—er, *Maverick* gets to his scheduled appearances on time—er, comfortably, is important, too."

"You can't just stay with me the whole day?" Maverick asked. He scooped Gowdie off the back of the couch and put him on his lap like a cat. "You and this little guy?"

Nimue chuckled despite herself. Maybe he had a crush on Gowdie that everyone was mistaking for a crush on Nimue.

"I'd be happy to send someone from Guest Services, but—"

"No." Maverick's pets grew a bit rough on Gowdie, and the dragon's eyes grew wider. "No other witches."

Esther looked up from her phone at that.

Nimue quickly moved forward to extend her arms out for Gowdie, but Maverick's pets had eased, and he mistook her approach. He scooted aside to leave just enough space for her on the couch between him and the armrest.

She took the seat, sticking her legs together awkwardly in front of her. "I'll do my best to be here," she said.

The stiffness in Esther's shoulders slunk and she looked back to her screen. "I'll email you Mr. Vanedestine's schedule for the con, then. Unless you have the itinerary?"

Cassie did, but Nimue didn't want to bother her to ask. "Best send it again," she said, rattling off the human-compatible email address she used to redirect important human messages to her witch network perma-charm crystal. Ren had set it up for her ages ago, back when she'd been her grandmother's assistant.

Nimue's eyes darted to the clock, but there were still a few hours before Maverick was supposed to go to bed.

Nimue didn't want to spend hours here when she still didn't know what the others had found out.

How to approach the topic, though?

"Ask if they've had a chance to check out the Bessa yet," Gowdie suggested.

"Did you have a chance to check out the convention center yet?" Nimue asked, clutching the dress at her knees. It was hard to look into Maverick's smoldering eyes for long.

Gowdie flapped his wings and took off between Maverick and Nimue, breaking the eye contact and settling on a table behind Maverick.

"Uh, no." Maverick's leg bounced and he grabbed it, pulling it up to cross his ankle over his knee. "Haven't gone anywhere but here and the banquet hall yet."

"Oh. I think you'll like it. Can't wait to show you for your first panel tomorrow—"

"At ten a.m.," Esther finished for her.

"Right." Nimue tucked a strand of hair behind her ear, jostling her witch's hat. She looked at Esther. "What about you?" She gazed over her shoulders at Jaxson. "Any of you? The other two, too? Have you seen any of Cauldron Cove yet?" She felt dumb asking, considering she'd seen both Jaxson and Esther at Sylvie's Bakery. But she didn't know how else to get the conversation going.

The assistant and the bodyguard exchanged a look.

"Mr. Vanedestine has needed me," Esther said.

"I looked around town after we arrived, but then I went back on duty," Jaxson added. "Kovac and Davies took a brief tour of the convention center with your security team this afternoon."

Esther nodded.

"The ones with the briefcases on them all the time," Gowdie pointed out. He was poking his nose around a pile of boxes, bags, and other miscellaneous things. Half looked to be wrapped in pristine paper or tied with ribbons. The other half looked opened, as if someone had gotten bored of looking through a giant stack of birthday gifts partway through.

"My assistant told me you were late to the VIP dinner," Nimue said.

"As were you." Maverick leaned in, and Nimue found herself leaning back, but the armrest wouldn't let her go very far. His breath was warm on the air between them. "I looked for you."

"Oh, well, as I said, I'm quite busy during a convention." She cleared her throat. "And shortly before it. But you, uh, was your security team all back by then? You could have wandered around the Bessa or strolled around town—"

"Mr. Vanedestine likes to stay inside his hotel room," Jaxson said. "Davies and Kovac got back around 5:30—plenty of time to make it to the dinner on time—but Mr. Vanedestine still wasn't sure he wanted to go, so I excused them to their rooms for a break."

"How long of a break?" Nimue asked.

Jaxson's eyebrows squished together. Nimue supposed it *was* an odd question out of context.

"I just mean—couldn't have been for too long. My assistant saw you all at the banquet hall…"

"We got there around a quarter after six," Jaxson said.

So Jaxson had seen both men around 5:30… But not

necessarily around 5:50 and 6:00, when the murder had occurred and a briefcase-carrying man had been spotted at the Bessa.

Esther piped up, though her attention was still on her phone. "It was only the thought of maybe seeing you and your dragon that got Mr. Vanedestine to leave."

Still leaning over on the couch, Maverick shot Esther a glare, but she didn't seem to notice. Nimue took the opportunity to stand when a bag or something crumpled rather loudly under Gowdie's feet.

"Gowdie!" Nimue said. "Sorry. He seems to be playing around with your things."

"Those are just gifts." Maverick waved his hand. "Whenever I go somewhere, companies and fans and everyone send tons of gifts."

Nimue hadn't noticed them when she'd been in the room this morning. Or at least not such a giant stack of them.

Esther nodded. "They've been arriving all afternoon." She looked up. "And it's up to me to sort through them. I end up sending most to charity, frankly. We can't be handling most of that stuff on every trip. No room in our bags."

"And it's mostly junk." Maverick *tsked*. "Or stuff I have plenty of at home."

"Conventions offer exclusive items," Esther pointed out. "Which I usually have you sign and we auction off for charity."

Maverick nodded. "I'll sign 'em, I'll sign 'em. Why don't you bring me what you wanted me to sign?"

Esther put her phone down on the table in front of them and stood.

Gowdie was still crinkling paper. *"Nimue,"* he said, knowing only she would hear him. *"One of these open bags. It has something you need to see."*

Nimue walked quickly across the room, catching up to Esther. Esther shot her a curious look as Nimue leaned over and widened the opening of the bag Gowdie's tail stuck out of. She peered inside. Nestled among the red tissue paper was her bright-blue dragon... and a very familiar box.

She lifted the box out of the bag to examine the limited edition golden Superstellar-Man figurine still in box. No alarm went off, as the Protection Charm had either never been put on this particular figurine or the charm registered the toy was no longer property of the CES.

The box wasn't pristine. The seal at the top was sticking up, the tape having taken a bit of the packaging along with it. The part of the box that touted the fact that the figurine came with a real 1:36 replica of the Sword of Stellar Planet dipped in gold.

The toy sword that was missing from this particular figurine's hand, the plastic bubble with a slot for it empty.

CHAPTER TWELVE

"Do you know where the toy sword is from this figurine?" Nimue raised the limited edition golden Superstellar-Man figurine box in the air, her eyes darting to Esther, Maverick, and Jaxson in turn.

Jaxson stared at Nimue almost unblinkingly, a frown on his face that made Nimue think he had no idea what she was talking about.

"I'm afraid I don't know what you're talking about." Maverick looked back and forth between Nimue and Esther, but Esther was still sorting through some of the gifts, completely ignoring Nimue's question.

Gowdie popped out of the gift bag and soared over toward Esther, who was in the midst of untying a ribbon over a box. He stuck his head in through the ribbon's curls and she startled, letting out a yelp.

Nimue took advantage of her distraction to show her the figurine box.

"What?" she asked, taking the box from Nimue and looking it over. She grimaced.

"Do you know anything about the missing sword with that figurine?"

Esther handed the box back to Nimue. "I didn't even know it *had* a sword with it." She looked over her shoulder at Maverick. "Is that the sword that was the big deal in one of the movies?"

"The Sword of Stellar Planet," Maverick confirmed.

"Right." Esther started stacking her arms with various items—books and boxes and T-shirts, by the look of it—and walked back toward Maverick. Though she stumbled at one point, she managed to place everything in front of him and then walked across the room to a small open suitcase propped up on a luggage rack in the corner and took out a black felt marker.

"There's supposed to be a sword with this figurine," Nimue said. She wanted to know why Esther had seemed almost repulsed when she'd thrust the box at her before, too.

Esther uncapped the marker and handed it to Maverick, who picked up a book and opened it up to sign inside.

"*Oo, autographs!*" Gowdie said, flapping his wings and flying over.

"That's right," said Maverick, chuckling as Gowdie landed on the pile of goodies and spread out his wings. "Little guy wanted an autograph, too, right?"

"Um, yes," said Nimue. *Gowdie, I'm trying to get them to focus*, she thought to her familiar.

Maverick finished his signature and then ripped the page out of the book as Esther reached forward and winced.

"That was a limited edition book reprint of issue 100 of *Superstellar-Man* printed just for this convention," Esther explained.

Gowdie took the page and cuddled it, rubbing his cheek all over it.

"And now it's a limited edition reprint missing its title page." Maverick scribbled in the book again. "Someone will buy it."

"This figurine is also exclusive to the con," Nimue said, clearing her throat and lifting the box high into the air.

Maverick smirked as he looked up at her and closed the book, shoving it down the table toward Esther. "If you love it so much, you can have it."

"Mr. Vanedestine," Esther started, "that could fetch a high price at auction—"

"And now it's a present for Dee-Dee."

Nimue was about to protest, but she was soon distracted by Gowdie doing a little dance of joy on the table.

"I wasn't asking for—" She stopped talking as Gowdie's thoughts blasted into her head.

"The figurine! The figurine! I'll share it with Willow if I have to." His eyes went wide as he stared at Nimue. *"Oh, please, Nimue! Please!"*

"Um, yes. Gowdie really wants it. So thank you." She took careful steps toward the couch and handed Maverick the box timidly. Gowdie flapped his wings excitedly. "Could you sign it, maybe?"

Esther *tsked*. "That could have raised hundreds—maybe over a thousand—for a charity…"

"So I'll donate a few more thousand to the charity you had in mind." Maverick took the box from Nimue and beamed at her. "I'd rather make this particular fan happy."

He scribbled across the box with his marker.

"Thank you," Nimue said, clearing her throat. Esther's jaw was set as she stared at her. "Gowdie is very grateful." She pointed at the box. "Do you see the sword that's missing, though? Any idea what could have happened to it?"

"She's just going to resell it," Esther said.

Gowdie's jaw dropped. *"I would not!"*

Nimue quirked an eyebrow at the assistant, who crossed her arms tightly over her chest. "Why would I do that?"

"You seem overly concerned with the toy's condition," Esther pointed out.

"Don't pay her any mind." Maverick slid the box on the table over to the dragon, who draped his arms around it, the piece of paper with another autograph squished against the box.

"I don't even care that it's missing the sword," Gowdie said. *"I just wanted this figurine."*

Didn't Nimue know it. *The sword could be with Cary and Zelena right now,* she reminded Gowdie in her head. *And it could have been used to kill Glinda.*

Gowdie winced and pulled back from the box just slightly, staring into the golden face of Superstellar-Man.

"Maybe we should complain to whoever gave it to me," Maverick said to Esther.

Esther walked back to the table stacked with gifts and

sorted through a few bags until she found the right one. "It's from the CES," she said. "Mia Estrada, President, it's signed."

Mia. Of course. She would have been able to authorize setting aside some of those figures for gifts or for the Comic Enthusiast Society itself. She wondered how many weren't at the booth and magicked with the Protection Charm.

She chuckled. "Like Mr. Vanedestine wants a solid gold figurine of himself. Tacky," she muttered.

"It's not tacky! It's glorious!" Gowdie hugged the box again.

Was that the entire reason for Esther's clear distaste for the item? She found it gaudy?

"It's not possible it was sent intact but someone took the sword out?" Nimue asked. "It was actually quite sharp. I just worry that whoever has it would have to be careful with it."

Esther wrinkled her nose. "A sharp sword? With a toy?"

"It's a collectible!" Gowdie stuck his tongue out in Esther's direction, but the assistant didn't seem to notice.

"It's a collectible," Nimue repeated. "For adults."

Maverick was busy signing more things at the table, stretching out a white Superstellar-Man T-Shirt and scribbling his name with a little more effort than usual. "Comic fans and their weird, little toys." He looked at Nimue, putting the cap on his marker. "Though thank goodness for comic fans, or my movies would bomb. I just didn't peg you for one, sweetheart."

Nimue bristled at the term of endearment, though a

small part of her actually didn't *mind* hearing it from this gorgeous celebrity's mouth. But then the rational part of her reminded her that it was completely inappropriate. *And* she'd seen him curled up on the hotel hallway floor. People couldn't help their fears, of course, but it hadn't exactly made for the most romantic first impression.

"My daughter and ex are more interested in comics. And my familiar." She gestured to her dragon, who nodded. "But I do see the movies." Well, she'd seen a number of them.

Maverick leaned back on the couch, hugging his ankle to the opposite calf once more. "So you *are* a fan?"

"Yes, of course," she said quickly, not understanding why she kept letting herself be distracted.

She turned to look at Esther, who was back to sorting through the boxes and bags. "Is there not a chance, then, that you opened up the figurine and took the sword out?"

"Just my signature will add to its value," said Maverick. "Even if it's not mint condition."

Gowdie hugged the box again. *"We're not selling!"*

"It wasn't me," said Esther brusquely, lifting a box of what appeared to be a plain, white handkerchief—albeit a fancy one, judging by the package—and tossing it unceremoniously to the ground. "I haven't had a chance to sort through the items yet."

"When did the figurine come?" Nimue asked, her eyes turning pleadingly toward Jaxson when no one else had answers for her.

Jaxson gripped his wrists. "They were coming all afternoon. I couldn't say. Davies or Kovac would take them in every time there was a knock at the door and do a cursory inspection to make sure there was nothing… unsavory among them."

Esther froze.

"Is that a concern?" Nimue asked. "That someone might send something dangerous?"

"Of course it's a concern!" Esther whirled in Nimue's direction. "Mr. Vanedestine is *famous*! He has overly zealous fans and he has crazy stalkers and he has estranged fam—"

"*Esther*," Maverick snapped, his tone deeply serious.

Esther flushed and whirled back to the table, this time gathering all the tossed tissue paper and wrapping paper and funneling it into a nearby trash can.

Gowdie cocked his head. *"Was she about to say 'estranged family'?"*

It wouldn't be entirely out of the question. Nimue knew some celebrities had families who wanted things from them only after they'd hit it big. Or maybe, conversely, Maverick had gotten a bit of a big head once success had hit and *he'd* angered *them*.

"And don't forget he's so afraid of witches," Gowdie said, chuckling. *"Maybe some run in the family. I could almost see why he's so paranoid about them if he angered one."*

Nimue's jaw dropped a little. A witch for an estranged family member would explain a bad case of strogaphobia indeed. But, then again, it wasn't like witches and warlocks *often* went around terrorizing humans, even the ones that irritated them. The Councils made sure of that. And if his fear was actually *rational*, why risk coming to a town full of witches?

At the very least, his mom couldn't have been a witch,

or he would have been a warlock himself. A warlock didn't pass on his magic genes to human children, though…

She studied Maverick, but he made a great show of stretching and standing up.

"So… the other two guards might have taken the sword?" she asked, trying to focus on one issue at a time. Maverick's personal grudges—or the grudges against him —were unlikely to have anything to do with the death of Glinda Redferne.

Esther *tsked* again as she picked up the box with a handkerchief in it. "You're free to ask them tomorrow if they took your toy."

Nimue frowned and glared at the young assistant. There were slight bags under Esther's eyes, and Nimue wondered if she was just tired. But Esther hadn't been so rude the last time she'd seen her. Then again, the young woman had mostly been focused on getting Maverick through his panic attack.

"They wouldn't have been messing with the contents of the gifts," Jaxson said as Maverick passed him and headed for the bedroom door. "If they found anything suspect, they would have reported it to the rest of us."

"Doesn't mean they didn't sneakily grab the sword and slip it into their pocket," Gowdie pointed out.

But Nimue had to wonder… why? Unknown motives for targeting the poor Director of Guest Services aside, would that have made the attack on Glinda premeditated? But why involve the toy sword at all?

There were so many other ways to kill a person. And if targeting a witch, well, a limited edition miniature golden toy sword would have been Nimue's last pick for a weapon, even if she'd had no access to charms herself.

"Unless the murder wasn't premeditated," said Gowdie.

Then why take the sword at all, for any reason? Nimue thought back.

"Nimue," said Maverick, yawning in the bedroom door. "I'd hate to ask you to leave already, but I do feel like getting started on that rather personal to-do list Esther leaked to you." He playfully shook his head in his assistant's direction and she winced, jumping into action and gathering the items Maverick had signed and left on the coffee table. Gowdie clutched tightly to his paper and box, watching Esther warily, but Esther never tried to take the items from him.

"Yes, of course," said Nimue numbly. "I'll let you get your rest and see you tomorrow." She bent down to pick up the figurine box, taking Gowdie up along with it.

"See you tomorrow." Maverick smiled dazzlingly, and Nimue couldn't help but be reminded of the confident Colton Carter in the Superstellar-Man movies.

"Thanks again." Nimue shook the figurine at him clumsily, causing Gowdie to let out a little "whoa" as he struggled to clutch on to the box. "Good night," she added to Jaxson and Esther, though only Jaxson offered a quick nod, a brief smile. Esther walked the signed items back to the larger table full of gifts, as if Nimue weren't there at all.

Nimue let herself out as she heard the bedroom door close behind her.

"Can we drop this off in your office?" Gowdie asked,

nuzzling his cheek against the box. *"I don't want it to get lost."*

"Sure," Nimue said aloud, making brisk moves toward the elevator. "We need to check in with Soren and Zelena anyway."

Her witch network perma-charm crystal blinked red at her wrist as she stepped inside the elevator. A woman wearing generic comic-book-design leggings and a white T-shirt was already on the elevator. Comic book fans certainly stayed active at a con, even when there were no panels and the showroom floor had yet to open.

She sorted through her messages since the woman's attention was drawn to her phone. She noticed out of the corner of her eye that the woman seemed a little fascinated by Nimue's projected screen coming off the crystal strapped to her wrist, though.

There were plenty of messages waiting for her, but she zeroed in on one from Soren.

"Meet us in the office ASAP," the message said curtly. Nimue wondered if that meant Ren was back in control, and if so, why he'd come back. *"We have a problem."*

What possible problem did they have that Nimue wasn't already fully aware of?

CHAPTER THIRTEEN

This time of night, most of the Bessa should have been in the dark, but at some point, Zelena or someone had turned on most of the lights, making the floating candles and other less picturesque sources of light brighter.

It felt disconcerting for Nimue to walk through the hallway on the employee floor late in the evening and find her eyes watering as they adjusted to the brightness after stepping out of the teleportation pad from the Southern Hotel.

"Now I see why we don't have conventions at night," Gowdie muttered. Nimue cradled him in her arms, a position he rarely deigned to let himself be carried for long, except that he was clutching to his signed paper and figurine and needed the assist.

"That and we need to be able to sleep sometime." Nimue yawned despite herself, her heels clomping against the floor. She could feel fatigue weighing down on her body, but there was no way she could sleep just yet.

She envied the staff that had already gone home on time because *someone* needed to be well-rested for the start of con tomorrow.

As she passed the employee locker room—open, but no one in sight—and made it to the Head Witch General Manager's office, Nimue slipped past Cassie's empty desk in the waiting room and stepped inside into her and Soren's office.

As she suspected, Ren was back in control, sitting behind his giant mushroom-shaped desk with his hair slicked back and a scowl pinching his brow. Zelena stood behind him, projecting an image to show him out from the witch network crystal at her wrist. As always, Messenger the sloth hung from her neck. Nimue spotted Balfour draped across the back of Ren's tall desk chair.

"Nimue." Ren nodded from behind his steepled fingers, his elbows on his desk in front of him.

Nimue blinked and tried not to think about all of that ridiculous talk about crushes and romance. Even Maverick's supposed flirtation had sort of dried up quick enough. There were other things to worry about. Nimue extended her hands to drop Gowdie and his prized items down on her own giant mushroom desk, a perfect copy of the other item of furniture, even if the collection of framed pictures and assorted office supplies and paperwork was more personal. It was perpendicular to Ren's desk, which had been Bernadette's originally, his back to the large, wall-sized window overlooking Lake Salem. Nimue's desk faced the bookshelf crammed with books and other small knickknacks across the other side of the office.

"What are you looking at?" Nimue asked, coming around behind Ren's desk to stand beside Zelena.

Zelena scowled as she stared at the picture, continuing to wave her wand across at it as it changed to different overhead shots of locations throughout the convention center.

"Nothing," Zelena said. "That's the problem."

Zelena's image kept changing, from one part of the convention center to another. "The perma-charm History Charm crystals were useless," she muttered.

Nimue glowered at her for just a moment, then looked back at the convention center images. "Did Cary touch base with you?"

"Yes," Zelena said. "I have the toy sword in my office. The blood does match Glinda's."

Nimue bit her lip. "Maverick and his team claim they were in Maverick's hotel room at the time of the incident —though I didn't talk to two of his bodyguards, who were touring the convention center earlier in the day. We even saw them on a History Charm a few hours before Glinda died."

Zelena nodded. "I was with them. Saw them through the teleportation pad back to the Southern Hotel at least half an hour before the… incident."

"Did they do anything strange when you were with them?" Nimue asked.

Zelena frowned. "They were pretty quiet, for the most part."

"Quiet?" Gowdie said in Nimue's head. *"Does that sound like that Davies to you?"*

Not really, she thought back. That one had been plenty

talkative around her. "They didn't have any security questions for you?"

"Well, not a question about security. One did ask in particular to see the Comic Enthusiast Society booth, I remember that."

"To steal a toy sword?" Gowdie asked.

Hmm, Nimue thought back. *Would they even need to? Remember, they had access to Maverick's figurine.* She spoke aloud. "And what did they do there, at the CES booth?"

"Look around," Zelena said. "I warned them not to touch anything. I wasn't sure if Morpheus had put an anti-thief charm on any of the items there, but I knew he was going to, so just to be on the safe side."

"And they didn't touch anything?"

Zelena tapped her chin and Messenger echoed her gesture. "No. In fact, we were only there half a minute when one of them seemed eager to get on with the tour. Get it over with, even. Said they had to be back before their boss had dinner."

"They asked to see that booth, looked around real quick, then were quick to leave?" Nimue asked.

"Yeah..." Zelena nodded. "I didn't think much about it. Just escorted them to the nearest teleportation pad and saw them off."

"You didn't follow them all the way to their rooms?" Ren asked.

Zelena shook her head. "No. Why would I?"

"Well, there's a chance..." Nimue walked over to her desk and gestured to the box Gowdie was still hugging. "So Davies and Kovac didn't touch any of the figurines in the CES booth. But Maverick got his own limited edition figurine only accessible to the CES until tomorrow. No one claimed to have touched it—except maybe those two bodyguards I didn't talk to—but it's missing... that golden sword."

Ren let out a deep breath. Nimue still wondered what had happened to switch him back out with Soren. Soren had been doing such a good job tackling the stress of this situation.

"Zelena, didn't you walk past the hallway where we found the sword earlier in the day?" He gestured at her projected screen. "With those two bodyguards on the tour?"

Nimue came back around the desk to take a look.

"Well, sure." Zelena waved her wand and the image changed to the hallway in question, brightly lit. "It was at least an hour before the incident, though. And before we saw the CES booth." Sure enough, Zelena was escorting Davies and Kovac through that very same hall, both with briefcases in their grips. Zelena was talking and they walked through at a steady pace, not stopping, but both men looking around.

"Can you look closer when they get to about here?"

Messenger shook her head slowly, wagging her finger in Nimue's direction, but it was Zelena who spoke, naturally. "No. These perma-charm crystals don't allow for three-dimensional inspections like a *real* History Charm."

Nimue squirmed under her glare.

"But they do allow for much faster combing through footage," Ren said, and Nimue was grateful he was backing up her idea. Not that he'd ever been against it, though. In fact, though he was still sometimes hard to read, Ren had been downright agreeable whenever she'd pitched an idea lately.

Granted, they hadn't been as outlandish as some of her ideas for Bookshop Con had been.

"Have someone on security examine the moment in question, see if the toy falls to the ground from one of the bodyguards as they pass by," Nimue said.

"Hours before Glinda is even attacked?" Zelena asked, incredulous.

Nimue nodded, not taking his eyes off the projected image. "Cover all our bases."

"How do you think Glinda's blood got on the sword?" Ren asked, though he at least didn't sound like he thought she'd taken complete leave of her senses.

Balfour purred loudly.

"Balfour thinks you're being obtuse," Gowdie translated for Nimue.

Balfour growled at him.

"Quiet, girl," Ren said, offering her a quick pet.

Nimue grimaced. "Maybe the bodyguards dropped it, someone picked it up, used it, and put it back where they found it. I don't know. I just think we need to check on every lead, no matter how much it doesn't seem to make sense. A lot about this doesn't make sense."

Messenger nodded grimly and Zelena pinched her lips.

"Messenger agrees with you on that," Gowdie added.

"You said you don't have anything on the footage that can help?" Nimue asked. "Nothing revealing who that man was at the end of the hallway? Or anyone closer to Glinda on the showroom floor?"

"Show her the man you tried to follow," Ren said.

Zelena waved her wand and the image fast-forwarded. No one passed by the hallway where the sword had been found between the time when Zelena and Maverick's bodyguards had walked through and the time of the incident. Nimue supposed that made sense, as the convention wasn't yet open and only set-up crew and some VIPs would have been present at all. Night fell in the image and the hallway got darker. Then there he was. The man appeared up at the top of the stairs. Walked across the hallway—briskly, but not as if running full-speed from the scene of a crime he'd just committed. Then he stilled at the juncture between that and the other hallway.

"This is when you were flying through the air," Ren said.

"More like 'tumbling.'" Gowdie snickered, and Balfour may have joined in, judging by the rumble of her purr.

"His attention was drawn by the ruckus, the voices, so he stopped," said Zelena. "But then I appear from the same direction he'd come from." She stuck her chin out toward the image and another not-clear silhouette appeared at the end of the hall. Though, since Nimue knew it to be Zelena, her brain was better at filling in that information.

The man in the hallway looked over his shoulder and started running. Zelena followed, paused—that was when Nimue told her to go after him—and she did.

But the man was already at the teleportation pad at the end of the hallway, rushing through.

Zelena on the screen wouldn't have noticed that since

she was still a little behind. She paused at the teleportation pad as she reached it, then looked in either direction around it, her witch network projection screen lit up. She picked a direction and ran, but the man was gone.

"What color did the teleportation pad glow?" Nimue asked. Then they'd know the man's destination and could follow the perma-charm History Charm records after that.

"Unclear," Ren said. "We can have someone History Charm there to find out—"

"But there doesn't seem to be much point," Zelena said. "The lighting isn't good in that hallway at that moment. The moon shines in from the atrium over the showroom floor *just so* to obscure it."

"What about all the other pads shortly after he vanishes?" Nimue asked. "Comb through them all, one by one?"

"We did." Zelena grunted. "I put my team to the task first thing. Nothing."

"Which means... he took the pad to somewhere else outside of the Bessa," Nimue concluded. "Where else do the teleportation pads go?"

"The hotel," said Ren quickly. "We don't have perma-charm crystal surveillance there, but I'm already planning on having someone do a History Charm at the pad there at the time in question."

Nimue tapped her finger to her lips. "Where else, though...?"

"That's it," said Zelena. "At least for members of the public."

"But not... the staff," Ren said quietly. "Anyone with all-access badges."

"Florence's clinic!" Nimue shouted. "That's the only other place, right?"

Ren nodded. "We still have to call in the rest of the staff."

"We can't let them sleep?" Zelena asked, yawning as if on cue. "We need an alert team tomorrow."

"I can talk to Florence," Nimue offered. "She's already aware of the situation. She was here when that man teleported out of the Bessa, but we can do a History Charm and see what it turns up."

Ren sighed but tilted his head slightly. "Good idea."

Their eyes met. Nimue smiled slightly despite herself. Ren's eyes widened and he focused once more on the screen. "And as for the man's entry…"

Zelena waved her wand and rewound the image. This time, it switched to the bottom of the staircase—there was no image of the staircase itself—and a dark figure approaching it. He walked backward.

"He doesn't come from the showroom floor," Zelena said. "He comes from this pad."

Sure enough, the man walked backward into a teleportation pad.

Nimue stood there, tapping her finger against her lip. "He jumped into the Bessa, went upstairs, got chased, and jumped out? What? To take in the view over the showroom floor from the balcony up there?"

"Apparently." Ren frowned. "Though it's possible his original entry point was from somewhere else in the Bessa."

"Which means he could have been on the showroom

floor during the time in question." Nimue thought about that. "What color was the pad this time?"

"Yellow, we think," Zelena said. The words came out sour on her tongue.

"Florence's clinic?" Nimue reiterated. "It wasn't Florence coming in herself?"

"Maybe. But we don't think so, though it's hard to tell in the dark. Maybe the color isn't captured correctly," Zelena said. "We can have someone do a proper History Charm to check it out."

Ren swirled in his chair to face Nimue properly. "We haven't installed perma-charm crystals in that part of the Bessa yet."

"Oh, right." Nimue frowned. Her grandmother could only make so many perma-charm crystals for them at a time, and there wasn't really anyone else in town up for the task. Besides, she had other interests and other crystals she was interested in crafting. They'd prioritized the higher-traffic areas when setting up the dozen or so Bernadette had been able to make for them in time for Comic Hero Con.

Messenger *tut-tutted*.

"More History Charms to be cast," Gowdie translated for her. *"And security is already spread thin."*

"What about Glinda?" Nimue asked. "What was she up to before she bent down to pick up that pin?"

Zelena waved her wand and the image changed to Glinda on the showroom floor. Then it moved backward like it had in Ren's History Charm, down to her picking up that pin. Before that, she browsed through some aisles of the showroom floor, looking left and right.

"Doing her pre-con sweep," Zelena said, just like Nimue had suggested. She let out a deep breath. "Linden often did a sweep of the showroom floor the night before a con. Sure, the maps in the con guides can show a con-goer where to go, but Guest Services does a better job of helping the guests if they also just *know* where the booths are and what they offer."

Nimue kept her mouth shut regarding Zelena mentioning Linden and watched Glinda move backward through the showroom floor. Before that, she'd been up in the lobby at the front desk. The image showed her talking to Humphrey, another member of the Guest Services staff, at the desk where badges were distributed and customers could come with questions. He'd appeared—walking backward—from the teleportation pad, which clearly flashed red, meaning he'd gone to the employees-only floor after talking to Glinda, probably to grab his things, drop off his badge in his locker, and fly his broomstick home.

Before that, the two had conferred at the lobby desk for hours. On occasion, they greeted a guest who came in from the teleportation pad—it flashed black, meaning the hotel—or the front door to pick up a badge. Early birds who paid extra could get their badges before the convention began. But they'd only be allowed access to the Bessa's lobby and the hotel lobby. The teleportation pads didn't work beyond that until a guest wore a convention badge, and they didn't unlock to con-goer activity until the start of the convention. Other than for the VIPs, who got their badges almost as soon as they arrived.

"Nothing unusual, then," Nimue said.

Gowdie let out a little sigh. *"Poor Glinda."*

They even saw—at quick speeds—afternoon turn back into morning in the projected image, and Florence walk into the lobby from the teleportation pad, which flashed black, with a bag full of Sylvie's pastries in one hand and a paper cup of coffee in the other. Humphrey was already behind the front desk, having apparently arrived before her. He reached into the bag, rummaged around, and pulled out an éclair.

"That would have been not too long after we saw her at the bakery," Nimue said.

"You saw her this morning?" Ren's head whipped around.

Nimue shrugged. "Sure. At Sylvie's."

"And nothing seemed… unusual?" Zelena asked.

"No." Nimue tapped her finger against her mouth. "Should it have?"

"Where's the other coffee?" Gowdie asked.

"Pardon?" Nimue asked.

"Glinda had two coffees, I assumed for her and Humphrey. But she just has one now, and she never gave it to him. Just an éclair. Then she drank the coffee herself."

Nimue hadn't been paying close enough attention to notice that. Was it relevant?

Messenger croaked something at Zelena, perhaps translating Gowdie's message to Nimue.

Zelena finally set her wrist down and tossed her other arm in the air, disturbing the projected screen and projecting it in the window behind them instead. "We're grasping at straws here! I don't know. I just wondered *why* someone might have wanted to kill her. I thought…

If she knew she was in danger, she might have been acting differently."

"If she knew she was in danger, she would have told you," said Ren softly.

Nimue opened her mouth to speak, but she noticed a single tear falling out of Zelena's eye. She'd had a rough month.

"Were you and Glinda close?" Nimue asked.

Zelena shrugged. "I suppose. She worked with Linden for all those years, you know… We had her over for dinner a few times. And we went to school together, her and I."

That reminded Nimue. "With Clarke and Esmerelda?"

Ren's brow arched up.

"Yeah." Zelena shrugged again. "But it wasn't like we were the best of friends, us three or anything. Glinda and Esmerelda were probably closer back then. Until their big fallout."

Nimue looked to Ren for answers, but he simply shrugged, leaning back in his chair with his hands steepled in front of his face.

Balfour purred, rubbing the back of his head and almost looking as if she were whispering in his ear.

He frowned. "Glinda and Clarke were a couple in school?" he said aloud. "And Esmerelda dated Glinda's brother?"

Zelena nodded. "They dated for years even beyond that. But then one day, they all just stopped being friends. Gossip was Esmerelda and Clarke had been cheating on Glinda and her brother. How they were now a couple. We soon found that part, at least, to be true. Never pried about the cheating rumor."

"Esmerelda told me they'd been close once, her and Glinda. That they'd grown apart. She didn't mention anything about stealing her boyfriend." Nimue looked to Gowdie for confirmation. Clarke perhaps being extra upset about Glinda's death made more sense now.

Gowdie nodded.

"You'd have to ask Soren if he knew this," Ren said simply. "He… got tired. The stress was just a bit too much for him."

Nimue was trying to pay attention, but her eyes were stuck on the image Zelena's witch network perma-charm crystal still projected, only crookedly onto the window behind her, this time moving forward and repeating what they'd just seen.

Not only had Humphrey not received one of the coffees Sylvie had implied had been for him, he'd chosen the éclair, not the cruller, hadn't he?

CHAPTER FOURTEEN

Nimue thought she might swing by her house and change—she couldn't use her Transformation Charm to turn her fancy dress back into her more comfortable uniform dress until sunrise, since she'd already used it once today, just like she'd used up her Undo Charm. And it was too personal, too inconsequential, an issue to ask Ren or Zelena for help before she'd left.

Maybe if it had been Soren, he would have understood.

So she'd grabbed her broomstick from the locker room and was riding it to Florence's, having sent a quick note via the witch network crystal to tell her she was on her way.

"Do you really think Ren will follow up with Soren's mom and dad and ask about them cheating on their respective part- ners all those years ago?" Gowdie asked, tilting sideways as he soared closer.

He was cradling his figurine, the autographed piece of

paper left behind on Nimue's desk to give to Graves next time they saw him, because they'd planned to swing by their townhouse. "He seemed annoyed I even suggested it might be important," Nimue pointed out. Her voice was loud, the streets quiet, as she sped with her body hugging the broomstick tightly for better aerodynamics. They'd skip the scenic route this time, heading straight to Florence's clinic over the sidewalks below. She didn't want to lose much time, considering she could have just teleported there.

"Well, I guess they do have a lot of other stuff to follow up on," Gowdie agreed. He flapped his wings with great force, aiming for one of the few buildings on this block with lights still on. *Floral Clinic.* Where witches and warlocks went for what ailed them when their own home remedy charms wouldn't do the trick. A pun on Florence's name and the décor.

Nimue leaned up, dragging the shaft of her broomstick up to slow her pace and begin her descent.

There was a corral for visitors' broomsticks out front that was currently empty. Nimue set hers in the nearest spot and stepped inside the clinic, the bright-blue flowers on vines framing the door shifting aside to let her in. Gowdie swooped down, his wing clipping one of the vines, and managed to stutter to a stop on her shoulder, the figurine box bonking the side of Nimue's head. She'd left her witch's hat in her locker, or it might have tumbled up with the force of his uneven landing.

"Sorry," he mumbled, straightening up. *"I didn't account for the extra weight in that high-speed landing."*

Nimue stepped into the reception area, and the

blooms of all colors and shapes and sizes turned slightly to watch. These were no ordinary flowers, and they wouldn't irritate anyone's allergies. Florence and her team had raised them with a combination of charms to make them hypoallergenic and even more alive than the average flower found in a park or garden.

"Florence?" Nimue called out. She didn't think anyone else was on duty this time of night. There was an emergency perma-charm crystal to touch on the front desk to send an instant message to the Head Medical Witch, and witches could always alert Florence and her team via the witch network crystal to anything that needed attention after-hours. It was a rare day when a witch had a medical emergency she couldn't handle herself after hours.

The bulk of the medical witches' work was done at the Bessa, with human con-goers. They typically addressed exhaustion and dehydration or overheating, the occasional injury or more serious medical emergency.

And twice now, dealing with the bodies left behind at the Bessa after a death.

"Nimue." Florence's voice carried down the hall. "We're in my office."

"*'We'?*" questioned Gowdie.

Nimue headed down the hall. She'd been here a few times—Willow had gotten all her checkups here while growing up—so she knew Florence's office was at the end of this hallway. First, though, she passed the teleportation pad that connected the clinic to the Bessa, with the right clearance on the perma-charm crystal affixed to an individual's badge. This was where Nimue would have exited if she hadn't decided to take her broomstick so she could swing by her house afterward. Still, considering the crisis going on, she'd kept her employee badge on the lanyard around her neck.

The clinic wasn't too big, though there was a floor upstairs that was more open for any more complicated treatments, akin to human surgery on witches. Those occurred very rarely, though.

The door was open.

"I needed to ask you if you know—" Nimue stopped herself.

In front of Florence's desk—a dark wooden desk adorned with more blue flowers on vines that grew up and around its surface—sat Dr. Choi, his hands folded over his lap.

"Dr. Choi," Nimue said. "I would have thought you'd be in your room at the hotel this time of night."

"Henry was supposed to exchange notes with me this evening. Well, we have been talking all evening about his position and the work we do here." Florence sighed. "Despite everything else going on. I didn't feel like there was much else I could do to help once we got Glinda… settled."

Henry frowned. "Tragic. Simply tragic. I didn't know her, but I know what it's like to lose a colleague. I've been working too long not to." He nodded solemnly, his focus on the desk in front of him, as his fingers gripped the staff badge hanging from the lanyard around his neck.

"Well, it's… It's not how I would have wanted your first day," Nimue said, swallowing. Gowdie flapped his wings and landed on the empty chair beside Dr. Choi, still clutching the figurine in front of him.

Dr. Choi observed the little dragon, taking in the box he was clutching that was about the dragon's size, but he didn't mention it. "I wanted to go, see if I could help. But Florence instructed me to stay here."

"You were here when we called Florence to the Bessa?" Nimue asked. She looked at Florence. The Head Medical Witch hadn't mentioned that, but she didn't seem to pick up on any of Nimue's curiosity.

"I didn't know what we'd be walking into," Florence said. "Besides, Dr. Choi is here to help with the human con-goers, provide some expertise about what kinds of treatments they expect from experiences in their own towns, tell us anything we might have overlooked about human anatomy."

"Though I *am* curious to learn about witch treatments," Dr. Choi added. "I knew it might be too presumptuous of me to accompany a medical witch on my first night. So I waited here." He smiled broadly, then his smile fell. "Until she came back with that poor woman." He wrung his hands together, and Nimue found herself staring at the movement. Dr. Choi seemed to notice and immediately stopped. "It's just... I've never seen a deceased witch, is all. Nothing strange about me being nervous about that."

Gowdie cocked his head. *"Did anyone say he was nervous?"*

No. No, they hadn't.

"Dr. Choi agreed with me," said Florence. "Her throat

was cut with a thin, sharp object from right to left. That was the cause of death."

"Tragic," Dr. Choi added once more. He caught his breath quickly.

"You were here, then?" Nimue asked. "At the clinic, for most of the day?"

Florence nodded. "Dr. Choi hasn't left my side all afternoon, not since he arrived here."

"Came here straight from the hotel room. Florence and her team have been instructing me all day. Haven't even had a chance to explore the rest of the town yet. By her side all day."

Gowdie sent a wary eye his way. *Why is he talking so rapidly? Like he's hiding something?*

"By each other's side all afternoon and evening—except for when Florence was called to the Bessa," Nimue pointed out.

Florence nodded glumly, but Dr. Choi actually *jumped* in his chair.

As if he'd been found out or something.

Nimue frowned. "And you've both been here since?"

"Yes," Florence asked. Her lips pursed as she looked up at Nimue. "Why do you ask? Why are you here, anyway? I thought you wanted the results of the Origin Charm on that pin." Florence tapped her wand against her perma-charm crystal on her wrist and the witch network projected a screen. "I'm not *greatly skilled* at them, so you may want the security team to run a second attempt, but I did see something of note." That got Nimue's attention.

She walked around the desk to stand behind Florence

and look at her projection. "What am I looking at here?" It was a table, perhaps? And a stick?

"*A wand?*" suggested Gowdie, peering up at it from the chair across the desk, his chin skirting the top of his figurine box.

"I can't tell exactly where this is, or who's using that wand," said Florence, confirming Gowdie's adroit theory. As the Head Medical Witch spoke, her hat shifted aside slightly, her leech poking her head out from under the brim. "But its origin… is from a witch or warlock, with roots in Cauldron Cove. I could feel that sort of energy from the Charm I cast."

In the image, which Florence must have recorded from her Origin Charm, smart witch—the wand tapped the table and a shiny glint of gold appeared from nothingness.

"The Create Charm," Nimue said.

Dr. Choi chuckled nervously. "Witches can create something from nothing? Marvelous."

"Well, the size and value of the thing is determined by the witch's skill," said Florence. "And it helps—but isn't always necessary—to have materials nearby. But a small pin should be doable for a skilled witch, especially if some gold is already on hand."

"Oh?" Dr. Choi observed. "Is there a witch jewelry shop in town?"

"No," Nimue admitted. "Though that doesn't mean there aren't plenty of witches with gold jewelry." Nimue chewed on her lip, thinking about it. Who knew what each witch in town had in their homes, but almost anyone with a wedding ring likely had some gold on them. Then there were the witches who'd had gold chains Nimue had noticed just today, like Glinda and Clarke and Esmerelda.

"Did you notice the gold chain Glinda had on her collar?" Nimue asked Florence.

The medical witch frowned. "Sure. Did you want an Origin Charm on that, too?"

"No, I suppose not," Nimue said. But something about it needled her.

"Oh!" Dr. Choi slammed a fist against his palm. "What about those exclusive golden figurines your little dragon has one of here? Maybe a witch made it from that?"

Florence and Nimue both looked at Dr. Choi curiously.

"What's he talking about?" Florence asked, looking up over her shoulder at Nimue. She lowered her wrist, first dismissing the projected image.

Gowdie lifted his figurine box in the air. *"Tell her about the ultra, limited-edition Superstellar-Man figurine that I got autographed,"* he said to Florence's leech.

The leech bobbed her head toward her witch.

"You knew the figurine was exclusive to the con?" Nimue asked the human doctor.

Gowdie shot him a curious look.

"Oh, uh—I assumed." Dr. Choi laughed again, awkwardly. "It being so shiny and all."

"Did he hope to get one, too?" Gowdie proposed.

But Nimue didn't ask. He hadn't brought that up as his reason for knowing about the con-exclusive figurine, outside of Gowdie carrying one with him, and he *could have* if that were the case.

Dr. Choi shirked back under Nimue's penetrating

stare. She didn't even have to say a word and he was babbling.

"Well, I mean, conventions like these—especially with comic-loving nerds—"

"Geeks," Gowdie corrected, even if the doctor couldn't hear him. *"Or just awesome fans, preferably."*

"I know they have exclusive items," the doctor continued. "And that toy looks so shiny, so of course it had to be a rarity?" He sat up straighter, his mouth hanging open. "Oh! And the pyramid display! That draws the eye and tells me the toy is a big deal for the convention—"

"Dr. Choi." Nimue cut him off with a hand through the air. "You said you still haven't had a chance to tour the Bessa?"

Dr. Choi's breath cut off sharply, his rambling extinguished.

Nimue turned to Florence quickly. "No one else has been here that you know of? After you went to the Bessa to get Glinda?"

"No…" Florence said. "Though you'd have to ask Dr. Choi. He's been here the whole time."

At least part of that was true. Whoever the man with the briefcase had been whom Nimue and then Zelena had chased through the Bessa in the dark, he'd maybe teleported from Florence's clinic in the first place, and he'd teleported somewhere else *before* she'd returned. Even if it had been back to the clinic, he could have been long gone out the front door by the time she'd gotten back.

But Dr. Choi was supposed to have been here. He would have at least *heard* someone running through the hallway. Most likely.

Except that, if he'd never been to the Bessa…

"How did you know the figurines were stacked in a pyramid?" Nimue asked the human doctor. "Did you happen to see that display at the convention center, from the balcony overlooking the showroom floor?"

The doctor's tawny face turned a shade of green.

He bent down, picked up a *briefcase*, and jumped to his feet, running down the hallway before anyone could think to stop him.

CHAPTER FIFTEEN

Nimue stared at the retreating human doctor in shock for half a minute.

But Gowdie was quicker on his feet. Or wings. Leaving his precious figurine behind, he soared into the air and went after him, which got Nimue's feet moving, too. Witches and their familiars could only be a certain distance apart at any time.

"Dr. Choi?" Florence asked into the darkened hallway, likely as flabbergasted as Nimue had been.

But she'd seen it. His *briefcase*. And if he was the only one who would have witnessed the mysterious figure leave from the clinic in the first place and he hadn't *said* anything… Did it not stand to reason Dr. Choi himself was the man in question?

Despite her high heels slowing her down a touch, Nimue caught up to Gowdie just as the front door to the clinic opened and Dr. Choi turned left down the sidewalk.

"But Florence was with him during the murder!" Gowdie shouted in Nimue's mind.

They burst through the door and Nimue snatched her broomstick out of the corral. "Maybe so, but he's clearly hiding something!" she shouted into the night.

Dr. Choi wasn't elderly, but he wasn't a young human by any means. And Nimue could be remarkably fast on her broomstick.

She and Gowdie were on top of Dr. Choi and in front of him, whirling around to face him, in a matter of seconds.

"Dr. Choi!" Nimue shouted, her nostrils flaring. "What are you doing?"

Dr. Choi let out a yelp and clutched his briefcase to his chest.

Gowdie exhaled a little burst of flame into the night and Dr. Choi screamed more, cowering on the sidewalk and raising his briefcase over his head as if to protect himself.

Nimue smirked at Gowdie and lowered to the concrete, one high heel toe landing first.

Florence appeared from behind the doctor, taking a few deep breaths. "Henry?"

Dr. Choi peeked out from behind his briefcase at the sound of her voice, just as Gowdie landed on the top of Nimue's upside-down broom, which she held in one arm, the other hand on her hip.

"Don't hurt me," he pleaded, squeezing his eye shut again. "I can explain."

"That's all we wanted you to do," said Nimue. "Why did you run away? From *witches*?" When she said it, it sounded like something that might have proven Maverick's worst fears right, but Nimue had just meant, how had the man *expected* to get away from witches chasing after him?

"Then again, he has before. At the Bessa," Gowdie pointed out.

There was that.

Florence bent down to help Dr. Choi up by the arm. He accepted her help, then hung his head, his shoulders slumping as he seemed resigned to his fate.

What kind of fate was the man expecting? What had he *done*?

"Let's sit over here," Florence suggested, pointing across the street to the edge of the large park in the middle of Cauldron Cove. Since no human vehicles were allowed within city limits—there was a large parking lot just outside of town where transportation witches would pick up visitors and bring them into town in broomstick-led flying carriages—there was no need to look both ways as the group headed for the wooden bench. Since the entirety of the park was like a slice of a forest in the middle of a city, it was almost like they'd taken a break in the middle of a forest hike, except for the fact that straight across from them was a line of buildings a number of stories high.

Nimue shivered in the chill autumn night air in her low-cut dress. Florence spared a glance as she sat next to Dr. Choi and seemed to notice. "Is that your usual outfit transformed?"

"Yeah." Nimue wrinkled her nose. "Hasn't been the most comfortable outfit to wear in a crisis, but I used my Transformation Charm for the day to put it on, and my

Undo Charm on something else. I was going to head home to change."

"May I?" she asked.

"Thank you. Please," Nimue responded.

Florence removed her wand from her holster and waved it over Nimue. "Transformation Charm."

Nimue's dress sparkled in a red light, the fabric re-weaving itself into her usual dress with black bodice, red skirt, and red, puffy sleeves. Even her pantyhose transformed into her usual black-and-white tights.

Dr. Choi adjusted his glasses up his nose, his mouth shaped into a little "o" as he watched the magic transform Nimue's dress, preserving her modesty all the while, naturally.

"Much better," said Nimue.

Gowdie nodded. *"I still want to swing by the house to drop off my…"* His jaw dropped. *"My figurine!"*

"We'll stop back at the clinic and get it," Nimue promised, keeping her voice quiet.

Nimue shifted to stand in front of Dr. Choi, still leaning on her broomstick like a walking stick of sorts, her dragon settled in the twig-like bristles.

"You were in the Bessa a few hours ago," she said, brooking no argument. "Why? And why did you run—both then and now?"

Dr. Choi sighed, holding on to his briefcase against his chest and focusing on the floor. "I really need this job."

Well, *that* didn't explain anything.

"You're not a suspect for murder if Florence vouches for you," Nimue said. She looked to the nurse witch, who nodded. "But Witchy ExS likes to be able to *trust* its staff, witch or human."

"I… I'm leaving a lot of debt behind in my old life. My house was foreclosed on, my car impounded. I declared bankruptcy. Here, I won't need a vehicle. And I'll make enough to get my own place over time." He looked back up at Florence. "And I've always found witches and warlocks fascinating. It's not often there's a position for a human in one of their towns, let alone one I'm uniquely qualified for. The timing of this job posting was just uncanny. I was looking to start over."

"And we were impressed with your resume," Nimue said, looking to Florence. She'd been the final decision-maker on the matter.

The nurse witch nodded emphatically. "A bankruptcy wouldn't have mattered to us. Like you said, this place could allow you a fresh start."

"So I thought…" Dr. Choi sighed. "To tell you the truth, I have—I *had* an issue with gambling. I've been working on it for years now. Seven months, I haven't bet a thing."

"That's good," said Gowdie, though only Nimue could hear him. Florence's leech jumped down from under her witch's hat and Florence cupped her hands out to catch her without even hesitating.

Dr. Choi stared at the leech out of the corner of his eye but kept talking. "I just panicked. I knew Florence asked me to wait for her at the clinic, but I also knew, from her orientation, that my staff badge would get me into the convention center, even after hours." He pulled his badge, hanging from its lanyard around his neck, out from behind his briefcase. "I knew something was wrong, the way she left in a hurry, and I didn't want to get in the way, but I thought... I thought I could take a look around, and if she needed my help, I could offer it."

The leech squirmed in Florence's hands.

Gowdie translated. *"She said that Dr. Choi would have seen the convention center tomorrow. What was the hurry?"*

Florence repeated as much to her colleague.

Dr. Choi used the back of his hand to wipe his brow. "I-I wasn't in a hurry. Um. But when I saw that witch tumbling through the air at me—"

"That was me," Nimue admitted.

Dr. Choi's eyes widened. "Yes, well, I—I didn't want to get caught where I shouldn't have been. So I just ran back through the nearest teleportation pad and thought of the clinic." He smiled haltingly. "Sure enough, the pads work just as Florence promised they would."

Nimue started pacing back and forth. "So you want us to believe you were just overtaken by curiosity to see the Bessa and find out what emergency Florence was dealing with, then you regretted it once you realized you might get caught, and you ran? Then you ran again when you realized you *were* caught?"

"I can't lose this job." A sigh escaped his lips. "I know I seem guiltier running like a fool. I just wasn't thinking."

The leech shimmied in Florence's hands again.

"Where were you headed now?" Florence translated for it. "Where could you run *to*?"

"Back to my room at the hotel," Dr. Choi admitted. "I thought—well, I figured I *had* lost the job. I needed to get out of here. It wouldn't be the first time I'd run from someone angry at me."

Nimue arched a brow. "You mean, you literally *ran* from someone after you before?"

"Well… No." Dr. Choi tugged at his collar. "I guess I didn't really get away from him, either."

Nimue frowned, ceasing her pacing. "Whom did you run from before?"

"A-A man I owed money to. My credit was shoddy by then, so I couldn't get a bank loan. I thought I had a sure-fire way to win it back, but…" He shook his head. "I was a fool."

Nimue frowned. "But this man you were running from before—is he still after you?"

Gowdie studied his witch. *"You're thinking that has something to do with Glinda's death?"*

Just exploring all possibilities, Nimue thought back to him.

"No, I-I paid him back," Dr. Choi said. He wasn't exactly proving to be the most trustworthy of humans here, but Nimue would take him at his word for now. He sighed. "After I lost my house, I sold my practice to another doctor and made sure to clear things with the man—with interest. I really do want a fresh start."

"Something still isn't adding up here," Gowdie said, tapping a talon to his thin, reptilian lip.

Florence's leech started squirming in her palms, the movements accompanied by a squelching sound.

"Uh-huh," Gowdie agreed with her. *"Hmm…"*

"What?" Nimue asked, her gaze darting from Gowdie to the leech.

"Epona says you should tell Nimue what you told me earlier today," Florence says. "About Maverick Vanedestine."

That got Nimue's attention.

"Patient confidentiality," Dr. Choi said, looking at Florence strangely. "I only consulted with you for a second opinion."

"If it's at all relevant to the crime that took place in Cauldron Cove today, though, I need to know," Nimue said simply. "Remember—this is a witch town. Human laws aren't the standard."

"Well, it's not a *law*, per se, but I could lose my license for sharing information about a patient."

"Even if you just see the man one time?" Nimue asked.

Dr. Choi frowned. "Frequency of visits wouldn't have anything to do with it. Even if it had been just one time."

"'*Even if*'?" Gowdie repeated.

That wasn't the first time he'd met with Maverick Vanedestine as a patient?

But Dr. Choi hadn't come to Cauldron Cove from Hollywood. Where in the world would he have met Maverick before…?

"I don't have to worry about medical licensure. Not via human rules, anyway," said Florence, turning to face Nimue. "Henry told me… He'd been asked to look at Maverick before."

Dr. Choi winced, clutching his briefcase harder to his chest.

"When?" Nimue asked. "Where? By whom?"

"By the guy I owed money to," Dr. Choi said, his facial

figures sagging. "I don't know his name. I knew him by 'Pound.'"

"'Pound'?" Nimue asked. "What does that mean?"

Dr. Choi shuddered. "I heard all sorts of explanations. Best one was he took your flesh by the pound if you crossed him." He pushed his glasses up his nose again. "He offered a slight discount on my debt if I'd take a look at a guy 'freaking out' at his West Coast house, he told me."

"Where was this?" Nimue asked.

"L.A.," Dr. Choi said. "Pound has places all over, including Chicago, where I'm from. I was in Las Vegas at the time and Pound knew it. It wasn't too long of a drive."

"Why *you*?" Nimue asked, as Gowdie echoed the same question in her head. "There are plenty of doctors in Los Angeles—"

"He wanted to keep it quiet. Especially given the fact that the man in question was… Who he was."

"But why was he *there*?" Nimue asked. "Maverick, I mean?"

Dr. Choi shook his head vehemently. "I knew better than to ask questions. Of anyone. I only asked as much as I dared to try to ascertain what was wrong with the man. But of course I recognized him right away. Who wouldn't?"

"You said he was having a severe panic attack then," Florence said.

"Yeah. Worse than what I saw here. Nobody would tell me what had triggered it. I asked Florence…" He looked at her and she nodded. "Well, even at the time, I suspected the man may have been charmed by a witch. But no one explained what had put the famous actor in that position, why he was at Pound's house, none of that. I didn't see any witches there, but I was ushered straight into Pound's living room and then out again, so I didn't really get a chance to look around."

"How did you treat him?" Nimue asked.

"Like I would for anyone with severe PTSD. Sedatives. A recommendation to see a therapist and start on anti-anxiety medications." He grunted. "Some tips for relaxation—meditation, mindfulness, exercise. But no one was really listening at that point. Pound just wanted to know if he would be 'all right.' If he could keep 'making movies' and 'making money.' I said, sure, with proper therapy. The problem didn't seem physical." He shuddered. "I… I suspected but wouldn't dare say that something had been done to the man. Maybe he owed him money, too, and he wouldn't pay—and this was Pound's 'pound of flesh,' so to speak. I resolved then and there to give up gambling cold turkey and find a way to pay the man back."

Gowdie *hmmed*. *"Would the star of the biggest box-office record-smashers of all time need to go to a loan shark for money?"*

I wouldn't have thought a doctor would need cash, either, Nimue thought back to him. *But it's not always so simple when something like addiction is involved.*

Nimue started pacing again. "When I sent you to check on Maverick today, did he recognize you?"

Dr. Choi shook his head quickly. "I'm certain he didn't. He'd been too panicked back at Pound's house.

And none of those people—those bodyguards, that little assistant—were with him at Pound's place. He didn't seem to have anyone there for him."

He chewed his lip. "He *did* seem improved since I'd last seen him. I tried to prod casually about it, ask if he'd been seeing a therapist and taking medications. He has been and he's been taking anti-anxiety meds. It's just that sometimes he still experiences enough stress to trigger an attack. I asked what had caused it, how long he's been this way, and he didn't answer." Dr. Choi smiled slightly. "But it's a good sign he was willing to confront his fear and come to a town full of witches. Sometimes exposure therapy works best to make the biggest dent in an anxiety." His chin trembled. "So… you have me on the ropes. If I lose this job, I have nothing. If you report that I shared this information with you, I'll lose my license to practice in the human world."

"You're not fired." Nimue *tsked*. "Not *yet*. Unless I find you're hiding anything else relevant…"

Dr. Choi gulped and lowered his chin behind his briefcase.

"Either way, I'm not reporting the medical privacy issue to the human medical professionals," Nimue said. Dr. Choi visibly relaxed. Nimue turned to Florence. "So when he asked—did *you* think the man had been charmed?"

Florence frowned. "I told him I'd have to examine the patient myself. It's possible—charms can do almost anything, as you well know—but there are many human methods of inducing fear in a person. Including torture."

Gowdie shuddered. *"Not Colton Carter…"*

"It's Maverick Vanedestine, not Colton Carter," Nimue pointed out. She thought about it. The doctor had said there hadn't been signs of any physical harm done to the man. But then again, couldn't a witch heal a good number of wounds? But that would point to a witch being involved either way.

Nimue's witch network crystal beeped at her wrist and she brought it up, finding a message from Cassie.

Comic Enthusiast Society checked out, she'd written. *They weren't in town when the crime occurred and Klaus Fowler verified picking them up in his carriage at the time in question outside of town. They checked in right as the dinner was about to start.*

Klaus was Witchy ExS staff member Morpheus Fowler's father, the head of the transportation witches around town. They didn't work for Witchy ExS, but they worked with them, and Nimue definitely trusted any alibi they gave. *The briefcases just had a bunch of Comic Enthusiast Society paperwork inside*, Cassie continued. *And business cards, things like that.*

Nimue wondered how she'd asked the men to let her search their cases.

"What's in your briefcase, Dr. Choi?" she asked.

The doctor blinked and lowered his briefcase, then popped it open. It was full of folders and medicines and bandages, things that might have been found in a first-aid kit. That explained why he'd brought the briefcase with him to the Bessa in an emergency, at least.

"Florence, can you keep an eye on our human doctor?" Nimue asked her. "Just until we've cleared this case."

Florence nodded, then looked to Dr. Choi, who sunk in his seat but nodded back. "I won't let him out of my sight," she said.

It would be a long night for them all.

"I'm just going to get Gowdie's figurine from your office and we'll swing by my house. I need to check in with Ren, Zelena, and Cassie." Nimue started walking and Florence stood.

"Are we alerting the rest of the staff yet? What about Bernadette?"

What about Bernadette indeed. Nimue's second major convention as co-Head Witch General Manager and her second murder on site. But if Bernadette could help solve the case…

"We'll alert everyone once Ren and I have made that decision together," Nimue said grimly. "I need to update them all that I found our briefcase-carrying mysterious figure from the Bessa." She glowered at Dr. Choi as he stood meekly and he flinched. "And that he didn't commit the murder at least."

Dr. Choi's eyes widened and he nodded emphatically.

Nimue held his stare a moment later, then slipped on her broomstick, gliding the short way back to the clinic.

She waited out front while Gowdie flew back in to get his figurine, sending a quick message to Ren, Zelena, and Cassie about what she'd discovered about their human doctor new hire. She left the details about Maverick off the message, at least for now.

"Nimue?" said Gowdie through their mind connection. The door to the clinic opened and he headed back out, clutching his figurine in his hands. Florence and Dr. Choi

arrived just at that moment. Nimue stuck her broom out to stop them, concerned about Gowdie's tone.

"There was a door open that wasn't open before," Gowdie said. *"And I looked inside. I think... I think Glinda's body is missing."*

CHAPTER SIXTEEN

Florence wrapped up her History Charm, after following the illusion of Glinda's body as it floated up into the air, lifeless, and then floated to the teleportation pad, disappearing within. The color shone brown, which indicated the Bessa lobby.

Massaging her temple with one hand, Nimue thought out her emergency message to Ren, Cassie, and Zelena explaining all of that.

What do you mean, her body floated? Where was the witch or warlock casting a Hover Charm nearby? Ren wrote back almost immediately.

I don't know, Nimue thought to her witch network message. *I didn't see one. Just like we didn't see anyone cutting Glinda's throat, either, I might add. Can you just check? The body would have passed through the lobby no more than ten minutes ago.*

I'll check. Give me a minute. Ren's message ended.

"Do you want something for your headache?" Florence asked, her wand at the ready.

Nimue looked from Florence to Dr. Choi, who stared at the teleportation pad in the hallway of the clinic as if it might suddenly open up a portal to a murderer's den. It just might, actually, based on how things were going.

"I need something to help me stay up all night," Nimue said.

"You'll crash at sunrise when the charms reset," Florence warned her. "Exhaustion will catch up to you."

"That's fine," Nimue said. "I can cast another one then if I need to."

Florence pursed her lips for a moment. "As long as you don't make a habit out of it. More than one witch has keeled over dead from relying on too many charms like that."

"Believe me, I am going to sleep as long as I can as soon as I can," Nimue promised.

Florence nodded, waving her wand over Nimue. "Awake Charm."

Nimue soaked in the magical stimulant, feeling her headache and achiness retreat. She wasn't tired at all anymore.

"Awake Charm? That's like an energy drink?" Dr. Choi asked. Neither witch knew what he was talking about. "I didn't think it was a good thing Esmerelda had a charm that could give her a burst of energy like that, but I'm not familiar with what witches can handle."

Right. Esmerelda's admission about the perma-charm crystal in her necklace. Nimue didn't have time to worry about that just now. Especially since she'd just had an Awake Charm performed on herself. It'd be a bit hypocritical of her to disapprove. "We need…" Her voice caught in her throat. "We need to find these villains and fast—before the convention opens."

"And if you don't?" Dr. Choi asked.

"The convention goes on," Nimue said grimly. "The cauldron beneath our city needs happy con-goers' energy, and that's why we can't make this public. But I'll never forgive myself if the killings continue—not to mention, that'll be the end of our city. No one will want to come for a convention here after several murder sprees."

Gowdie, still clutching his figurine box, floated in the air beside her. *"Um, I don't know if this is relevant, but I heard it again. That fizzling sound. As soon as I entered the clinic the second time to get my deluxe figurine. Followed by a flash of dull light. I didn't think much of it at first."*

"The light was the teleportation pad?" Nimue guessed.

"Probably." Gowdie nodded. *"Did you notice anything weird about Glinda hovering in the History Charm?"*

"You mean, beside the fact that she *hovered* on out of here with no witch around?" Nimue deadpanned.

On Florence's shoulder, her leech made several squelching noises.

Gowdie nodded enthusiastically. *"Yes! That's it. It didn't really seem like a Hover Charm had been used, did it?"*

"What do you mean, it didn't seem..." Nimue squeezed her jaw shut and thought back. In the History Charm illusion capturing what had happened here, Glinda had hovered off the table, hovered out the door, then went around the cor—

No. She hadn't smoothly gone around the corner, had she?

"She kind of dipped when going around the corner," Nimue said aloud.

Florence nodded. "That was strange. A Hover Charm wouldn't make something loll down and then back up like that. It goes straight up, as high as the witch wants the object to go, and stays that high until an Undo Charm is cast."

"It looked like two people were carrying her," Dr. Choi said. "At least to me." With one hand, he let go of the briefcase he cradled against his chest and pushed his glasses up his nose. "Not that I understand anything about witch charms. Isn't there one that might... make people invisible?"

Nimue and Florence's eyes widened as they turned to one another.

A witch's skills were limited mostly by practice and knowledge of what could be done. And the fact that they could draw on magical energy and only cast one of each charm per day until the next sunrise.

A witch without practice or clarity could attempt a charm and it could simply not result in the intended magic.

Nimue waved her wand at herself and pictured it. Really *pictured* the possibility of something she'd never done before. Never had reason to need before. "Invisible Charm."

At first, she was sure it wouldn't work. She'd only rarely heard of such a charm being used before. But then her left hand flickered, and she could see the sterile clinic floor beneath it, even with the hazy outline of her fingers.

"*Nimue?*" Gowdie asked cautiously.

The outline of her fingers disappeared, leaving nothing at the end of her long limb. She could still feel it there. She could flex her fingers. But she couldn't see the hand at all.

But then with a *crackle*, the hand came back into view.

"Whoa," said Dr. Choi, taking in a sharp breath.

"Failed charm," Florence said. She screwed up her lips. "No practice?"

"Who would need to practice *that*?" Nimue said. "A thief?"

"*A spy?*" quipped Gowdie.

Nimue's jaw dropped. "Zelena was a spy. Decades ago."

Florence's face greened. "You can't think… Not both her *and* her husband."

"She grew up with Glinda, too!" Nimue said. She bit her lip. She couldn't picture Zelena doing such a thing, surly as she was. But she wouldn't have pictured Linden doing such a thing, either.

And then there was the fact that she was supposed to be on her best behavior, considering what her husband of eighty years had been up to under her nose, when she'd been proclaiming her ignorance? Didn't that kind of make her the *least* likely suspect?

"Which then means she could take advantage of that cover and actually commit crimes, knowing no one would suspect her," Gowdie said. He frowned. *"I know Messenger makes for a slow-minded familiar, but I didn't pick up anything suspicious off her. Not like I did when they were starting to suspect Linden last time."*

"And I just included her on the message to Ren…"

Nimue bit her lip. "But she would have expected me to either way. It would have been suspicious if I hadn't."

"No." Florence shook her head vehemently. "She didn't do this."

"Whoever she is, she didn't do it alone," Dr. Choi said.

Nimue turned to him.

He flinched. "I just mean, it was *two* people carrying the body, surely?"

Nimue let out a sigh. He wasn't wrong.

"Don't tell anyone," Nimue said, turning to Florence and Dr. Choi in turn. "Stay here." She frowned. "Do you still have that pin Glinda picked up?"

Florence jumped into action, checking around the medical slab. "No." She shook her head. "They must have taken it along with her."

Nimue ran a hand down her face. She'd been hoping someone else more skilled with Origin Charms than Florence might have been able to trace a specific witch's signature on it.

Dr. Choi raised a hand shakily. "About that…"

Florence and Nimue both whipped their heads around to face him.

He winced, and his voice shook. "I noticed as soon as Florence put it to the side of the body to perform her magic on it. But I couldn't say… Well, you know now."

"Spit it out," Nimue said, all but grinding her teeth in impatience.

Dr. Choi flinched again. "I thought once I told you about *Pound*—"

Gowdie let out a little burst of flame, causing Dr. Choi to stop talking. *"Hashtag! Hashtag, Nimue!"*

"You lost me," Nimue admitted. Then she remembered the discussion they'd had earlier. "Hashtag? Hash brown?"

Gowdie rolled his eyes. *It's only been called a hashtag in the past few decades or so. Humans and their internet speak.*

"Okay..." Nimue said. "And it used to be called something else?" She frowned. Witch education was quite a bit different than human education, but she *had* seen that before. "It's a number sign. Also known as... a pound sign!"

Dr. Choi nodded grimly. "It's Pound's calling card, so to speak. He leaves a golden pin with the pound sign behind anytime he wants someone who owes him money to know he's watching. Or that he..." He swallowed. "He did whatever thing happened where it was found."

"*Pound* murdered Glinda?" Nimue shrieked.

"Well, no, I don't think." Dr. Choi stumbled over his words. "But he could have ordered it done. I doubt he does his dirty work himself."

"Why?" Florence asked. "I admit I didn't know much about Glinda's personal life, but witches in Cauldron Cove don't need human loan sharks. We always chip in if anyone needs more money, witch or human currency. There'd be no need to hide that."

Nimue nodded. Both forms of currency were accepted in Cauldron Cove to accommodate so many human congoers. But most of Glinda's bills would have been in witch currency, considering she lived here. And no witch went without in a witch town. It was simply an unwritten rule. The only danger was if they moved out to human cities and lived by human rules and human currency.

Human bills had been an unpleasant part of living in Huntsville with Greg. Nimue had had to work at a library for a bit to help make ends meet.

But even then, if the witch still had connections back home to a witch town, the witches would generally rally to help them out.

"Aren't you forgetting something important?" Gowdie said. *"Glinda found that pin. Before she died. It wasn't left behind like some proof-of-murder calling card."*

Nimue let out a deep breath as Epona translated Gowdie's comments for Florence, no doubt. "So Glinda might have just stumbled onto it. Whatever crime Pound or his people were announcing."

The room went quiet.

"What other crime?" Nimue finally asked aloud after a minute.

"It could just be him saying 'I'm watching you,'" Dr. Choi guessed.

"Watching whom, then?" Nimue asked.

Nobody had an answer. Dr. Choi shook his head. "Not me. I swear, it's all over between him and me."

Nimue's witch network perma-charm crystal flashed red and she checked to find a message from Ren. *Had to track down Zelena, but we looked over the History Charm footage. Glinda's body did show in the lobby. Hovered in from the teleportation pad all on its own, hovered right back into the teleportation pad. No sign of any witch or warlock around. Color capture on the body's destination was off again, thanks to the shadows and the moonlight. Don't know where they went, but we're checking all the pads now.*

Nimue relayed the message grimly. "The lobby was

just used to cloak their real destination," she concluded. "They got lucky that we couldn't see the color the pad flashed in the lobby." She sighed. "Was Zelena involved? Why did Ren have to 'track her down'?"

"You mean, besides the fact that she's busy with a security issue?" Florence asked wryly.

Nimue wasn't so sure the answer was that simple.

"What are you going to do now?" Florence asked.

"If I tell Ren all of this right away, Zelena will find out," Nimue said. "First… First I need a plan."

"We need to drop off my limited-edition figurine, too," Gowdie insisted. *"You promised."*

Nimue shot him a look. He kept flapping his wings but didn't seem to cave.

"Fine," she said aloud. "And then we're messaging my grandmas."

"You think they're awake?" Florence asked.

Nimue checked the time on her witch network screen. It was nearing midnight.

"I hope so. Or I might have to fly over there to talk to them in person." Her witch network screen lit up with another message. It was from her Grandma Prue.

We're headed to your place, she'd written. *Sorry it's so late. If you're asleep, we'll just leave the latest batch of perma-charm History Charm crystals on your porch. Bernadette finished up another half dozen and was sure you'd want them installed before Comic Hero Con.*

"We've got to go," Nimue said quickly to Gowdie. "If we move fast, we can catch my grandmas at my place."

CHAPTER SEVENTEEN

N imue flew to the street in front of her townhouse, her eyes darting briefly to the "FOR SALE" sign on the townhouse next door—looked like her neighbor hadn't found someone to buy the place yet, though it'd just been for sale for about a week. She managed to get home just in the nick of time, as she spotted her Grandma Bernadette and Grandma Prue walking away from her front door, which had a basket on the porch in front of it, and about to mount their brooms.

"Grandmas!" she shouted, going in for a landing.

Tired from all the flying while carrying his figurine box, Gowdie had perched on the bristles at the back of her broomstick.

"A little easier!" he shouted at her in her mind. *"Take the landing a little easier. Precious cargo back here."*

Nimue took his concerns into consideration and softened her descent.

"Nimue?" Bernadette said, leaning her broomstick back against the exterior of Nimue's house. "What's going on?" she asked in her merry, soprano voice. It was just one more disarming thing about her because she was always all-business. She'd lived so long, she had the appearance of an older human, complete with all-gray, long hair pulled to the side in a low ponytail and wrinkles on her rose-toned skin. Her blue eyes were a lot like her granddaughter's, and Nimue always felt like she was looking at her future when she looked at her grandma.

Nimue glanced to the neighbors' townhouses on either side of hers. Her one neighbor had already moved out earlier in the week to go live with her son in a human town in another state and no lights were on in the other townhouse, but she still didn't want to have this conversation in her front yard. "Come inside." She tapped her wand to the perma-charm crystal that kept her front door locked.

Her grandma Prue was the first to follow her. She, too, had lived long enough to show signs of aging, though there were a number of decades between her and her partner. She'd married Bernadette a few years after Bernadette had lost her first spouse, Nimue's grandfather, who'd died long before Nimue had been born. Her copper complexion was wrinkled, particularly around the eyes and mouth, and her black-and-white, curly hair fell over one shoulder.

"Why are you still up?" Prue asked. "Still preparing for the con tomorrow?"

"It's worse than that, I'm afraid." Nimue gestured to her living room, setting her broomstick against a wall in the entryway.

Gowdie took off and went straight upstairs with his

precious box. Naismith and Dunlop, her grandmothers' matching golden lovebird familiars, tittered sleepily and perched atop Nimue's fireplace mantel, nuzzling cheek to cheek. The logs caught aflame as soon as Nimue neared, sensing her need for warmth after a long, horrid evening.

Bernadette came in last, carrying the basket full of additional perma-charm History Charm crystals Prue had promised in her message.

"You seem stressed, but you don't even look tired," she said, putting the basket down on Nimue's two-seater dinette set. She peered closer at her granddaughter. "Have you used an Awake Charm?" Her tone implied a mild rebuke.

"I know they're dangerous, but it was Florence herself who cast it on me," Nimue said. "Please. Sit." She gestured to the brown loveseat couch and kitty-corner matching armchair.

Prue and Bernadette exchanged a glance but sat together on the couch.

Nimue started pacing and wringing her hands. "There's been another murder at the Bessa—and this time, it was one of our own."

She watched as her grandmothers' faces went from shocked to saddened as she explained everything she knew so far.

Ending with her suspicions about Zelena.

"No," said Bernadette simply, her lips pinched. "Not her. If you'd have told me you suspected Linden last month, I wouldn't have argued with you, but Zelena, I trust completely."

Nimue's jaw dropped. She certainly would have said

vice versa about the two in question, considering Linden's perfect customer service demeanor.

Then again, she'd slowly uncovered the fact that he hadn't been so kind to his underlings. And he had a self-loathing that had extended to a hatred of all witches.

She decided to listen to what her grandmother—who'd worked with Zelena for over half a century—had to say.

"Zelena Varlett has worked her entire life to get out from her grandmother's shadow," Prue explained. She'd never worked for Witchy ExS, preferring a more freelance existence before her retirement like Nimue's parents and other grandparents, but she'd known her wife's co-workers well.

"Gala Varlett was Bessa Toothaker's rival," Nimue said.

Naismith chirped from atop the mantel, flapping his wings.

"But she was also her best friend," Bernadette said simply. She squeezed her legs together and closed her eyes, taking a deep breath. She'd known these women personally. "Gala was jealous of my mother's accomplishments, I have no doubt. *She* had hoped to found this town, you see. They'd moved here together, had worked with the human peoples already settled, gifting the land with magic with which to aid them, and carved out a small slice of the area with their permission to create a witch town."

"They each had their respective husbands by then," Prue added. "Though they hadn't yet had children."

"By the time I was born, the city was founded, the

cauldron that provides our cove's magic sunk beneath the dirt and sediment. But there was always... a tension between the two friends."

"And you don't think that tension could have passed down to Gala's granddaughter? That, maybe, she hoped to get some sort of revenge on behalf of her grandmother?"

"By killing *Glinda*?" Prue's brow wrinkled.

True. Nimue didn't know if Glinda had been a purposeful target or if she'd just been in the wrong place at the wrong time, but...

"With another murder, there's another chance for a convention to be a disaster," Nimue said. "And if a convention is a disaster, the whole town is destroyed. And a Toothaker, as co-Head Witch General Manager of Witchy ExS, would get blamed for it."

Bernadette *tsked*. "Don't take the weight of the world on your shoulders, dear. A convention's success depends on the entire town—and you had nothing to do with this disaster."

Nimue let out a sigh and settled on the armchair beside her grandmothers, clutching her hands together between her knees. "I just... can't help it. There've been smaller conventions without incident, but this is my *second* convention with a murder since I've taken up the position of co-leader." She wiped a tear from her eye. "And Glinda. That hits hard, it being one of our own. Maybe even more than one of our own being a killer. But if another one of us did this deed..."

Prue reached over to pat her back, as Gowdie flapped his wings and flew down the steps, his figurine put away upstairs. He bristled at the sight of his witch so forlorn and quickly made his way over, settling in her lap and rubbing his head against her abdomen.

She laughed despite herself, patting his head. His scales were cold beneath her now-warmed fingers.

Get your toy all nice and settled? she mentally asked him.

"*Found him a nice perch in my cat-tree castle. Can't wait to show Willow. Especially how it's signed and everything.*"

"Well, I'll tell you one thing," Prue said. "You've referred to yourself as a 'co-' leader more than once in this conversation. I think you've really stepped up over the past couple of weeks. *Especially* considering all these disasters." She got up. "Let me make you some tea." She looked to Bernadette, who nodded at her, and slipped past the staircase into Nimue's kitchen.

Bernadette slipped down the couch to sit closer to her granddaughter.

"Grandma, what do I do?" Nimue said softly. She was a parent herself, but she felt like a child in that moment. Vulnerable and small. "Should we tell the rest of the staff?"

"Not yet," Bernadette said. "Let them sleep—at least one more night of peaceful slumber." She sighed. "You told me what you know. Let's go over what you don't."

"Why Glinda?" said Nimue to start. "Was she targeted or silenced because she stumbled onto something?"

"And the pin," Bernadette added. "Was she killed because she picked it up? Who dropped it? Was it someone this 'Pound' gangster sent? And why is Pound possibly involved at all?"

"Who dropped the toy sword we think was used to kill her?" Nimue grimaced. An invisible person running it over Glinda's neck made more sense now than a hovering sword. The cut had been too precise for that. "And what two witches are involved?"

Bernadette blinked. "*Two* witches?"

"Well..." Nimue leaned back on the couch. "Two people were carrying Glinda. If they were both invisible rather than using a Hover Charm, there had to be two witches casting the charm. One Invisible Charm per person. Either for themselves or on two other people who did the actual carrying."

"What about perma-charm crystals?" Bernadette asked hoarsely.

"Being talented at casting Invisible Charms is rare, I give you that. It'd be weird to have two witches who can do it skillfully working together. But perma-charm crystals for Invisible Charms are even rarer, don't you agree?"

Bernadette's expression grew stern, her jaw clenched as her eyes darted downward, like she was thinking.

Nimue leaned back, still stroking Gowdie, letting all of the information she had filter through her.

She knew who the man with the briefcase was. Did that clear the Comic Enthusiast Society and Maverick's bodyguards—the other men about the same height and shape with briefcases she'd initially suspected—entirely of involvement?

Maverick's bodyguards were the most likely to have stolen the toy sword. Assuming the one missing from Maverick's—now Gowdie's—figurine box was indeed the item in question.

If an invisible person had been carrying it down that hall, they could have dropped it at any time before Dr. Choi had appeared and not been visible via History Charm.

So what else did she have to go off of? The Pound pin.

Someone at this convention had a connection to Pound—other than Dr. Choi, who claimed his business with the man was done. Then there was Maverick, who was keeping his connection secret.

Maverick, whose strogapohobia might have been caused by Pound himself.

Which probably meant Pound had worked with at least one witch since even before this convention. *Something*—a charm or a witch or warlock acting menacing— had to have instilled this fear into Maverick.

"What if instead of this pin just acting as a 'message' to someone who owed Pound, Pound's associates wear this pin to identify themselves?" Nimue asked aloud.

"Seems a foolish thing to do, wear a mark on your sleeve or lapel like that," Gowdie said.

Naismith chirped from the mantelpiece.

Gowdie nodded. *"But sometimes groups are foolish out of some sense of pride,"* he translated.

Nimue smiled at her grandmother's bird.

"Yes, so… Someone working for Pound is here. Has been here since this morning—yesterday morning," she said, checking her witch network quickly and seeing it was now getting late past midnight. "And they dropped it before the murder."

"Someone who went on a tour of the Bessa," Bernadette said. Prue returned with a tray with three mugs on it, and her lovebird flapped his wings to settle on her shoulder, nestling his cheek against hers.

"Who went on a tour of the Bessa?" Prue asked, not entirely caught up.

"Not the Comic Enthusiast Society members, other than Mia herself," said Gowdie as Prue passed out the teacups.

Nimue took hers and blew on it, the lavender and chamomile aroma settling into her senses. "And not Maverick. His bodyguard and assistant said he was inside his hotel room until dinner." She froze, the teacup halfway to her lips.

"Nimue?" asked Prue, settling down on the couch beside Bernadette.

"Two of Maverick's bodyguards were taken on a tour —by Zelena," she added.

Bernadette scowled over the top of her teacup. "But Zelena is innocent."

"We'll see," muttered Gowdie, and he looked to Dunlop to see if one of the lovebirds would tattle on him. They didn't appear to just then at least.

"Maybe." Nimue put her teacup back on its saucer. "But those two bodyguards also have to explain how the golden figurine in Maverick's possession came to be missing its sword. Considering that was the murder weapon." She took a quick gulp of her tea, eager to get it down and get back out there to start investigating.

Her grandmothers exchanged a look and both put their teacups back on their saucers.

"What is it?" Nimue asked.

Bernadette set her full teacup down on the table in

front of her and took out her wand. "Undo Awake Charm," she said, waving it over Nimue.

"What…?" Nimue felt herself lose all of her energy. She suddenly became very sleepy.

"Nimue?" Gowdie asked, his back stiffening.

Her head lolled. Her grandma had undone her Awake Charm. And the tea… The tea was a sedative. Not a strong one, per se, but in her already exhausted state…

"Rest, dear," Bernadette said, taking the teacup from her and passing it back to Prue. Nimue's eyes could barely stay open. "We'll keep investigating while you sleep. Hopefully, it'll all be settled in the morning."

"Grandma…?" Nimue asked, but she was already sinking back into the chair.

Bernadette's face was grim. "If this is what we think it is, it's safer for you not to get more involved."

"Nimue!" shouted Gowdie, the chirping of lovebirds ringing out in Nimue's ears as exhaustion took over her.

CHAPTER EIGHTEEN

Buzz. *Buzz. Buzz.*

A familiar, if grating, sound echoed in Nimue's ears. She blearily opened her eyes, her neck immediately jolting with a flash of stiffness and pain. Rubbing her sore muscles, she shot up—and realized sunset was streaming through her window.

The witch network perma-charm crystal at her wrist blinked rapidly with a red light, but it wasn't what had made the buzzing noise. It was her human smartphone, sitting on the coffee table in front of her. Next to Gowdie, curled up in a feline manner beside it.

He popped up, a bleary eye blinking. *"You're awake!"*

"What...? What happened?" She massaged her temples and thought back to last night.

"Your grandmas put you to sleep!" Gowdie shouted. *"I couldn't leave the townhouse—too far from you, and you weren't budging off that chair. And familiars can't use the witch network. So I went to get your smartphone, and I was*

going to call Willow at first—but then I thought you might not want to freak her out like that, especially since I still doubted your own grandmothers would hurt you—so I had to think about who in town could even answer."

He was speaking a mile a minute and Nimue was finding it difficult to keep up. She reached for her wand at her hip, still in its holster and even jabbing into her side. She was about to cast an "Awake Charm" but stopped herself. She'd just used one the day before, and she knew her grandmother didn't approve of relying on such things—

Her grandmother. Who'd put her to sleep, just like Gowdie had said.

"We didn't have her number, so I had to be coy about it," Gowdie said. *"I texted Willow on the pretext of telling her about getting the limited-edition Superstellar-Man figurine, signed and everything, and casually asked for her number. Of course, she still clearly found it weird, especially since she knew it was so late here, so I had to pretend Spandemager had an interest in this figurine and I'd wanted to let him know. And now, I've been waiting for hours, but I bet she was asleep, so—"*

Nimue shot to her feet. "What are you talking about? Whom did you text?"

As if on cue, there was a knock at the front door, and Nimue, frozen for a moment with indecision as to her next course of action, found the continued knocking most urgent. She went to the front door and opened it to find Merga Arriens, a witch about her daughter's age who worked on the showroom floor and often was in charge of the hovering item storage in the lobby. Holding her broomstick brush-head up in one hand beside her, she was wearing all black, her snow-pale skin popping out in contrast, her red hair hanging in gothic waves over her shoulders. Her familiar, Spandemager, a miniature red llama, frolicked to and fro behind her across the cobblestone path.

Merga examined Nimue from head to toe, pulling a human smartphone out from the pouch at her hip. "You texted me? Six hours ago? I didn't see it until I woke up, sorry." She leaned around Nimue. "You said it was an emergency?"

Gowdie flapped his wings and flew out to meet Spandemager, landing in his fluffy fur. While it was true that Cassie wasn't much older than Merga and that Nimue appreciated Gowdie being coy about the situation to Willow—who was halfway across the country in human college and couldn't have rushed home to help—she wouldn't have relied on Merga to handle this extreme crisis. She wasn't even sure what Ren had decided to tell everyone about Glinda. Hadn't he noticed she'd gone AWOL?

"It's all fine now, thank you," Nimue said quickly. Her eyes widened when she caught a glance at the time on Merga's phone screen. Seven-thirty. Half an hour until Comic Hero Con was due to begin. "We're late!" she shrieked, as if the convention were the only thing she had to worry about.

Merga fumbled to put her phone back into her pouch. "Well, I mean, I woke up with enough time, but I didn't expect for you to summon me to your *house*."

"I'm not upset with you," Nimue said quickly. Spandemager was nodding his head, which he'd turned and aimed at Gowdie, the two lost in conversation. "I-I overslept. Gowdie was trying to wake me up and couldn't think of how else to do it. I apologize, and thank you. Gowdie!"

"Overslept? But didn't he send the text at like one in the mor—"

Nimue rushed inside, grabbing her own broomstick from where it leaned on the wall. Flapping his wings, Gowdie soared through the front door and settled on her shoulder. *"Spandemager says no one got any message about anything out of the ordinary. He wanted to know why, but I told him to stay tuned. I wasn't sure when you were revealing this to your staff."*

Nimue turned around, to find Merga shrugging and getting on her broomstick. Once the younger witch had taken to the air, she reached a long arm down and snatched Spandemager by a clump of fur, dragging him beneath her as they flew off toward the Bessa. As her familiar, he wouldn't weigh that much, but he was one of the larger familiars around, despite his relatively small size compared to an actual llama.

Nimue followed suit, stepping outside and about to saddle up, when Gowdie stopped her. *"Wait! Willow is expecting a text from you."*

Nimue chewed her lip. She didn't have time for this, but she wouldn't let her daughter worry, either. Besides, texting… She hated it, but it would allow her to quickly ease her daughter's mind without giving away how panicked and lost she truly felt.

She bolted back inside and picked up the buzzing smartphone.

Willow had written, about to head to class, telling her to have a good first day of Comic Hero Con.

"Thank… you… dear…" Nimue said aloud. She frowned when the words changed to "thank you, deer" on the phone screen but kept going. "Will… be… Busy. Leaving… phone… At… home."

Gowdie peered over her shoulder, and Nimue assumed he was about to make a wry remark about how the "AutoCorrect" had mangled another one of her text messages to "will be bussy," so she sent the text quickly before they could debate it. Instead, he reached a talon out and made a swiping motion across the air, changing the text to a news page. "Check out that human news entertainment section headline. Anyone look familiar?"

Nimue frowned, swiping at the headline that had popped up at the top of her screen.

With the article, there was a picture of a large fence joined with a gate, the very top of a terracotta roof visible some distance behind it. Maverick was smiling broadly in front of the gate.

"'Maverick Vanedestine's Hollywood Home Exclusive Tour,'" Nimue read aloud.

She skimmed the rest of the article, struggling to get the screen to move through the text at just the right speed. "He gave a tour of his place last week, I see. Looks like typical rich-guy stuff."

"Isn't it weird a man so afraid of witches, he'd curl up into a ball on a hotel floor just puts his whole house layout out there for all to see?"

"I guess. But it's not like a witch after him would need the blueprints to scare him. It's probably just normal human-internet stuff." Nimue looked out at the street through her still-open front door. The broomstick carriages were out in force, bringing thousands of con-goers to the convention center, likely joining the already thousands who were lined up and ready to go.

All when there was a murder to solve. Or was there?

She put the phone down on the coffee table and brought her wrist up, projecting her thoughts at the witch network crystal to sort through her messages.

There were so many.

She brought up the latest from Cassie.

"Can you stop by Ms. Estrada's room before you shadow Mr. Vanedestine for the day?" she'd written. *"I'd ask Mr. Southern, but I still can't get a hold of him, either. Where are you two?"*

Nimue's breath hitched and she glanced at her list of messages from Ren. There wasn't any she'd missed while she'd been asleep. He still hadn't found out where Glinda's body had gone after it had left the Bessa lobby, after all this time?

Cassie? she thought-wrote into her witch network crystal. *What have I missed?* She decided to let her in on the most important bit of information she'd yet to share— Cassie was already in this deep. She hesitated, unsure about betraying the grandmothers like second and third mothers to her. *My grandmothers visited last night. They were acting suspicious once I told them everything I knew about Glinda. Then they sedated me and told me it was too dangerous for me to investigate. Have you seen them?*

Nimue was about to turn back to her broomstick, not more than a moment after she'd sent the message, when the yellow circle of a Communication Charm materialized in front of her, an illusory portal opening between them. Cassie appeared on the other side, the office behind her, bags weighing down on her eyes. "Miss Toothaker!" The color had drained from her face. "You've been *sedated* all evening?"

Nimue bit her lip. "Yes. What have I missed?"

Cassie scoffed and Laveau, her familiar ferret, sighed as he drooped himself over her shoulder. "Well, now that I know your grandmothers were up to no good, I'm even *more* worried."

"Why?" Nimue felt a sudden drop in her stomach. "Have you seen them?"

"I have." Cassie shook her head. "Several hours ago. They met Ren and me here, told us you were so exhausted, you were going to sleep a few hours and they'd step up to help with the investigation in your stead."

"*Uh-oh,*" said Gowdie. He flapped his wings from Nimue's shoulder.

"They left with Ren right away, and I haven't been able to contact him since. I couldn't even get my Communication Charm to work with him before sunrise—I didn't try again this morning, though, figured I'd use it on you." She stared bleakly ahead of her, into Nimue's face. "The con is about to start."

"I know," Nimue whispered. "Can you hang in there? Make sure it's all ready?"

"Humphrey can't handle Miss Redferne's job. I've told

him she's out sick—but that just made it worse. Everyone knows witches rarely get sick." She grunted. "Should have said it was a family emergency."

"I'm sorry to ask this of you, but please hold down the fort. I'll find Ren and my grandmothers—did you say you wanted me to visit Mia Estrada?"

Cassie massaged her temples, closing her eyes. "I can't spare a moment. She keeps calling the office. She wants an update—I can't... I don't know what to tell her."

"I'll handle it," Nimue said. "You handle the con. Best you can." She bit her lip. "Cassie, we can do this."

Cassie grunted and waved her wand at herself. "Awake Charm."

They were turning into a regular bunch of Awake Charm addicts.

"Be safe," Nimue said.

Cassie nodded and waved her wand, dismissing the Communication Charm.

Gowdie flapped his wings and landed on the coffee table beside the smartphone, clicking the screen with his talon as it buzzed again. *"Did your grandmothers put Ren to sleep too?"*

"I can only hope that explains why he went missing." She clenched her fist. "They like him. They wouldn't hurt him. They wouldn't hurt anybody."

Gowdie frowned. *"But they'd knock them out without their permission, apparently."*

That was *not* like anything her grandmothers had ever done before. Not as far as Nimue knew.

So... why?

Nimue snatched her wand out of its holster and waved it in front of her.

"Communication Charm," she said, picturing Ren, then Soren for good measure in case he was currently in control.

The charm formed a circle in front of her and then... fizzled. Without ever making the connection.

"How...?" Nimue asked. Cassie was right. The charm wasn't opening a connection to Ren. Even if a person was sleeping, the charm was supposed to open a connection, alert them to the need for communication.

The only time it didn't work was when...

"A witch or warlock is dead," Nimue whispered harshly.

"Or they're passed out so deeply that a Communication Charm has no hope of rousing them," Gowdie pointed out. *"No need to jump to the worst conclusions yet."*

That was true. Nimue took a deep breath. She didn't know what to prioritize first—but she also didn't know where to look for Ren. She'd start at the Southern Hotel and ask his parents. Or try his quarters in the hotel basement. She'd never been there, but she knew that was where he lived. And there was Mia and Maverick to worry about—

"Nimue," said Gowdie, peering down at the smartphone. *"I think we missed something in this photo when you were looking at it the first time."*

Nimue cocked her head but picked up the phone to see what he was looking at.

In the story about the tour of Maverick's Hollywood home, there was something strange worked into the metalwork of the gate, right behind where Maverick had struck a pose.

Four lines, two horizontal and two vertical at a slight angle.

"*A pound sign,*" Gowdie said. "*On Maverick Vanedestine's front gate.*"

CHAPTER NINETEEN

"*I* *suppose we already knew Maverick and Pound were connected,*" Gowdie said as they stepped into the Southern Hotel lobby, broomstick in Nimue's hand. The lobby was packed with con-goers at the currently open breakfast bar, milling about in the lobby talking and lining up in front of the skywalk and teleportation pad entrances, just waiting for the convention to open. Nimue chanced a quick glance at her witch network crystal, summoning up the time. Only ten minutes until con opening now.

Even if she weren't worried about her conversation with her familiar being half-overheard, Nimue wasn't sure he could hear her if she spoke aloud, so she thought back her reply to him. *But if it was a matter of owing Pound money, why get the symbol metal-worked into his gate?*

"*Maybe it's like a sign to the world: Someone who owes Pound big time lives here.*"

Nimue smiled flutteringly at a man dressed as Supervile-Villain, Superstellar-Man's greatest rival, as she slipped past him to reach the front desk. *That's a lot of time and money spent on something one would hope you'd eventually get out of. Like Dr. Choi did. Owing money to a shady man like that.*

"*True, humans can't just wave a wand and make a change.*" Gowdie curled one front foot into a fist and slammed it against the palm of the other. "*Maybe he hired a witch to do it!*"

Nimue shot him a look. *Maverick. With strogaphobia. Hired a witch for a gate change.*

"*Or Pound did it for him, kind of, like, a reminder he owes him. Plus, we don't know when his fear of witches started. Maybe the gate design was done before the incident Dr. Choi witnessed.*"

Maybe, Nimue thought back. She wasn't going to hesitate to grill the man, celebrity VIP or not, next time she saw him.

She checked her witch network crystal as yet another message flashed in. It was a reply from Zelena. She'd carefully worded an inquiry about everything's status to the Director of Security—she still wasn't completely sure the witch was innocent, not if her own grandmothers were clearly hiding something, too—and Zelena had replied back at last.

Bernadette told me to leave it to her and Ren, she wrote back—and Nimue wondered if her zealous Director of Security would really be fine with passing over responsibility for *anything*. Then again, she'd always clearly respected Bernadette. *I'm to focus on the con itself and any potential new issues. So far, so good. We're ready to go.*

Nimue grunted and wrote back a curt "okay" before

focusing on what was right in front of her. She'd just have to discover Zelena's alibi later. Truth was, Witchy ExS needed a professional of her caliber to handle security at this convention about to start.

Though the line at the hotel front desk was long, Fidelity and the other witch helping customers barely sparing a glance her way as she approached, Nimue leaned over on the small space left beside a woman in an anime-design hoodie. "Fidelity, can you get Esmerelda or Clarke here for me?" When the anime-loving woman gave her a sidelong glance, Nimue cradled her staff badge out in front of her. She'd never dropped it off at her locker the night before because she'd never exactly planned to take the hours-long slumber she'd been subjected to, and she'd thought she'd be at her investigation all night.

"Sure," Fidelity said quickly, Rhutwine the lizard familiar sticking out his tongue as he spoke. "Assuming they can spare a minute." He handed the woman in front of him a keycard with a broad smile and wished her a pleasant stay before tapping the witch network crystal at his wrist and quickly sending a message. "She'll be with you in a moment," he told Nimue, then he turned to face the next guest.

Nimue thanked him and stepped aside, moving closer to the elevators, which had lines of their own forming. Most people ignored Nimue at first, but when their gazes slipped her way, they'd do a double-take, speaking in whispers to the people beside them. Gowdie preened, spreading his wings and soaking in the attention. Nimue was used to it, even down to the scrape of Gowdie's outstretched wing against her cheek.

After a moment, one opened and Mia Estrada, still in her Megastellar-Woman costume, stepped out, four men of various heights and shapes right behind her.

Mia looked as if she hadn't slept a wink. Nimue doubted she had.

"Didn't Cassie ask you to speak with Mia this morning?" Gowdie reminded her.

Nimue bristled and stood straighter. She simply didn't have time—even if normally, making sure the convention's paying client was taken care of would have been one of her foremost priorities.

"There's one of them!" Mia's voice carried over the crowd as she spoke over her shoulder to the four men behind her. They made a beeline straight for her, cornering Nimue in a little alcove beside the elevators that was about as private and quiet as one could find in this busy lobby.

"Ms. Estrada," Nimue said, clearing her throat. "I'm afraid you'll have to forgive none of us coming to see you earlier. As you know, we've had a *number* of important things to see to." She arched a brow and then looked over Mia's shoulder at the men behind her. Had Mia told her fellow CES board members about the murder?

She and Ren had asked her not to spread the news, but Mia had been left unattended, without updates on the situation, all night. Nimue could hardly blame her if she'd spoken to the others about it. Frankly, they all deserved to know.

Mia's pale-brown complexion paled even more as she fidgeted her hands together. "Yes, I wanted to know… if that *little emergency* last night had been taken care of yet."

So she hadn't told them?

"Unfortunately, no," Nimue said. "But it's my highest priority right now."

One of the men, one of the two rather burly ones Nimue had fleetingly thought could have been the man at the end of the hallway last night, grunted. "What's this? Something that will affect the con?" His long nose wrinkled, his pale brow already dotted with a sheen of sweat amidst the crowd of the lobby. He wore the same Superstellar-Man shirt as the other three, and Nimue could read the "Comic Enthusiast Society: CES" logo more clearly under the image now that they were all so close. They were practically surrounding her against the wall.

Mia looked about to faint as the other men mumbled. Nimue specifically picked up one, a rather short, balding pale man who stretched his T-shirt a bit more than the rest, muttering, "Never should have elected a woman to head the CES."

Nimue stiffened. Wasn't that what Mia had told her, but she'd been too overwhelmed by Mia's nervous personality to truly process? This convention had to go right because she was the first woman head of her group. Because she, even if unfairly, had something more to prove.

Witchy ExS had always had a woman in charge before this, and witch society was matriarchal, which Nimue knew most human society was *not*, but Nimue still felt some kinship about needing to prove oneself capable of being in charge.

"The convention is going to be fine," Nimue promised, though she felt like she was relying on pure bravado making that statement just then. "And it's about to start—you'll miss it."

Gowdie let out a little spurt of fire to punctuate her statement, and three of the men's eyes widened as they focused on the dragon perched on Nimue's shoulder.

The fourth, Nimue noticed, didn't so much as blink. He focused instead on Nimue herself. Almost as if… he could tell she was lying. That something was still off.

Nimue stared back. She'd briefly seen him in the lobby last night, along with the bald man, talking to Esmerelda once Nimue had finally made it to the dinner. He was tall and thin, with just a few signs of aging in his rosy skin. He seemed a bit older than the rest of them, though Nimue would have pegged him to be in his fifties at the latest. Some white worked its way through his blond hair, and his cheeks were rather gaunt, highlighting the noticeable spiderweb wrinkles around his eyes. He almost looked out of place in the Superstellar-Man T-shirt he and his fellow board members wore. In fact, it was clearly several sizes too large, appearing overly baggy on him. He hadn't yet put on his VIP badge, which dangled from a green lanyard in his hand.

Nimue felt herself shirking under his glare.

The elevator opened nearby and out stepped Esmerelda at the front of a group of con-goers.

Nimue seized the excuse to lift her hand into the air. "Esmerelda!" The sultry older witch noticed her and headed her way. "If you'll excuse me, Ms. Estrada and gentlemen." Nimue nodded at them, staring at Mia in particular. "Please enjoy the con. Leave everything to us and relax."

Mia's shoulders rolled forward, visibly relaxing, and Nimue offered her a smile. Not even a murder could jeopardize Mia's commitment to making this convention a success—and since Cauldron Cove itself depended on that, Nimue couldn't help but feel the same.

"Oh! Excuse me."

Jostled by a group exiting another elevator nearby, Esmerelda bumped into the back of the tall, thin member of the Comic Enthusiast Society who had unsettled Nimue so. The lanyard, which he'd been about to slip around his neck, almost slipped out of his grip, but he caught it before it fell. The witch turned on her charm, her deep-red lips in a wide smile as her long fingers landed over her heart, her wedding ring glinting in the overhead light. "Bit crowded in here, you understand. You hold on to that." She nodded at his VIP badge, which he successfully managed to slip around his neck this time. "Why, one could lose track of *anything* at a con with so many people. Of course, if you don't want to lose *something important*, you can always count on me to keep it safe for you." She glanced at Nimue. "We offer safes in every room as an optional add-on, you know."

"Of course." The man smiled tightly. If even Esmerelda's less-than-subtle charm didn't move the man, Nimue wasn't sure he was capable of showing an emotion other than glowering.

Esmerelda bristled, fluffing her hair, and turned abruptly to Nimue. "You called me, dear? Is this about Soren?"

Nimue waited a beat for Mia and her board members to file toward the skywalk, and then another moment more as the crowd started cheering because the skywalk entrance opened and the teleportation pad started flashing, indicating entrance was now allowed by the general public into the Bessa.

"Do you know where Soren is?" she said loudly to be heard. "Is he all right?"

"Oh, yes, yes. No need to worry." Esmerelda bit her lip and turned over her shoulder, watching the crowd as it dissipated in multiple directions toward the convention center. Some even opted to walk out the front door and approach the Bessa in a more traditional human manner. Or perhaps they hoped the wait would prove shorter, since so many were enthralled by the idea of instant teleportation or walking across the invisible platform through the sky. Still, now that the pathways were open, the lines were moving pretty quickly. Esmerelda didn't turn back until Mia's group had gotten up to the skywalk. "He's in his apartment downstairs, sleeping."

Nimue did a double-take and Gowdie flapped his wings, focusing on Esmerelda's familiar. The snake hissed back at him. "But the con just started. And we had…" She lowered her voice. "Last night's crisis to deal with."

"Oh, I know, dear, I know." Esmerelda sighed. "He made himself *sick* over it. When Bernadette and Prue brought him back home, I took their advice and put him straight to bed. He's going to have to take today off, I'm afraid." Her snake, Faulkner, nodded, revealing Esmerelda's gold chain and perma-charm crystal.

Nimue couldn't decide if it was a good or a bad thing that Esmerelda wanted Soren to rest and hadn't thought to boost him with her Awake Charm perma-charm. Probably good, considering her grandmothers might have just forced them both asleep if Esmerelda had tried in their presence.

What could her grandmothers be thinking? Where *were* they?

"But Florence can stop by, or someone else on the medical staff—"

"It's not *that kind* of ailment, dear," Esmerelda said. Fidelity waved at her from the front desk and she waved back, mouthing what Nimue took to mean "Just a minute" at him.

She turned back to Nimue. "I know you'll forgive me if I have to hustle. Large conventions are always our busiest times. But let me say this much, Nimmy: Have you ever seen Soren at his worst—his very worst? Since the accident, I mean?"

"I…" Nimue bit her lip. "I can't say I have."

"Well, when it all gets to be too much for him, his body gives out. It's hard enough handling the two souls in one body—but add crisis on top of crisis on top of that, and you understand." Esmerelda straightened up, fanning her face. "I really do think that's why he wasn't given the Head Warlock General Manager position alone. Bernadette understood that about him and knew he wouldn't be able to be there at all the times the job demanded."

Nimue frowned. She'd never known Soren had a medical condition that might require time off like that— and she didn't like the insinuation that that was the *only* reason Bernadette had decided the two would share the job. She wouldn't have minded that being a factor, but she wondered why no one had ever made her aware of it.

Then again, Ren didn't like to show weakness.

"Can I see him? Go over some things while he rests in bed?" Nimue asked.

Esmerelda shook her head vehemently. "Oh, no, no. Please let the dear rest. He'll be up and back as soon as he's recharged himself, you'll see."

"Okay…" Nimue frowned. As long as Ren was safe. "But where're my grandmothers now?"

Esmerelda smiled as a couple of guests walked by, staring at Nimue's dragon. "I'm afraid I can't help you there. They dropped Ren off hours ago and took off to the skies. Now if you'll excuse me." She set off toward the front desk, where Fidelity pointed at something on his witch network screen.

Nimue took a deep breath and looked around. There were still con-goers in the lobby, though the number had diminished since the convention had started.

"Now what?" Gowdie asked. *"You know, even if Ren is sleeping, Balfour is sure to be awake if her warlock is sick and she's worried about him. We can talk to her—"*

"But it sounds like he wouldn't know anything more about the case if my grandmothers brought him here right away." She *tsked*. "I wonder if they knocked him out, too, actually, knowing his parents wouldn't find it suspicious if he has this medical condition. But bottom line is, as long as we know he's safe… I guess he could use the rest for a bit longer."

"So look for Bernadette and Prue? Check in on the conven-

tion and see how Cassie is doing? Zelena? Florence and Dr. Choi?"

Nimue checked the time again. She'd be two hours earlier than he'd be expecting her, but... "Let's go talk to Maverick. I want to know what Pound might have to do with any of this."

Gowdie grimaced. *"Well, at least I got my autographs before we started grilling him. Try not to upset him too much. Fans are awaiting his first event."*

Oh, Nimue knew that. But if Maverick had had anything to do with Glinda's murder, then he wasn't going anywhere at all. The giant cauldron would just have to understand, somehow.

CHAPTER TWENTY

T aking a deep breath, Nimue knocked on the front door to Maverick's room.

"Maybe they went out for breakfast," Gowdie suggested, even though Maverick had been rather reclusive thus far.

"If so, we can follow some other leads." She glanced at her witch network crystal. Comic Hero Con had begun a few minutes back, and she hadn't been at the Bessa to see the crowd rush in, one of her favorite moments of any packed convention.

The cauldron beneath the town positively bubbled over with the thrill of it each time. She felt it now, even from here.

Nimue was about to leave when the door whapped open, Esther on the other side. She hadn't been disturbed in her pajamas or anything—in fact, she looked more put-together than she often did—and a smile lit up her face before she turned over her shoulder. "Mr. Vanedestine! Your witch escort is here."

Nimue tried not to bristle at the term "witch escort"

before she stepped inside. On either side of the room, Kovac and Davies milled about, dressed in dark suits and watching Nimue carefully as she stepped past. Neither was holding a briefcase, but a briefcase was positioned on an item of furniture behind each of them. Jaxson was nowhere in sight, but neither was Maverick Vanedestine himself.

That was, until Maverick padded out on bare feet from the suite's bedroom, wearing nothing but a white, terracotta robe parted just so at the chest to reveal a swash of chestnut-brown hair.

Gowdie's eyes widened. *"They don't show that in any of his movies. He must wax as Superstellar-Man."*

Nimue arched a brow. *Thanks for the information,* she thought back to him. Now it was going to be a bit harder not to think about Maverick Vanedestine's broad chest. Just a bit.

"Nimue!" he said, holding his arms wide. "Welcome. We didn't expect you yet. Have you come to join us for breakfast?"

Nimue's stomach was empty, but she was also running around on too much adrenaline to care just then. "No, thank you. I just needed to touch base—before you head to the convention."

Maverick's posture grew stiffer, a slow smile growing on his lips as he sat down on one of the sofas in the suite. "Okay?"

Esther made her way to stand behind Maverick, picking up an electronic tablet left on the coffee table and holding it between her hands but looking over it, as if ready to take notes.

"What are we talking here? Some ground rules?" Maverick shrugged. "If this is about my, uh, medical issue, I can assure you I'm feeling a lot better today—"

"I'm glad to hear it." Nimue's eyes flicked to Davies and Kovac, then to the briefcases behind them on a luggage rack and a dresser, respectively.

"We already know they weren't the man with the briefcase you saw at the Bessa last night," Gowdie said, picking up on her curiosity.

But we don't know they weren't the men carrying Glinda's body out, she thought back. *Or that one of them didn't take that sword from the toy to use as a murder weapon.*

"Deluxe figurine," Gowdie muttered back to her.

"First off, can I see inside those briefcases your security carries around?" Nimue gestured to either one. "Security protocol, you understand."

Davies scowled as Nimue stepped closer to the briefcase he'd had with him, moving just a step to the right in order to block her from proceeding.

Maverick chuckled. "Oh, let her, Davies. Would it be so different any human-led con? They usually check bags."

"Not for VIPs." Davies growled. The words were rough on his tongue, as if he had limited ones to speak each day and they cost him dearly to speak them.

"Well, *that* doesn't look suspicious," Maverick said sarcastically. "Let her look."

Davies sighed, then stepped to the TV stand and scrolled through the numbers on the locks to pop open the top. He stepped aside, clutching his hands together and glowering down menacingly all the while.

Gowdie looked up at him and let a little fireball pop out of his mouth for good measure. It dissipated almost instantly.

Davies actually flinched, though.

Gowdie laughed smugly as Nimue took a look inside. There was a Taser, a weapon Nimue knew some humans relied on that was usually non-fatal but could kill in certain circumstances. It was cushioned inside a large, fitted piece of foam so it wouldn't roll around. Nimue lifted her wand out and pointed at the box. "Do you mind if I dig inside some more?"

Davies snatched the Taser out of the suitcase and into his hand. Either accidentally or intentionally, he hit the weapon's trigger and it crackled in the air. Nimue glowered back. She was certain this consummate professional wouldn't have activated the Taser on accident.

She waved her wand over the briefcase. "Reveal Charm."

She heard a feminine gasp from behind her as the molded cushion stretched up and out of the briefcase, revealing the briefcase itself without any lining. It was, of course, only an illusion, one that revealed the briefcase's secrets to Nimue. There appeared to be none.

"Boss won't let us carry any other weapons, but he gets all kinds of crazies after him," Davies snapped as Nimue's wand stopped moving and the illusion faded. He put the Taser back into place and slammed the brief-case shut. "It's just a precaution."

"'All sorts of crazies,' huh?" Gowdie pondered. "Like a loan shark's goons?"

Nimue walked over to Kovac, and she found the

second bodyguard quiet but rather more cooperative. The case's contents were identical, and this time, Nimue rummaged around by hand, poking the lining, but she didn't feel anything hard. The lining slipped free at her tug, and she made sure nothing small and thin was hidden on either side of the case.

Maverick cleared his throat. "You didn't use magic to check the second case."

It *was* rather more cumbersome to check the second case by hand, but Nimue finished up and nodded at Kovac, who returned his Taser to its cushioning, that strange glint from behind his sunglasses catching the light.

"It's no secret that witches can only perform one of each charm a day," Nimue said as she walked back toward Maverick. She watched Davies and Kovac out of the corner of her eye. They weren't off the hook yet.

"Right. I knew that." Maverick swallowed. "Unless they have one of those diamonds—"

"Crystals," Nimue corrected. "A perma-charm crystal. They're difficult for most of us to create and awfully expensive to buy from those of us who have the talent for making them."

"Right, right." Maverick frowned. "They seem to use quite a few of them on sets, though."

"Hollywood could afford them," Nimue said stiffly. "You could, too, I'm certain of it."

Kovac let out a little cough, covering his mouth.

Maverick's face grew green as he stared up at her. Nimue hadn't been expecting quite that reaction.

She wrung her hands, looking back and forth at Esther and the bodyguards. "Mr. Vanedestine—"

"Maverick," he corrected.

She ignored that. "I'm afraid I have a *sensitive* issue to speak with you about, related to con security. And I don't know if you want your staff present."

Davies's brow arched as he took a step closer. "If it's related to security, his security team should be aware—"

Nimue held two of her fingers up and then crossed them with two fingers from her other hand, forming what she hoped to resemble a pound sign.

Tendons strained on Maverick's neck as his lips clamped together. "Esther, Davies, Kovac. Take fifteen."

"But, Mr. Vanedestine—" started Esther, her gaze darting accusingly toward Nimue.

"We can't—" started Davies.

"*Now*," Maverick insisted.

The two bodyguards exchanged a look and Esther swept past, her tablet clutched to her chest. "I'll go find Jaxson," she muttered. "See what's taking so long with that coffee."

"We'll be right outside," Davies said. "*Right outside.*" The repetition seemed like a threat, directed at Nimue. Gowdie let another fireball rip, but this time, Davies didn't flinch. The two—bulky man and little dragon— scowled at one another for a moment before the body- guard turned and left with his companion.

Once the door had shut behind them, Nimue turned back to the celebrity, whom she was surprised to find leaning back in the couch, stretching his arms out in either direction across the top of it, crossing one ankle over the other knee, thankfully revealing a pair of boxer shorts as the robe slipped back.

"So. You want to discuss our mutual associate?" Maverick didn't seem at all the nervous, even shrunken version of himself he'd been around witches before. "I must say, he has good taste. A little less intimidating than I'd have expected at a glance, but I know you're hiding some real fire power there." He smirked and nodded toward the wand on her holster.

"Uh, what is happening here?" Gowdie asked.

This wasn't how Nimue had expected things to go, either.

So what direction did she take this conversation? What would lead to her discovering what she needed to know—and fast?

She took a seat beside the movie star, pressing her legs together and leaning in beside him. "I did some digging, Maverick, and I noticed on one of those 'house tours' celebrities take part in that there's a very interesting sign *charmed* into your front gate."

Maverick pursed his lips as he studied her. "I take it you owe our common associate, too, then?"

"So he's verifying he owes Pound?" Gowdie proposed. *"What? Money? Even though he's a famous actor?"*

Nimue tilted her chin up, trying to play it cool. "Maybe it's more of a cooperative relationship. I *am* in charge of the biggest witch expo service in the nation." *Let him infer what he wants from that,* she thought to Gowdie. She'd just said two sentences. She hadn't outright *stated* they were connected.

"You also forgot to mention you're not solely in charge," Gowdie said.

"A cooperative relationship?" he said, the jaw at his muscle twitching. "That so?"

"Maybe it is." Nimue smiled grimly. *Now what?* she asked Gowdie in her head.

He flapped his wings and landed on Maverick's thigh. The celebrity softened and started petting the blue dragon's cold scales. "I don't know what it is about this little guy, but he definitely relaxes me."

"I'm adorable," Gowdie said matter-of-factly, blinking his eyes rapidly up at Maverick.

He seemed to be helping Maverick let his guard down.

Nimue cleared her throat. "So you did what you were asked. To pay off that debt."

Maverick stiffened and took the bait. "My men did." He was quick to add, "They didn't know *why* I wanted the pin there, of course."

Nimue bit the inside of her cheek. The Pound pin Glinda had bent down to pick up right before she'd died? He'd wanted the pin on the showroom floor?

Gowdie *hmmed.* *"Maybe it wasn't supposed to be there, exactly."*

"The pin was found on the showroom floor," Nimue said succinctly. No need to mention Glinda and her death unless the man slipped out with it himself.

Maverick blanched, his hand freezing atop Gowdie's head. "It wasn't supposed to be on the floor. But I wasn't the one who put it there. I stayed here all last night, like I was told. Maybe-Maybe they dropped it. They didn't tell me they messed up. Though I thought… They were acting a little off when they got back last night."

"So did they go back to put it where it was supposed to be?" Nimue asked, hoping he'd tell her precisely where that was.

"I-I don't know." Maverick started petting Gowdie again. "I guess not, if you found it on the floor. I can ask."

"Wait." Nimue held up a hand. So much for hoping he'd spill more information about *why* he'd asked his "men" to plant a Pound pin at all, and precisely where. "What about the toy sword?"

Maverick tapped his fist against his lips. "Toy… sword?"

Nimue frowned. "You remember when I asked who might have handled that golden Superstellar-Man figurine before you gave it to Gowdie? And you said your bodyguards?"

"Oh, yes." Maverick nodded. "And it was missing something. But I didn't tell them to do anything with it, I swear." He swallowed. "Was that a mistake? Who was that a gift from? Esther told me, but I don't remember…"

"The Comic Enthusiast Society," Nimue reminded him.

Maverick's grip on Gowdie stiffened. "I shouldn't have given that away, should I have?"

Gowdie frowned as he looked up at his witch, his jaw dropped in horror. *"Don't let him make me give it back!"*

Nimue refrained from rolling her eyes. "It's with me, remember? It's fine. But I need to know who took that sword out of that box."

"It wasn't me," Maverick said quickly. His brow was

beginning to dot with sweat and Gowdie flew off his lap and back onto Nimue's shoulder. "I swear. Whoever messed up, it wasn't me." He raised both hands up beside his face and put his foot back on the ground, scrunching up. "Please don't hurt me."

"I'm not going to hurt you," Nimue said gently. Perhaps too gently for the charade she was trying to pull off. So his strogaphobia was real, as was Dr. Choi's account of the man perhaps having been tortured by a witch or warlock? What was it he'd said? That Pound had asked the doctor to treat Maverick in Pound's own home?

"Maverick," she said sternly, taking what control she could of the situation. "Have you ever met Pound himself?" Maybe he'd explain who had tortured him and why.

Maverick's posture relaxed, his head coming out from behind his arms. "Of course I have…" His brow wrinkled. "Everyone he considers a *friend* and not just a patsy who owes him money knows that." His voice grew louder. "And why would he even need *my* help here if he had you? What kind of game are you playing?" He leaped to his feet.

"Mr. Vanedestine, I'm the co-Head Witch General Manager of Witchy ExS, and if you've been involved with any sort of crime here—"

"Out!" he shouted. "Get out! Before he *really* finds out I messed up!"

The door to the hallway burst open, and in stepped Jaxson, flanked by Davies, Kovac, and Esther, each holding a cup of coffee from Sylvie's Bakery.

"Boss?" Jaxson asked quizzically.

"I need her out of here." Maverick ran a hand through his hair and then turned on his heel. "And don't let her in again."

Davies grinned and stepped forward, Jaxson following a step slower on his heel. Kovac didn't head in her direction, instead making his way toward the luggage rack, where he'd stood before.

Nimue was amused they thought they could force her to go anywhere. But she stood anyway. "I was just leaving." She didn't let anyone approach and walked right past them, but once she was in the hall, she turned around.

"I need to speak with you," she said to Davies. "It's a matter of con security."

Davies cracked his knuckles as he stood in the doorway. "I ain't speaking to no one the boss doesn't want me to."

"You are if you don't want your VIP all-access badge revoked this instant," Nimue said.

Davies grinned. "You'd do that? And cancel Mr. Vanedestine's appearances? Rumor tells me you can't *afford* so many disappointed fans, now can you?" He glanced to Kovac and made a gurgling, bubbling sound with his tongue. "The cauldron under our feet and all."

Nimue frowned. It wasn't a *secret* that Cauldron Cove had been built on a giant cauldron, but no one really talked about the fact that it fed off happy con-goers' energy. That wasn't something the witches and warlocks who lived here put on the brochure.

"I'll talk." Kovac stepped past Davies and out into the

hallway, ignoring the way Davies's jaw went slack. "Will that satisfy?"

"Maybe." Nimue glanced at Davies. She wouldn't get much out of him without some sort of forcible charm anyway.

"You'd better not say anything the boss wouldn't want you to—" started Davies.

Kovac shut the door behind him, cutting his colleague short.

He gestured across the hallway. "My room."

Nimue nodded and let the man retrieve a perma-charm-crystal-embedded keycard out of his suit pocket and unlock the door. He held it open for her and she stepped inside.

Only the second she stepped inside, she saw it. Gowdie gasped.

So brazen. That didn't bode well.

Nimue turned back, withdrawing her wand from her holster, aiming to charge right through the bodyguard.

But that was when she ran straight into Kovac's Taser, which sent a painful, jilting shock through her body.

CHAPTER TWENTY-ONE

Nimue groaned. She rubbed her eyes with the base of her hands and then shot up, her eyes wide open.

She'd been shocked. In more ways than one.

"Nimue!" Gowdie flapped his wings and panted, flying onto her lap. *"I burnt that big thug with my flames, best I could while he carried you over to this bed, and I pecked at his face, but he slapped me clear across the room."* He did his best to look tough, but he cradled his elbow as he spoke. *"I didn't wake up until just a few minutes ago, but I've been calling out for help. We really need those witch network crystals to work for familiars somehow, too."* He tsked. *"Second time in less than twenty-four hours."*

His eyes scanned slowly to the other full-sized bed in this hotel room.

Where Nimue saw exactly what had shocked her into turning around and trying to run back outside the room in the first place.

There lay Glinda, still at peace, her hands crossed over

her abdomen. Atop her hands rested her familiar Titan beetle, deceased once his witch had died.

Her neck had even been cleaned. Nimue saw no trace of a wound.

Someone had arranged the two of them peacefully like that. Someone with magic who could have erased evidence of a wound.

Of course, someone had brought her here from Florence's clinic to begin with.

Someone like Kovac, apparently. He'd been prepared to lead Nimue into this trap.

She patted her holster desperately with one hand as she cradled Gowdie to her side with the other. "My wand! He took my wand!"

Gowdie frowned. *"But he didn't take your witch network crystal."* He nodded at her wrist. *"That means he either didn't know what it was or he thought you'd be out long enough for it to not matter."*

Nimue checked the time. She'd been out a few hours. It was already noon. Her message inbox was full to capacity, and she hardly knew where to start.

There still wasn't anything from Ren, though, which worried her.

She had a choice before her. Contact Cassie and check in with her—at least she trusted the witch, even if she knew her assistant had her hands full overseeing Comic Hero Con in her and Ren's stead—or trust that Zelena had nothing to do with this.

There were messages from Zelena. She opened the latest one.

Where are you? she'd written. *Why is everyone missing?*

What's going on? How can I shut down this convention when so much depends on it—

Zelena, she thought to the crystal.

She might not have fully understood what her grandmothers were up to, but they had a point that she'd been too quick to assume an invisible witch or warlock meant Zelena.

True, Linden had seemed above suspicion, too. But she'd worked closer with Zelena. And the witch had seemed genuinely disturbed by her husband's betrayal.

A pop and a crackle rang out and a circle denoting a Communication Charm tore an illusion into the air in front of Nimue.

Zelena's haggard face appeared on the other side. She was on the employee-only floor of the Bessa, the showroom floor of the convention in full force down below her.

"Where have you been?" she nearly shouted. "I've been looking all over for you. I tried Communication Charm after Communication Charm and nothing happened. I thought..." She bit her lip and Messenger, her familiar sloth, reached up an arm and slowly, slowly tapped her cheek, as if offering comfort.

"I was attacked. And my wand was stolen," Nimue said simply. Knowing Zelena had saved her daily Communication Charm to try it over and over for Nimue —it didn't count as a use if the charm didn't connect— made her feel a little guiltier about ever doubting the witch. "And I found Glinda."

Zelena blinked. "Where? We didn't see her body exit on any of the History Charm perma-charm recordings in the Bessa a second time."

"That's because she exited at the hotel. You better come," she said, providing her with the room number.

Fully caught up, Zelena stood in Kovac's hotel room with Nimue, barking orders into her witch network crystal non-stop.

Cassie had been caught up, more or less, and thankfully didn't have anything out of the ordinary to report about the convention so far. She hadn't seen Ren or even Nimue's grandmothers. Some of Zelena's security team were headed to where Maverick was currently due—signing autographs after a panel about the Superstellar-Man movies. A panel that Mercy, the Panel Programming Coordinator, reported to have gone off without a hitch. They were on high alert for Kovac specifically.

Zelena crossed her arms as she stared down at Glinda's prone body. "Why didn't you check in with me? You woke up *hours* ago."

"I didn't know where she'd been taken then," Nimue protested. She fidgeted in place as she stared down at Glinda beside Zelena. "And then I was knocked out *again*—"

"But you could have done a re-group with me earlier." Zelena's eyes narrowed on Nimue, as Messenger's did the same on Gowdie in echo of her witch. "And don't tell me you thought I was too busy."

Nimue squeaked. "Okay. I'll lay it out there. I knew a witch or two who could turn themselves or others invisible had to be involved. It's a tricky charm."

"And you assume only a former spy could have mastered it?" Zelena grew unnaturally silent for a moment, staring down at Glinda. There was a knock on the door and Nimue welcomed the opportunity to open it.

Florence waited on the other side, along with another medical witch from Florence's team. Of course. The normal shift would have been working by now. Nimue was so used to the secretiveness of their earliest attempts at solving this crime that she'd half-expected to see Dr. Choi standing alongside Florence.

"Come on in," Nimue said to their grim faces.

The other medical witch, whose long, brown hair was pulled back into a ponytail, put her hands over her mouth as she stared down at Glinda. Tears dripped from her eyes and a neon-yellow hamster familiar, who'd been riding on her shoulder, nuzzled its face against her cheek. "Flo-Florence told me. It's just… Seeing her like this…"

Nimue nodded. "It doesn't make sense," she whispered. Gowdie flapped over from where he'd been resting atop the TV in the room, his shoulder all better thanks to a graciously donated Heal Charm from Zelena. He landed atop the headboard of the bed on which Glinda rested, then locked eyes with Nimue.

"He wants to know how we intend to get her back to Florence's clinic without anyone seeing," Nimue translated aloud for him after he'd spoken to her. "Now that the con is in full swing."

"We can leave her here," said Florence grimly. "But at least one of us should stay with her, I think."

"Someone on the security team, too. Then we can

arrange transportation of her after the con closes for the day. Once we have whatever monster did this in custody." The knuckles on Zelena's hand gripping her wand went whiter. "We need to let Clarke or Esmerelda know."

Florence and the other medical witch did a cursory exanimation of the body, making note of the neck wound that had been magically healed. But Nimue knew a witch or warlock was a part of this crime by now. And Kovac, clearly, was working with the magic user in question.

"So there's at least one witch in this Pound criminal's organization," Zelena said.

That was the crux of it. Pound had wanted something done at this convention, and that had led to Glinda's death. Either intentionally or incidentally.

The crackle of an opening Communication Charm beside Zelena drew everyone's attention. She stepped back, her face grim. On the other side was Charity McAllister.

"Boss," she said. "We asked Mr. Vanedestine and his team to follow us after his autograph session ended. They're all here." She motioned behind her.

They were in an empty conference room, not unlike the one that Tituba used for the Con Suite with free snacks and water for guests. Maverick sat with his ankle crossed over his knee, the foot still on the ground bouncing and his arms crossed tightly over his chest. Davies stood behind him, Jaxson on the other side. Esther walked back and forth just out of sight, talking on her smartphone, though Nimue couldn't hear what she was saying.

"I want my lawyer," Maverick said, all charm and anxiety gone from his face as he jeered at the open Communication Charm with a tight upper lip. Charity's familiar, the pink chimp, Lucas, did a little dance complete with chimp noises in front of the movie star, his frustration clear on his face.

"We don't use human courts with human lawyers in Cauldron Cove," Zelena said, her chest puffing up. "And you're in *our* jurisdiction."

Maverick's face blanched, and his lip trembled, but he quickly recovered. "You can't hold me here against my will."

"I can and I will," Zelena started. "Nimue's told us all about your involvement in the crimes committed here—"

Nimue stepped up and held a hand out to her. "Where's Kovac?"

Charity frowned and looked to someone just out of sight of the Communication Charm's circle. Probably another member of the security team. "No one else was with them," she said after a beat.

Davies scoffed but didn't say anything.

Jaxson flinched.

"Jaxson?" Nimue asked. "Please. It's important."

"He's off-shift," Jaxson said simply. Davies glowered at him, as if that had been some big secret to be guarded. "He's probably in his hotel room."

"He's not in his room," Nimue said. "Because we are." Nimue took a deep breath. "With a dead body."

Zelena grumbled, but Nimue watched the reactions on the other side of the portal. Jaxson's razor-sharp features slackened, his jaw dropping. Even Davies's furrowed eyebrows softened a little. Esther, still pacing and on the phone, hadn't seemed to have heard Nimue.

And Maverick started taking shaky, audible breaths. Louder and louder. He jumped to his feet.

"Mr. Vanedestine!" Esther cried, pulling the phone away from her ear. "It's fine. Your lawyer says to stay put, not say a word—"

"I didn't know he wanted someone *dead*!" The handsome actor put both hands on his head, threading them through his thick hair. "He never—How could he?"

"Talk," snapped Zelena, even as Maverick's own security team attempted to corral Maverick into a sitting position, the convention security team coming into view and holding their wands out threateningly.

"Give them a minute," Nimue said to Zelena. They waited for Maverick's very real-seeming panic attack to subside. But now that Nimue knew he had some connection to Pound, she couldn't be sure what to believe.

"Mr. Vane—*Maverick*," she said softly once his breathing had grown shallow and everyone had moved out of the way of Charity's Communication Charm. "Please. It was one of our own staff who was murdered— and it happened last night."

Maverick was shaking now, holding his stomach as he hunched over, his eyes seeming a bit glossy as he stared at the ground. That was some improvement, Nimue supposed.

"The reason why I interrogated you the way I did— why I asked about Pound... We're pretty sure he's involved. As well as Kovac." Nimue's eyes darted to Davies, who swallowed.

"Could your gut instinct to hate Davies more than Kovac have just been down to his personality? He's not totally exuding 'criminal mastermind' or anything. Maybe he's just a grumpy bodyguard," Gowdie offered.

Nimue *had* rather forgotten to pay much attention to Kovac with Davies being all aggressive and angry in her face all the time the two were around.

"So did you send Kovac to 'plant the pin' somewhere on the showroom floor?" Nimue asked. "Or was it both Kovac and Davies?" Jaxson was out of the question. He hadn't been on the showroom floor taking the tour Zelena had offered the night before.

Davies's eyes shot tellingly to the ground.

"I didn't murder nobody, okay?" Davies spat. "I don't need no lawyer around to tell you that."

"Double negative," Gowdie said, amused.

I think he really means he didn't kill anyone, Nimue thought back to him. Though it'd be a clever way for a murderer to admit his guilt and still maintain innocence at the same time.

"Zelena," Nimue said, turning to her Director of Security, "you mentioned that when you gave Davies and Kovac the tour last night, they were especially interested in the Comic Enthusiast Society booth. The one with the limited-edition figurines."

"Yeah. Though they only stayed a minute. One of them said 'the boss' had one of those figures back in his room." Zelena scowled. "I don't know which one said it, sorry. They look too alike."

"We do *not*," Davies protested. "And it was me who said it, all right? Didn't mean anything other than it meant. Kovac and I did our inspection of the gifts the boss received. Kovac made a point of looking closely at that one. It stuck in my head."

"He's spilling the beans now. Suddenly Mr. Chatty Cathy." Gowdie chuckled.

Nimue didn't hesitate to take advantage of the man's newfound need to spill the truth. "So Kovac took the toy sword out?"

If Kovac had Glinda's body here, it stood to reason he'd been at least one of the people who'd transported it here. Which meant he could turn invisible himself or knew who had turned him invisible. Which meant he was the number one suspect for taking that toy sword and dragging it over Glinda's throat.

"I don't know what you're talking about." Davies fluffed a hand in the direction of the open Communication Charm, his expression growing dour. "But if anything was missing from that box, it was him who took it, not me."

"'He,'" said Gowdie. *"'He' who took it."*

Nimue shook her head slightly. This was no time to correct the man's grammar.

"Okay, then let's forget that." *For now,* she silently added. "You knew about the Pound pin, didn't you?"

Davies's eyes darted to Maverick, who had his head in his hands, his elbows resting on his knees. Esther sat beside her boss, talking to him quietly.

"Yeah, I knew about the pin, you happy?" Davies crossed his arms. Maverick didn't react to his confession.

"And your *boss* wanted you to put it… somewhere in the CES booth?" Nimue had no other guesses, if the bodyguards hadn't shown a particular interest in any other part of the showroom floor.

"Yeah," Davies spat. "Only I didn't have it on me when I got there. And before you ask, I don't know *why* I was supposed to do it. I just do what the boss asks."

"You—a member of Maverick Vanedestine's security team—didn't know Maverick had been threatened by a loan shark criminal known as 'Pound'?"

Jaxson's eyes widened, and Maverick's head snapped up.

Davis's chin dipped to his chest. "Well, I never said I didn't know *that*."

Jaxson whirled on him, his jaw clenched. It seemed this was news to at least one of the bodyguards.

"How *did* you find that out if you weren't sent by Pound?" the movie star asked Nimue.

"Dr. Choi," Nimue said. "The human doctor I sent to take a look at you yesterday? He recognized you. From Pound's house."

Maverick looked taken aback.

"Mr. Vanedestine, what is she talking about?" Esther asked. She squeezed the phone in her hands. Nimue wondered if the lawyer was still on the other side of the line.

"Jig's up, boss," said Davies. He sighed. "Unless you want to go down for murder, too—which neither the boss nor I would ever do." He stared forward through the Communication Charm. Then he scoffed. "Look at me. Talking into a floating portal like this witchy way of life makes the least bit of sense."

Nimue ignored that comment, taking quick stock of

the room. Florence was comforting the other medical witch over in the corner, Zelena hanging back quietly behind Nimue, watching the men spill their guts over in the Bessa.

"Messenger says Zelena thinks you're making good progress here," Gowdie translated for her. *"She's letting you take the lead."*

The Director of Security's confidence in her raised Nimue's brow. She'd have to apologize to the security witch even more profusely later.

"I don't remember that doctor," Maverick said quietly.

"He thought you might not have. Seeing as how you were deep in the middle of an anxiety attack at the time." Nimue bit her lip a second. "I can't tell if you actually experience anxiety or if you're just acting, but if you don't remember Dr. Choi—and he seemed to think your anxiety has been real both times he's looked at you—"

"It's my dad, okay?" Maverick ran a hand through his hair. "He's the one who gets me out of sorts more than witches in general. I know I can't blame every witch or warlock for his awful acts."

"Your dad?" Nimue swallowed. What was it Maverick had told her? If she'd really known Pound, she would have known Maverick had met him. Everyone who knew Pound knew that.

"Because Pound... is your father?" Nimue asked aloud.

Maverick laughed, but it was bitter. "Dear ol' dad. He doesn't do favors without expecting repayment. Not even for his kid. Of course, he wasn't exactly *involved* much in my upbringing."

Jaxson narrowed on Davies. "And did you know this? That Mr. Vanedestine's father is some-some gangster?"

Davies lifted both hands in the air. "Hey. Not my secret to tell. But it's not the first time I've seen some dirty hands reaching into willing pockets around Hollywood. I don't pry."

"Don't you think I needed to *know* that as a potential security risk?" Jaxson asked.

So he truly was innocent of all of this, Nimue supposed. No one was *that* good of an actor.

"Up to the boss," Davies said simply. "I didn't know— I mean, Kovac was cheesed that I'd dropped the pin before we could plant it in that booth, but he said he'd take care of it. Told me this convention had to go *just right* and I'd screwed the pooch."

"Kovac was sent by my father," Maverick explained. "Acts as security while also keeping an eye on me." He frowned. "But Kovac keeps so much close to the vest. I never know what he tells my father. That's why I wasn't sure if you were a messenger my father sent or not. I thought maybe Kovac was being told to keep an eye on you, too. Who knows with my father? He has eyes everywhere, it seems. I just do as he asks of me."

"And he asked you to… plant a pin. At a comic convention booth," Nimue said.

"What good would the pin do? Other than sending a message," Gowdie said.

That was it. "Pound wanted to send a message… to someone with the Comic Enthusiast Society?" she asked aloud.

She turned to Zelena. The elder witch shrugged.

"I don't ask the details," Maverick said. "Besides, I left it to Davies and Kovac. I knew Kovac would get it done. Or so I thought. Looks like, judging by the dead body in his hotel room, things didn't go as planned. I wonder if my dad ordered the hit."

Nimue chewed the inside of her cheek. "It didn't seem like a premeditated murder…" She changed tactics, focusing on Davies. "So, when you said Kovac went back to find the pin, did he go alone?"

Davies nodded. "Said I'd messed things up already. He went without me. I don't know *what* he did after we parted ways outside of the boss's room at the hotel. I swear. I went into my room after that, and when Blevins knocked to get us to join the boss in the banquet hall at dinner, Kovac was back in his room, too."

"So it's possible he met up with the Invisible-Charm expert witch after that. They cast a charm on him, he went scouring the showroom floor after-hours without raising suspicion, only Glinda found that pin first."

"And he killed her for it," Nimue said softly aloud. "But why? Why would the pin mean anything to her? He could have just swiped it out of her hand while invisible, without hurting her—"

"Unless it did *mean something to her,"* Gowdie guessed. *"If she knew what that sign meant, she would have told you and Ren and Zelena, and then you would have known to be on the lookout for Pound at this convention."*

Her dragon familiar wasn't on the wrong track. Nimue was sure of it.

Davies's jaw clenched. "So it was Kovac who killed your witch. He's probably gone off our radar for a purpose, then. Maybe Pound ain't too happy with him, either." He looked around, a bead of sweat glistening on his brow.

Maybe, Nimue thought. *But why take Glinda here, to his hotel room? And who was the Invisible-Charm expert witch who helped him do it? Even if Kovac were such a warlock, he hadn't carried her body alone.* Someone *had helped him.*

Zelena spoke up for the first time in a while. "My security witches will protect you. Stay calm and stay there."

"Will they?" Davies said, taking a step back as he looked all around him.

"Pound's organization relies on a witch," Nimue pointed out to Zelena. "At least one."

"Just *the* one," Maverick said. "At least as far as I know—and one's plenty." He frowned. "When I said I can't blame all witches for his awful actions, I meant—"

But he broke off what he was about to say and looked overhead.

The floating candles responsible for the illumination in the conference room over in the Bessa flickered, the room growing dark and then light again.

"Charity?" Zelena asked.

But Charity and the other security warlock had their wands at the ready, both facing in the same direction. "Boss, something's off about the magic in this room—" Charity started.

The lights flickered out in that room in the Bessa entirely, and the Communication Charm portal crackled shut.

CHAPTER TWENTY-TWO

"Charity?" Zelena shouted, as if the witch could hear her all this distance away. Not with the Communication Charm closed. That meant Charity was distracted with something else or... Something had happened to her.

Zelena brought up her witch network perma-charm crystal and started shouting into it. "Security team: Code red! Room 334 of the Bessa. Suspects may be armed."

Nimue was a flurry of activity, bringing up her own witch network crystal and warning Cassie quickly first, followed by a general code alert to the staff.

Keep the con-goers calm, she added, emphasizing that point. *Incident is contained to Room 334 for now.*

"Stay here," Zelena barked to Nimue as she ran for the door. She turned over her shoulder to look at the medical team. "Can't spare a member of security to help guard Glinda just yet. You'll need to stay here as well."

"What? I can't." Nimue followed her outside the room to the hall.

Zelena whirled on her. "You don't have your wand. You've been attacked twice today already—even by people you trusted. You're a liability." Zelena's face was coloring red, her distaste for Nimue coloring her speech.

"I can help," Nimue insisted, grinding her heel into the carpet.

Zelena wasn't moved. "Stay here!" She took off at a run toward the stairs, presumably to the teleportation pad in the hotel lobby.

"Well, better than you two arguing about this all day," muttered Gowdie. *"We need everyone who can help at the Bessa fast."*

"And I can help—somehow," Nimue insisted. "Wand or no wand."

She was about to head in the same direction Zelena had gone when the door to Kovac's room opened and Florence stuck her head out.

"You're still here," she said grimly. "I know it won't work as well as your own for you, but I thought maybe…" She handed her a wand with both hands, as if offering an object of great reverence.

For a second, Nimue thought it was Florence's own wand and was about to demur in case there were any medical emergencies. But then she saw Florence's wand sticking out of the holster at her hip.

"Glinda's?" Nimue asked.

The leech familiar dangling out from the brim of Florence's witch hat made a squelching sound.

"Yes," answered Gowdie in translation. Florence's eyes were welling with tears and she couldn't speak.

"Thank you," Nimue said. "I'll take good care of it."

Gripping the unfamiliar wood in her hand, rougher than she was used to, Nimue headed to the stairs. She didn't want to deal with con-goers in the elevator when she was so panicked.

"No Hover Charm this time," Gowdie grunted as he took to the air, having read Nimue's mind when she'd looked down the stairwell and wondered if she could just leap and hover to a gentle landing at the bottom. *"Remember what happened last night?"*

True, she hadn't handled hovering with the greatest finesse. And that had been with her own wand.

Nimue hoofed it down the stairs the old-fashioned way, going over what she knew, as well as a few remaining mysteries with Gowdie to focus her mind.

"Kovac killed Glinda because she picked up the Pound pin Davies dropped earlier, the one they were supposed to use to send a message to someone in the Comic Enthusiast Society."

"Someone like who?" Gowdie asked.

"Well, the only one we know a bit is Mia. And she's…" Nimue stopped on a step, clutching the handrail with her free hand. Gowdie had to circle back, flapping his wings to stay in place.

"She's what?"

"She's overly anxious about this convention going well."

"That's understandable. Remember, she's the first woman head of the CES."

"Yes, but…" Nimue thought back. When Mia had been found at the showroom after hours, Nimue had believed she'd just been checking everything out one last time. But she'd seemed a little... off. And not just because she'd found out about a murder.

"How do you tell the difference between being off because of the shock of a murder and being off because of another cause anyway, though?" Gowdie rightfully pointed out.

"What if Mia was scared... because she suspected Pound's involvement in the murder? Because she knew about him? Was she supposed to get the original message, the pin in the CES booth?"

"A message threatening what?"

Nimue shrugged. "I don't know. Making sure this con is a success."

"Like she needed a threat to wish for that." Gowdie shook his head. *"So let's say she's involved with Pound. She owes him money. Maybe she said she'd pay out of the CES's coffers once this convention was over?"* Gowdie shrugged as he soared overhead. *"The con was going to be successful whether she was threatened to make it so or not."*

"But not *as* successful as it would have been without Maverick Vanedestine. Whose *father* is Pound. Maybe that's how she managed to get him to come in the first place! That's the connection they share."

"It's a huge comic book con, Nimue," Gowdie said. *"He's a huge comic book movie adaptation star. There doesn't need to be a special reason for them to have a connection other than that."*

"Sure, but Maverick had never been to a convention hosted in a witch town before," said Nimue. "And he even admitted that what his father wants him to do, he does."

"He's scared of him," Gowdie said grimly. *"The criminal had his own son tortured! Why?"*

"Maybe he owes him money, too," Nimue said.

"Really? With that mansion, he can't cough up the cash? Maybe he just owes him a favor." Gowdie flapped his wings quickly and flew in front of Nimue as they reached the ground-floor landing. *"Hey, where do you think the few Invisible-Charm-expert witches tend to work?"*

Nimue shrugged. "I never really thought about it. I mean, I guess a life of crime might suit, since you'd avoid detection on human surveillance systems. As far as legal applications, I don't know… Special effects? When a Hover Charm won't do, you could stand in a scene and carry something to make it fly or—" Nimue gasped. "Pound has his claws in Hollywood. Did he get his son an agent or a movie role or something?"

"Or the movie role of the decade in the most witchy-special-effects-heavy film franchise of all time."

"Okay," said Nimue, thinking as her boots kept clomping down the stairs. "So, Pound's guys are attacking Maverick right now." She chewed her lip. She really needed to get over there. She wasn't the most skilled combat witch, but she *was* co-Head Witch Manager…

Her eyes darted farther down the stairway. A gate blocked further descent, a sign posted "Employees Only Beyond This Point" on the small metal gate.

Ren's apartment was down there.

"Could be Kovac acting alone," Gowdie said. *"Though that doesn't track with him having help carrying Glinda away. You think he's the warlock?"*

"Maybe," Nimue said. She didn't have a Southern Hotel employee perma-charm crystal, so she took a running start and clutched the top of the gate, heaving one leg and then the other over it. It wasn't magicked to keep her out that way. Another security flaw to let someone know about, Nimue supposed. And why was it, as Cary had informed her, that Southern Hotel master keycards allowed hotel staff all-access to the Bessa, but the Witchy ExS staff badge didn't allow the same in the hotel? She'd had to ask Fidelity for help getting into hotel rooms for security reasons before.

Gowdie's jaw dropped. *"What are you doing?"*

"Getting Ren," she said. "Or at least checking in with Balfour, like you said we should. Nothing's adding up with him, either—or my grandmothers disappearing after they dropped him off."

Gowdie shrugged and flew over the gate without a single issue. *"We'll face this crisis as a team, right?"*

"Right." She headed down the last set of steps.

At the bottom of the stairs, a hallway stretched out. It was fairly dark, the light fixtures set to dim or overshadowed by a wide growth of vines and leaves growing out from tree roots. That made sense. The giant tree that grew up and through the entire hotel would have had a heavier presence here, in the basement floor.

"Glow Charm." Nimue flourished her borrowed wand and held it up, lighting up the path ahead a bit better.

Rather than fly to scout ahead, Gowdie settled on Nimue's shoulder, trying, it seemed, but failing to suppress a shudder. *"Bit dreary of a place to call home, isn't it?"*

Nimue nodded slowly. "Well, but it's sort of pretty. In a natural-campsite sort of way."

"Natural campsite perpetually at night," Gowdie added.

"So, if Kovac is a warlock who can cast the Invisible Charm," Nimue said, "who's the other witch?"

"We don't know *Kovac's a warlock,"* Gowdie said. *"Maverick insisted there was 'just the one' witch in Pound's organization before he was cut off. What if the sole witch has a perma-charm crystal and can just keep turning themselves and others invisible all day?"*

Nimue ground to a halt. "Then there wouldn't have been a need for there to be two Invisible-Charm expert witches involved at all! Humans could use the perma-charms by themselves entirely." She frowned as she lifted her leg high over one particularly gnarly root. "Being able to craft such a perma-charm would mean the witch in the organization would have to be skilled at both the Invisible Charm *and* perma-charm crafting."

"A double rarity. Even Bernadette couldn't pull that off."

"No, but she seemed to know who might… That was the tipoff for them! They *knew* right away!" Nimue shook her head. "I can't believe they knocked me out! I'm a grown woman." She shook her borrowed wand for emphasis in the air.

The borrowed wand lit up by the soft glow she'd charmed into it.

And that revealed, halfway down the side, an engraving in the wood. An engraving of a pound sign.

"Is that a sign from Pound? Like to tell us he condoned the *killing?*" Gowdie asked. He fluttered over to a nearby tree branch sticking out from the wall of the Southern Hotel's basement hallway.

"But it sounded like Pound *didn't* condone the killing. That Kovac might have acted on his own." Nimue cocked her head and she slowed to a stop. "The only other explanation I can come up with is that Glinda had this engraved into her wand long before yesterday."

"Meaning… Glinda worked for Pound?"

"How?" Nimue asked. "She had a full-time job here. But she must have had some connection to him." She gripped the borrowed wand tighter.

"So… what? She owed him, and he was branding her source of magic, more or less?"

"Or she flaunted the connection with pride."

"Because she volunteered to work for him?"

"Or for some other reason." Nimue walked forward again. This was the wrong time to marvel at Glinda's apparent connection to Pound. Only that meant she definitely *had* recognized that pin on the ground when she'd gone to pick it up. She hadn't just been picking up a lost item and gotten a look at the wrong thing.

She would have known what the presence of Pound's sign might have meant for the con. And she would have been likely to report it to Ren, Zelena, and Nimue—something she'd been unlikely to do if she'd thought it was just an innocuous misplaced item.

And if Pound didn't want Witchy Expo Services to know he or his representatives were doing something at this convention, it stood to reason he'd want to keep her quiet.

But if she had a connection with him... Maybe she would have kept it quiet anyway.

Nimue shook her head. She was losing track of the fact that the Witchy ExS team was dealing with a security crisis while she was contemplating things in a darkened basement hallway instead of actively getting the help she'd come down here to get.

She approached the nearest door. She knew Ren's parents lived on one of the upper floors of the hotel, so she was unlikely to get the wrong residence if she knocked on a bunch of the doors.

"You're knocking?" Gowdie asked. *"If he's out like Esmerelda said he'd be, then how will he—"* He stopped and perked up, his head arching. *"Try that door."* He nodded a few doors down.

Nimue didn't even ask why. The reason became clear enough as she approached.

A cat's meow—or more like a forlorn, garbled cry.

And songbirds. Instead of cheerfully chirping, though, they seemed distressed.

Nimue tried the door handle. It didn't move. "Unlock Charm."

This time, when she tried the handle, the door swung open.

She stepped inside, her borrowed wand at the ready.

It was a cozy apartment, though dimly lit and with only a small half-window toward one of the ceilings letting in any light from outside.

There was a TV attached to the wall, a leather armchair facing it with an end table with lamp and a hardcover book on top. The book was perfectly parallel to the edge of the table, and the whole area seemed neat and tidy.

Across from that chair was a blue plush sofa armchair, its armrests open to reveal a mess of clutter sticking out from it. There was a coffee-stained mug in a small drink holder, paintbrushes, pens, a notebook, and well-worn paperbacks piling up and out of the armrests.

"Ren and Soren," Nimue said quietly. That meant the warlock chose a different chair depending on which of them was in charge. She imagined Ren wouldn't want to share a chair with the messier Soren. They were an all-in-one odd couple of sorts. The open kitchen nearby told the same story. Half was gleaming and clean, the other half stacked with clutter. Though there were no dirty dishes. Perhaps Ren wouldn't abide that kind of mess in their shared space.

A feline hiss pierced the air and Balfour leaped down from above the refrigerator, jumping to the cleaned parts of the kitchen counter and then to the floor. She was more talkative than usual, her tittering meows in time with her bouncing footsteps in their direction.

"Slow down," said Gowdie, flapping inside and resting atop the plush armchair. *"You've been trying to reach some-one, and you can't leave your warlock—"* He started translating.

Balfour slammed into Nimue's shins, rubbing the top of her head against them. Nimue jolted, still unused to such affection from Ren's cat. Even when her warlock was Soren, Balfour remained aloof.

Gowdie's next words were drowned out by the shrieking chirps of birds, and two almost-identical golden lovebirds flew in from another room, zeroing in on Nimue and flying in rapid circles over her head.

That meant her grandmothers were nearby. No wonder no one had seen them all evening, despite what they'd seemed determined to go off and do.

Gowdie shot up into the air. *"They're all in trouble!"* He flew into the room the lovebirds—Dunlop and Naismith, belonging to Nimue's grandmothers—had vacated.

Nimue followed suit, the other familiars matching her pace.

It was a bedroom. Ren—or Soren, judging by the messy hair—was lying on top of a king-sized bed, just a little space between him and Bernadette and Prue, who were lying face to face, Bernadette's back to Soren.

All three were sleeping or…

Nimue nearly ripped the metal pull-string on the nearby lamp to bathe the room in more light and ran over to the bed. After examining each of them, she stood up straight and let out a deep breath. Of course they were still alive. Their familiars all were.

Balfour jumped up onto the bed and landed in front of Soren's face. She put a paw on his cheek and meowed in his face, as the lovebirds landed more lightly on their witches' sides, chirping rapidly.

Gowdie flapped over to land on the bed's headboard, looking down at them. *"Okay, one at a time. One at a time!"*

Nimue started shaking Prue lightly as Gowdie listened to the familiars explain everything. No amount of jostling roused either Prue or Bernadette. She headed around the bed and more reluctantly shook Soren.

"Okay," started Gowdie, all business, *"so Naismith and Dunlop fully admit to their witches being naughty and putting their granddaughter to sleep. They thought they'd take care of things before sunrise—that they could protect you and Ren from harm if you didn't get further involved."*

Balfour growled over at the birds, who jumped up and peeped.

"Yes, yes, they were misguided. And they put Ren to sleep with some tea, too."

"Does he have a medical condition that makes him collapse, then?" Nimue asked. She gripped Soren's shoulder and pushed it gently.

Balfour rubbed against her warlock as Gowdie nodded. *"He's got a good handle on managing symptoms. It hasn't happened during a crisis in a while. She knew something was off about him falling asleep after Bernadette and Prue's visit, and she tried to tell Faulkner, Esmerelda's snake, but Esmerelda..."* Gowdie gasped as the lovebirds kept shrieking. *"Esmerelda just put Bernadette to sleep herself once they'd come to deliver the sleeping Ren!"*

Nimue's jaw dropped. Ren was stirring beneath her—since his sleep had been caused by tea and not a charm, apparently. Still, with all the racket the familiars had caused, he hadn't been able to fully wake earlier?

She waved the borrowed wand over his bed. She was glad she'd saved the charm for the day. "Awake Charm."

"Soren? Ren?" Nimue called out as Ren's eyes began to flutter.

She turned to Gowdie. "But Esmerelda would have only been able to put Bernadette to sleep," she said. "She can't use a Sleep Charm twice—"

"She wasn't alone," Gowdie translated for a chirping Naismith. *"There was a second witch or warlock here with her. But no one could see that one. It was like they were—"*

"Invisible," Nimue finished for him.

Soren shot up on the bed, looking around blankly. He jumped to find Bernadette and Prue, of all people, beside him, then blinked harder to see Nimue standing beside his bed.

"What is going on?" His voice cracked. It was Soren, all right.

"Balfour, fill him in," Nimue said to the cat. The feline nodded curtly beside her, gave Nimue's hip a quick, seemingly grateful head rub, and sat on her warlock's lap, staring up at him.

"Esmerelda's working with the Invisible-Charm-expert witch?" Nimue said aloud.

Soren snapped up from looking at his familiar and stared at Nimue at that. "My mother...?"

He fumbled at his waist for his wand, which was nowhere to be found. He looked at the bedside table, the ground. Balfour jumped up smacked her paw atop his cheek, forcing him to look back.

"My mother took my wand? All our wands?" He stared at Bernadette and Prue beside him.

Nimue handed her borrowed one over to him. "It's Glinda's," she said. "I've had a few strange exploits myself. Wake my grandmother up? Then I'll catch you all up and see what they know."

Chewing on his bottom lip, Soren took the offered wand, waving it over Bernadette. "Awake Charm."

Bernadette shot up. Then it took another tense exchange and Bernadette borrowed Glinda's wand to use "Awake Charm" on Prue.

And all three were standing up and conferring with their familiars, Prue especially, but even Bernadette, sending a few guilty looks Nimue's way.

"I'm sorry, child," Prue said. "We only meant to keep you safe."

"We'll talk about that later," Nimue said. Then she caught them up with everything she knew—down to the crisis Zelena was handling without them.

"I take it you don't suspect Zelena anymore, then?" Bernadette asked, an amused hint of a smile on her face.

"I don't," Nimue admitted. She turned to Soren. "But Esmerelda…"

"We were worried about her," Prue said, adjusting her sweater. "We brought Ren back home to allow him to get some sleep in peace, but also to talk to her."

"Seems she was a step ahead of us, though,"

Bernadette said. She stared at the wand still in her hand. Glinda's wand.

"Zelena needs our help," Nimue said. "Then we can look into finding Esmerelda—"

"Esmerelda has our wands," Prue said. "We're not going to *be* much help, one shared, borrowed wand between us."

Bernadette was staring at the wand now, at the pound sign Nimue had just noticed.

"Glinda knew this Pound criminal," Nimue said. "Maverick's father."

Bernadette clutched the wand tighter and held it beside her thigh. "'Pound' is just a nickname," she said, which wasn't a surprise to Nimue, considering the strangeness of the name. "His real name is Vanedestine Redferne. And he was a warlock from Cauldron Cove."

Nimue's lips pursed. "Pound is… Glinda's brother?" Maverick's father was a warlock? Of course, warlocks who sired children with human women didn't pass along the magic gifts, whereas witches who had children with human men did. It was part of the reason why witch and warlock society was matriarchal.

And that meant… Pound himself was the one and only witch in his organization? He'd tortured his son with his own hands?

"I wouldn't send him *a card on Father's Day,"* muttered Gowdie.

"One and the same." Bernadette grimaced. "Not many people knew that when he left, he took up a life of crime among humans. But Glinda did. And so did Esmerelda."

"My mother? Knows a warlock criminal?" Soren

asked. He cradled Balfour against his chest, squeezing her a little tighter at the news.

"Your mother dated him for the longest time when she was younger," Nimue said. Apparently, that *was* news to Soren. Even if Ren had recently found out.

Bernadette took a deep breath. "And, son, sorry to break it to you now if your mother never saw fit to… But there were more than a few rumors that you were *that* warlock's son."

Nimue hadn't heard *that*. Soren froze, his mouth pursed in an "o." Balfour meowed. But before he could say another thing, his hair smoothed itself out, slicking back over his head.

Ren was back in control.

CHAPTER TWENTY-FOUR

"While this might prove fascinating," Ren said, petting Balfour, who was still clutched in his arms, "Soren confronting rumors of his true parentage doesn't help solve any of our current issues."

"It might," said Nimue softly. "If it's connected to Glinda's death in any way."

Bernadette frowned. "You said you think this bodyguard of the movie star, Kovac, is the murderer?"

"Yes. He's the one who went back to retrieve the pin Davies dropped. He had access to the deluxe figurine's sword, and he pocketed it for some reason—my best guess being that he realized it was sharp and small and portable because Maverick forbade his bodyguards from carrying anything other than a Taser as a weapon, and working with Pound, he probably didn't like not having something more lethal on hand. And the most obvious reason: He had Glinda's body in his hotel room."

"Why take it back in the first place?" Prue wondered. She held her finger out and her familiar, Dunlop, perched atop it. "If Vanedestine Redferne wanted her body, he'd get it in time, criminal or not. He's her only known relative. Well, I suppose other than his son…" Her eyes flicked toward Ren. True or not, there was at least Maverick Vanedestine, apparently. Nimue wondered briefly if that was a stage name or he'd taken his father's given name as his surname instead of "Redferne" for a reason.

Nimue supposed it helped hide his connection to Cauldron Cove. The Redfernes had been one of the first families to move to Cauldron Cove.

"Pound likely wasn't happy Kovac had made the call to kill Glinda," Nimue said, sure that referring to him as "Vanedestine" would just prove confusing, considering Maverick's presence. "Maybe Kovac needed some kind of insurance."

"Insurance Pound wouldn't seek revenge against him?" Bernadette asked. "But he'd be free to as soon as he had his sister's body in hand. This has someone else's hand in it. Someone gave Kovac the idea that taking Glinda's body would help him in some way."

"He *did* have to have help carrying the body…" Nimue said.

"I have another question," Gowdie added. While Balfour sat up on the bed now, Ren was scrolling through messages on his witch network crystal behind Gowdie, and Nimue stiffened in anticipation of the warlock alerting them that they were tarrying too long—though she felt that way already. *"If Kovac didn't hesitate to murder Glinda, why did he spare Nimue? He managed to knock her out with the Taser, but he just brought her to the bed and left her*

there, knowing she could wake up at any moment and ruin anything he had planned."

Nimue's jaw dropped. True, there was the chance that Kovac had gotten in trouble for killing one witch already, that he'd dropped the sharp toy sword, but that didn't seem reason enough to stop him. He could have killed her any number of ways. It certainly couldn't be the fact that he didn't *like* killing. There'd been little reason to kill Glinda in the first place as far as Kovac had known. She either wouldn't have known what the Pound pin meant and wouldn't have made a big deal of it—or she would have known and thus would have been scared into keeping quiet. Or even *wanted* to keep quiet, since it was her brother.

"What if whoever else he was working with… was the one who didn't want him to kill me," Nimue said softly. Ren looked up from his witch network crystal, slowly lowering his wrist.

"Just like Esmerelda knocked Bernadette and Prue out without intending to kill them," he said.

Nimue was surprised he was following along with her idea. She almost didn't have faith in it herself. But Ren thinking along the same lines meant she wasn't necessarily on the wrong track.

"Esmerelda likes us," Nimue said. "I mean, we're not close friends or anything, but she has hinted to me that Ren—er, Soren—might be interested in a relationship with me." Nimue felt her face heat as she quickly looked to the co-Head Warlock General Manager who'd driven her crazy ever since she'd moved back to Cauldron Cove.

Only he'd been proving a lot less aggravating somehow lately.

Ren was intensely focusing on the ceiling, the area behind his ears growing just a bit pink.

Nimue couldn't believe it.

But she shoved all that strangeness aside for the moment, ignoring Gowdie's sly laugh in her mind.

Bernadette grimaced. "It would explain why she knocked us out at all. And yes, we wanted to talk to her about Vanedestine—*Pound*," she corrected, following Nimue's lead on that.

Everything was confusing enough as it was.

Ren cleared his throat. "We got messages from Zelena," he said, nodding curtly to Nimue. "Though it seems like she just copied me on a message to you since she probably assumed I wouldn't answer."

Nimue quickly brought her witch network perma-charm crystal up and checked her latest message from Zelena.

Maverick Vanedestine is missing, the Director of Security had written. *Everyone else in this room is accounted for, but when the lights went out, Charity reports they were up against another witch. Charms were flying everywhere. The guard named Blevins positively identified Kovac appearing at their boss's side as well. But though he fought him off for a bit, and Davies tried to Taser him, Kovac got away with Maverick, whom he Tasered. Then the attackers retreated. Kovac never used magic himself.*

"Kovac has Maverick," Nimue said, relaying the message to her grandmothers. "And he's human, but he had help grabbing him from a witch."

She looked up and locked eyes with Ren. "Fidelity made a comment once that Soren's mom seemed to pop up and surprise him. And *I* just learned that a Southern Hotel master keycard gives the holder all-access to the Bessa, too."

Ren nodded. He'd probably never had a need to question the safety risks of such a thing before. Soren's family owned this hotel.

"Vanedestine Redferne could use the Invisible Charm," Bernadette said. "We thought it'd be a good skill for him to have when he moved out to Hollywood. *If* he'd kept his nose clean. Even back then, we wondered… Well, we weren't too surprised a few years ago when rumors spread he might have been dipping his toes into something like illicit loans."

"Pound works on the Superstellar-Man movies, doesn't he?" Nimue asked.

"I didn't see his name in the credits," Gowdie pointed out.

"He does work in movies even still. He needs some legit front for what he does." Bernadette sighed. "I'm not as skilled at the Invisible Charm as he is, but I'm one of the most talented perma-charm crystal crafters around." Naismith the lovebird cheeped happily from his witch's shoulder.

Nimue wouldn't begrudge her grandmother saying that. It was true.

"About twenty years back, before I heard rumors about his illegal activities, he paid his sister a visit for a bit. Even though I was busy with Witchy ExS at the time, he put in an order for a batch of perma-charm crystals, with him standing alongside me in the evenings over a series of weeks to provide the charm for each crystal. He was supposed to be expanding his special effects company with it. I couldn't resist the idea of humans relying on witches more for such a thing." Bernadette shook her head.

Gowdie flapped his wings excitedly. *"Crimson Fern Special Effects!"*

"Of course," Nimue breathed. "Crimson Fern. Redferne." She narrowed her eyes at Nimue. "So you're saying… He's one of the few warlocks in the world with a stash of Invisible Charm perma-charm crystals."

Bernadette nodded. "And as we can see, he hasn't been *just* using them for movies."

Nimue scuffed her shoe against the floor. "He passes out those crystals to his human grunts to use for criminal activity? Would they even work for a human?"

"Not as well as it would for a witch, but in this case, yes, I think so," Prue said softly. "He asked for them to be tailored that way, so he could hire humans for his special effects work, too. But maybe he asks them to use the perma-charms sparingly outside of work—to not draw attention except when necessary."

Nimue's mind raced over everything she'd seen on Kovac, searching her mind's eye for sign of a perma-charm crystal. He'd had a watch, but so had Davies. The only difference between the two of them, practically was—

"His sunglasses," she said aloud. "I thought one time there was a sort of strange sparkle behind them." She grunted. "I wish I'd paid better attention."

"Soren's mother's necklace," Ren added quietly. "I always knew it was a perma-charm crystal. She claimed it was an Awake Charm she used sparingly for busy times at work."

"She told me that, too," Nimue said. "You think it's a perma-charm Invisible Charm?"

"A gift from Pound?" Bernadette asked. "But I made those for him long after she and Vanedestine Redferne were a thing of the past."

"Were they ever… totally a thing of the past?" Nimue asked. "Zelena mentioned something about Glinda dating Clarke when they were younger, Esmerelda with Glinda's brother. And then Esmerelda was with Clarke all of a sudden after a few decades, leaving Glinda and her brother high and dry. But did they? What if there were still warm feelings between Esmerelda and Pound? Especially if… other rumors are true." She glanced at Ren guiltily.

"And what if there were *hard* feelings between her and Glinda, do you mean?" Ren asked, not seeming bothered by the insinuation that Pound might be his father. "Soren's father… Soren's only seen him once since Glinda died." Nimue nodded. She'd observed Soren interacting with his dad. She'd been just out of earshot when that had happened, before she'd attended the dinner. "Balfour told me. He didn't seem well. I didn't attribute it to Glinda's death because he hadn't reacted at first, not until the prep for the dinner had died down and he had a moment to himself."

"Maybe it didn't really hit him until then." Nimue frowned.

"'*Nuts*'!" shouted Gowdie. Nimue looked at him until he made it clear he was quoting Frone, Clarke's familiar. "*Short for 'Nutter,' maybe? She wasn't saying, 'Drat,' she was mourning for her friend, Glinda's familiar.*"

That actually made a lot of sense. Nimue wished she'd figured it out sooner. "Clarke knows something. I say we track him down and find out what."

CHAPTER TWENTY-FIVE

Though Bernadette was supposed to be retired, she'd gotten herself involved in this crisis to the point where Nimue didn't mind that she was the one to catch Zelena up. Rather than wait for their conversation via Communication Charm to finish, though, Nimue lowered her voice and whispered to Ren, "Should we go check on Soren's father?"

Stepfather, biological father… Whatever the truth was, the man had raised Soren. He *was* his father. Perhaps the warlock just needed a little time to process that.

"And the fact that his mom might have helped a murderer?" Gowdie added from Nimue's shoulder.

Ren nodded and looked at Balfour, who jumped to the ground and trotted alongside him as they headed for his front door.

"Nimue, Ren, wait." Prue shuffled over to meet them at the doorway, her eyes glancing back to Bernadette, who paced as she spoke to the Director of Security. "Pound's a dangerous warlock. That's why we didn't want the two of you to get hurt." Dunlop cheeped and fluffed a wing over Prue's scalp. "She regrets making those perma-charm crystals for him, you know. When she figured out his connections to crime a while back... Well, she just always hoped it wouldn't reach us here."

Nimue's voice lowered. "Why didn't she tell the Witches and Warlocks of the Greater Midwest? Or... whatever it's called where he operates?"

Prue sighed. "She didn't have proof, just suspicions. She'd seen that pound sign before, she knew he was one of the few warlocks anywhere capable of the Invisible Charm and that he was sitting on a stock of perma-charm crystals to cast it repeatedly... But he still had his special effects company, and she thought, surely, if the Witches and Warlocks of the Pacific Coast suspected it was a front, they'd put a stop to it all."

"Has he killed before?" Ren asked, clipped.

"Not that we know of, but he doesn't exactly appear all over the news."

"But she's afraid of him," Nimue said.

Gowdie nodded. *"Enough to knock these two out!"*

Dunlop chirped.

Gowdie translated. *"She knew what magic he had access to and was afraid of what he might be capable of. Especially after it was clear Glinda had already been murdered—though she didn't know it hadn't been by Pound directly."*

"Pound's not even here..." Nimue looked over to Ren. "Right?"

"I don't know what he looks like," Ren said curtly.

But her grandmothers did.

"We haven't seen him," said Prue. "But we weren't looking long before…" She gestured around her.

"Grandma," Nimue said, taking her Grandma Prue's hands in hers, "we're adults. Bernadette put us in charge of Witchy ExS for a reason. She has to trust us to be okay."

"You don't have your wands," Prue said, her voice cracking. She handed Nimue the one borrowed from Glinda. Bernadette must have passed it on to her.

"Thanks," Nimue said.

Prue reached into her pocket and removed a perma-charm crystal, placing it in Nimue's hand. "It's the only one I have on me. A perma-charm crystal for the Undo Charm."

"Handy," Ren said curtly. "I wonder if I should commission one—"

Balfour meowed.

Ren went quiet.

Gowdie giggled, a rough, throaty sound. *"She told him to focus on the crisis in front of us. She doesn't usually have to lecture Ren instead of Soren, does she?"*

Balfour meowed again, sticking her maw into the air, heading out into the hallway.

"Thank you, Grandma," Nimue said. "We're just checking on Clarke—we'll be fine. Meet up with Zelena to track down Maverick and our wands, and we'll reunite soon. We'll let you know if we find Esmerelda anywhere along the way."

Prue nodded, pulling her cardigan tighter over chest and Nimue heard the lovebirds' song grow quieter as she and Ren and their familiars made their way down the dark, overgrown hallway.

"Didn't you used to have a cozy, little cottage?" Nimue asked. "Right on the outskirts of town? Why move down here?" A branch nearly whapped against her face. "There's hardly any light here, and the trees could use some pruning."

"That was… Soren. Before. With Lydia."

Nimue winced. She'd just wanted to break the silence, try to stick to a less-frightening subject, and she'd foolishly forgotten all about that. "I'm sorry."

Ren grunted. "If Lydia Southern hadn't died, I never would have found a body to live in. I feel sorry for Soren, appreciative that it was a sacrifice I owe much to him and her for. But at least I'm here because of it."

Nimue frowned. "Where were you before then?"

"I can't say," Ren said simply.

He couldn't say because he didn't know… or because he'd been forbidden to for some reason?

They reached the end of the hall.

"Well, I'm sad the only way you could be here was with a death. But I'm glad you're here." Nimue stared up at the stairwell, which went on for seven floors above. The elevator didn't let out to this bottom floor.

Ren stumbled on the first step, his hand on the handrail catching him.

"Th-Thank you," he said, reddening. "I've felt it hasn't been my place to mingle with the townspeople, considering the circumstances of my coming here. And Soren wanted to hide away in his grief. We both found the basement suitable living arrangements. The cottage just reminded him of her." He started heading up the stairs, Balfour running up always only a step or two ahead, practically tripping him every few seconds. He walked confidently without ever kicking her, though.

"Is that why you threw yourself into your job?" Nimue asked. "Soren didn't work at Witchy ExS before I left town. Well, I think he did an internship after school, but—"

"He wanted to be a potions brewer," Ren confirmed. "A perma-charm crystal creator. He stopped caring about that… for obvious reasons."

Right. He and Lydia had been trying to brew something when she'd died. "Of course," she said. "But you wanted to stay productive?"

"I had to prove my worth," Ren said. He took a keycard out of the pouch at his hip and waved it over the employees-only gate in front of him. "To Soren. To this town. To Lydia's memory."

Nimue didn't know what to say.

Gowdie broke the tension. *"Glad you're not jumping over the gate,"* he teased.

Nimue rubbed her hip as they approached. Maybe he had a point.

"Balfour? Let's take the elevator," Ren told his familiar, who'd already started for the next set of steps. "It's quicker."

As Ren turned to the first-floor door, Nimue grabbed his elbow before he could push on it.

"You don't need to prove your worth," she said. "I know Soren appreciates you. I know it was only the accident that allowed you to inhabit Soren's body, but *you*

didn't have anything to do with hurting Lydia. You just…
appeared at the same time."

Ren swallowed as he looked down at where Nimue
touched him.

Suddenly conscious about all those rumors about his
crush, she dropped her grip.

"I appreciate that," he said softly. He took a step
forward. "I'm sorry. For all the times I've argued with
you. I was upset I had to share the co-Head Witch General
Manager position, it's true, but that wasn't about *you*. I
just thought earning that position meant I'd finally
proven…" He clamped his lips shut.

"You proved your *talent* and *aptitude* for the job. Your
leadership skills. That's all you had to do—for advance-
ment in your career. You don't have to justify anything
more than that."

Ren offered her a flittering smile. It was awkward…
but almost kind of sweet.

"You are the best co-Head Witch General Manager I
could have asked for," he said. "And I was foolish to ever
think I could handle the job alone."

"Well," said Nimue, tucking a strand of hair that had
escaped from her ponytail back behind her head, "back at
you. I shouldn't have assumed I could handle all of this
alone, either."

Balfour chirruped at their feet and Gowdie flapped his
wings. *"I know what you mean,"* he said to the cat. *"It's
weird for them to be getting along, isn't it? Weird for us to be
getting along, actually."*

Balfour meowed again, arching her back as if to

remind Gowdie one last time she was pretty tough. Then she relaxed and meowed up at her warlock.

Ren's eyes blinked rapidly.

"What do you mean, he should tell Nimue the truth about where he came from?" Gowdie asked.

Nimue cocked her head at Ren. Ren fluffed a hand in the air and spun on his heel, opening the door to the lobby without another word.

"Here," said Nimue, trailing after him. The lobby wasn't as crowded as it had been this morning, but there were still con-goers milling about. Over near the bar, a group of five costumed superheroes Nimue didn't recognize were getting their photos taken by a handful of other con-goers, both costumed and in street clothes alike.

Ren slowed down but didn't stop. She slipped the borrowed wand into his hand.

That got him to stop and turn around.

"We're a team," Nimue said, smiling. She showed him her closed fist, which held Prue's lent perma-charm crystal. "Let's each have something to work with."

Ren's gaze shot to the side briefly, then he stared back at Nimue, his eyes growing glossy. "A team," he repeated back.

Balfour purred rather loudly and wove around Nimue's legs. Gowdie got in on it, too, and took to the air, landing on Ren's shoulder.

Ren stared at the little dragon in shock.

"Let's do this!" Gowdie shouted, letting out a little roar.

The group of people posing for and taking pictures nearby all turned to look—and Nimue recognized Mia, no longer in costume, her Comic Enthusiast Society white T-shirt on in its place, as well as a pair of jeans.

Mia stared at Nimue and pushed her glasses up.

Ren followed Nimue's line of sight. "Head of the CES. Should we talk to her first?"

Why had Pound wanted to leave her a message—assuming Nimue was right about that?

"You check on Soren's dad," Nimue said. "I'll meet you."

Ren nodded. "Seventh floor. Room 701."

Gowdie flapped his wings and took to the air again. *"Wait a minute. You just said you were a team!"*

Balfour meowed from the floor as well.

"Divide and conquer," Nimue said. "We're good at that. Besides, nothing's going to happen to me in the hotel lobby. And Ren's just checking on Soren's dad."

Ren nodded and headed for the elevator.

Gowdie landed on Nimue's shoulder. *"You haven't seen enough horror movies."*

Nimue turned on her heel and headed to where she'd last seen Mia. The head of the CES wasn't there, though, the cosplaying group starting to disband.

"Did you see where that woman with glasses went?" Nimue asked one of the men in costume. "The one taking your picture?"

The average-sized man scratched his chin, a rather confused, relaxed look for a superhero. "The one with the Superstellar-Man T-shirt? I think she went to the bar with another guy in the same shirt?"

"Thanks," Nimue said, heading past the group and

into the darkened part of the lounge devoted to the hotel's bar.

Luckily, the nonchalant superhero had been right. It didn't take long for Nimue to spot Mia in a corner booth, one of the other members of the CES across from her.

Mia's gaze kept flicking back and forth between Nimue and the man across from her as Nimue approached. In the dim light from a lamp overhead, Mia's brow glowed with perspiration.

"Mia," Nimue said, glancing quickly at the CES Board member across from Mia Estrada. It was the skinny one, the one who looked a touch older than the rest of them. She turned back to Mia. "I was wondering if we might talk? Alone?" She lifted her eyebrows as if to convey it had something to do with the murder Mia had been so concerned about resolving. She didn't know how much she'd told the other members of the Comic Enthusiast Society yet.

Mia leaned back in the booth, a watery smile plastered on her face. "Oh, I think we can talk later, maybe, right? Depends on what else we have to do. Maybe when—"

But Nimue didn't hear the rest of her rapid babbling.

Something poked into her back, a quiet, high-pitched voice hovering in her ear. "Don't move. I have my wand in your back, and I *will* use it if you force me to."

Gowdie squeaked. The voice was hovering right over his head.

"I like you, Nimmy," said none other than Esmerelda. No one else called her that. Nimue dared to look out of the corner of her eye, but she saw no one. "But I won't hesitate to stop you however I must if you keep poking your nose into other people's business."

The table had gone quiet, both Mia and the other member of the CES staring up at Nimue.

"Now have a seat," barked invisible-Esmerelda, prodding at Nimue's back with the wand. "And don't make a scene."

CHAPTER TWENTY-SIX

"Esmerelda," Nimue said, looking up at the area where the voice had come from. She couldn't see the wand, just like she hadn't been able to see exactly what had cut Glinda's neck in the History Charm at first.

"Smart cookie," Esmerelda said.

The man from the Comic Enthusiast Society looked up in Esmerelda's direction, but he didn't seem startled at all. Sure, he was in a witch town at a magic-enhanced convention, but Nimue would have thought the disembodied voice could have warranted a *little* surprise.

Or fear. Like Mia was expressing as she clenched hard to Nimue's forearm as the witch slid down beside her.

"Sorry I didn't sense Faulkner until they were right up on top of us," Gowdie said. *"The snake is a sneaky little thing. The most I got was a little hiss. Like a can of soda freshly opened."*

A little hiss? Nimue thought back to him. *In other words, a fizzling sound? Like what you sensed briefly before we found Glinda's body on the showroom floor?*

Gowdie's eyes widened. *"Or when I entered Florence's clinic alone, right after the body went missing. Maybe I just missed them…"*

"The invisible witch was you," Nimue said aloud. Her eyes darted to the man from the CES, unsure how much she should say. "I know *anyone* with one of the rare Invisible Charm perma-charm crystals could have done it, but Kovac didn't work alone. At least not when it came to retrieving… the body. From the clinic."

The man looked from Nimue to Mia to the empty space where Esmerelda presumably was and even to Gowdie on the table between him and Mia. There were no drinks on the table, Nimue just noticed. A bit strange, then, for the two to be sitting down together at the bar, before they'd even ordered.

Nimue glanced to look for the bartender, but there was none.

"I told the bartender to take a break," Esmerelda said. "Create Charm." Nimue assumed Esmerelda waved her wand because a sign on a post appeared between the bar and the hotel lobby, probably indicating the bar was closed for a bit. "Give these two a little privacy. Though you can't stop yourself from snooping, can you?"

Mia gulped.

Nimue looked back and forth between Mia and her companion for the first time.

The man was so unfazed by this. He leaned his elbows on the table, resting his chin on his hands. The fine lines around his eyes popped as he narrowed his gaze on Nimue. A flash of Glinda's face, the way the spiderweb-pattern wrinkles around her eyes had often stood out to Nimue brought a truth to light.

"You… You're Pound. Vanedestine Redferne."

Gowdie's jaw dropped.

The man chuckled darkly and with a clack, a perma-charm crystal lodged in a golden locket on a chain appeared on the table. Esmerelda materialized into view as she slid in the booth beside him, her wand clearly now pointed across the table.

"I guess you already know too much." Esmerelda sighed. "As long as you keep my Soren out of it. If those two meddlesome witches hadn't knocked him out, I would have done it myself—just like I did to Clarke before that."

Nimue chewed her bottom lip. So Esmerelda didn't know she'd woken everyone up. She hadn't invisibly observed Ren walk through the lobby and to the elevators?

Nimue kept glancing at the lobby to watch for her grandmothers while she was at it. They didn't have their wands, either, but they would do what they could in a pinch.

She gripped the perma-charm crystal Prue had given her in her hand, feeling her sweat accumulate on the smooth, cold gem. "You have our wands."

She nodded. "Up in my room. I would have given them to you as soon as this was all over. If you'd just stayed out of our business."

Up in her room, Nimue thought to Gowdie quietly. *Where Ren and Balfour are headed.*

Gowdie just nodded. She supposed anything he

thought back to his witch could be overheard by Esmerel-da's familiar—or Pound's.

As Nimue moved slowly, ever so slowly, to tap the witch network crystal on her wrist with a finger still clutching the Undo Charm, Nimue glanced at Pound, but she didn't see a familiar anywhere.

"I'm not picking up on their thoughts," Gowdie said.

As if on cue, a slimy little forest-green snake popped out from beneath the collar of Pound's T-shirt. It wiggled and squelched.

Gowdie stiffened. *"She says her name is O'Leary. And she doesn't much like talking."*

No wonder you never heard her, Nimue said. *Ren,* she thought to the witch network crystal. As quick as she could, she told him about the wands and thought where she was and what she was up against, composing a message with her mind. Mia glanced down at Nimue's wrist under the table but didn't say anything.

Nimue focused on the two across from her. "Where's Maverick?"

"He's safe," Pound said simply. He held a hand out to his snake, and she slithered around an arm, writhing about. "He was getting a bit too talkative for my tastes, so I felt he needed a timeout."

"He's sleeping in my apartments," Esmerelda said simply. "I left Kovac in charge of watching him."

Nimue's breath cut short, and she did her best to keep her mind blank, not to convey that she was worried about Ren walking into a fight with just a borrowed wand that couldn't work quite as well with his magic. She could tell from the tension in Gowdie's body that he was trying to do the same.

She added Kovac's presence to the message and then quickly hit the witch network crystal again to end the message before anyone noticed.

She swallowed desperately, her throat suddenly dry. When she caught sight of her grandmothers exiting the stair landing out in the lobby behind Pound's and Esmerelda's backs, she quickly looked down. She couldn't risk shouting and getting their attention. They were probably on their way to the teleportation pad to join Zelena in the Bessa, or better yet, she hoped, to the elevators, to head where they'd last known Ren and Nimue to be heading. Maybe they'd help Ren, get their wands back, and head back down. She could hope.

Right now, she had a wand trained right at her—two, if Pound was likely carrying one—and her only defense was an Undo Charm perma-charm crystal in her grip on her lap under the table.

They had the advantage. They *knew* they had the advantage. Nimue could use that to *her* advantage, keep them talking and focused on her, so they wouldn't know that the others were awake.

"What has Mia got to do with this?" Nimue asked, glancing at the cowering woman beside her. When no answer was immediately forthcoming, she hazarded one of her own. "You wanted to send a warning to her," she said to Pound, straightening her back and meeting Pound's eye. "A subtle one. Only it wound up being not-so-subtle." She looked at Mia, whose head dropped down, then stared at Pound's CES shirt. "Are you really a member of the Comic Enthusiast Society's board?"

He smiled slyly. "Do I not look like one?"

"Nerds come in all forms, I suppose."

"Geeks," Gowdie corrected, even in the midst of all of this. *"Or just 'fans,' really."*

O'Leary writhed and hissed softly and Pound chuckled.

"You *are* a member," Nimue said. "You're in charge of Crimson Fern Special Effects, you work on the Superstellar-Man movies—I can see you using your influence to get on the board. And your son is in the movies."

"I suppose even bad guys can be comic fans," Gowdie muttered.

Both O'Leary and Faulkner hissed at that.

"The comic publishers work closely with the movie production company to discuss future installments," Pound explained. Nimue allowed herself a fraction of a second to check the lobby and saw her grandmothers were gone—though she hadn't caught which direction they'd headed. At least they were safe. "So yes, I channeled my *enthusiasm* for comics as well as my need to know how to design upcoming special effects for future movie storylines and found myself on the board of the nation's biggest fan group."

"Did you use your connections to get Maverick the starring role, too?"

Pound smiled. "Let's just say I opened the right doors for him. No one could deny me a favor. No one can replicate what I can on a set—an Illusion Charm doesn't transfer to film like a practical effect done with an Invisible Charm's assistance."

"That's what I *said!"* Gowdie shouted. Nimue refrained from rolling her eyes. He *had* said that, but it was hardly important right now.

"Still, he had to have *some* talent to get the job. Even with your influence," added Esmerelda. She slipped her free hand—the one not holding her wand toward Nimue —through Pound's arm. "Your children have all sorts of talents, don't they?"

Did Nimue dare ask about Ren's parentage? She didn't want Esmerelda to ask how she might have known about those rumors. Even if it was possible her grandmothers could have told her before tonight. If they had, though, she doubted she'd have been able to interact with Esmerelda without at least *some* of her awkward feelings slipping through.

"And Mia," Nimue said, focusing on the woman beside her. "You kept focusing on how this convention needed to be a success." Nimue pasted on a flittering smile. "Well, isn't it? Even when crises happen, Witchy ExS always delivers."

"So it would seem." Pound looked out at the somewhat busy lobby now, and Nimue was grateful her grandmothers had already passed through.

"I assumed it was because of what you said." Nimue spoke to Mia directly. "Your first year as head of the CES, the first time a woman was in charge, how your election wasn't unanimous and a poorly run convention would be just the excuse they needed to vote you out."

"Only it wasn't *just* my position as head of the CES at risk," Mia squeaked, the first time she'd spoken in ages.

Pound smiled. His teeth were perfectly straight, though slightly yellowed with age. "I never explicitly stated I'd take away anything more than that. And with that Pound pin in the CES booth, I simply sought to remind her that *I* made sure she won the election to be the first woman head of the Comic Enthusiast Society and I would be keeping an eye on her, even when I didn't appear to be there."

Mia whispered. "He influenced the vote. I didn't know what I was getting into when I agreed to do as he asked for the next convention. I didn't know he was a…" She yelped and shut her mouth tight.

"A criminal?" Pound provided for her. "A warlock? I'm never sure which is more likely to offend."

"So this all started with just a simple reminder that you're always watching." Nimue scoffed. "You could have sent her a text with a hashtag in it."

"A pound sign," corrected the warlock.

"That's not how he operates," Esmerelda said smoothly. "Besides, he needed to give Maverick *some* reason to show up here. If he knew he was doing a favor not just for his father, but for *Pound* himself, he'd buckle up and show up. The boy owes his father everything, down to that fancy home of his."

Pound preened. "It was his movie fortune that bought him that place, but I got him the role, didn't I? I left my calling card *in* the front gate one time I visited to remind him. A simple Transformation Charm."

Nimue decided not to further examine that father-son

toxic relationship just now. "Maverick had to keep an eye on Mia?"

"All he had to do was plant a pin." As Pound spoke, O'Leary slid down his arm and down his torso. "And be his charming self, making the fans happy. See, I may have made a mistake once, when it comes to the *reminders* I've given my son before."

"You hurt him," Nimue said simply, petting Gowdie in front of her with her free hand. "With magic."

Pound scoffed. "I knew the kid was talking too much."

"It wasn't he who told me."

Gowdie piped up in her mind. *"Don't get your source in trouble."*

Right. Dr. Choi was one of them now.

"So his strogaphobia is real," Nimue said before anyone could pry further.

"He manages." Pound scoffed. "Didn't even scratch him, really."

"Not physically, anyway," Gowdie said.

"He got a bit *overconfident* is all," Pound said. "Said he didn't need me now—that he already had the part and had for several movies—what were they going to do, recast him? I don't know about that, but I showed him they *might have to* if he *couldn't* play the part anymore." He shrugged. "Then I healed him. But the disappointment still couldn't quite get over it."

O'Leary slithered back up then, carrying something gold and shiny in the overhead light atop her head. Pound took it and pinned the gold pound sign pin over his breast, then pulled his wand out from his hip as

Esmerelda tapped the golden chain and locket she'd placed on the table.

"Do me a favor, sweetheart?" she asked.

Pound waved his wand at the golden chain. "Create Charm."

The gold chain separated from the perma-charm crystal embedded in it, then morphed into a Pound sign pin just like the criminal's, and he reached over to pin it at her lapel, but he clenched his jaw all the while, like it brought him no pleasure.

Throughout it all, there was always a wand pointed at Nimue, so she didn't dare move.

"You knew having a child with a human wouldn't pass on your gift," said Esmerelda, her nose in the air. "You never should have left me."

"*You* never should have dumped me for that pretty boy," Pound quipped. "I know you had some petty argument with Glinda, but that was no excuse."

"Four became two and two," said Esmerelda softly, her fingers stroking over the pound sign pin on her lapel.

"Is that what the pound sign means? Four witches?" Nimue asked.

"Two witches, two warlocks," said Esmerelda. "The two Redfernes and their lovers." She smiled at Pound beside her. "It was just a silly sign we came up with, representing our friendship. We all wear gold chains we can transform into our pound sign, four lines connected."

"Then you and Glinda had that falling out, and you cheated on me." He shrugged. "I didn't care that you told me you were pregnant after I left—it could have been Clarke's."

"He wasn't!" Esmerelda bit her lip as she stared at Pound.

"Yeah, yeah. A simple charm could tell." Pound chuckled. "Though Clarke didn't need one, did he? He did the honorable thing and married you before the kid was born."

"He's a good guy," Esmerelda said softly. "Better than I deserve."

"You built this place," said Nimue, trying to make sense of it all. "I know it was the Southern family legacy, but you came in here and you made changes and you made it for the better." Nimue's breath caught. "Why would you ruin it all for *him*?"

"No one was supposed to get hurt." Pound waved his wand at Mia. "This was all supposed to be a simple visit. Thought my oaf of a son would make the con-goers extra happy, get the cauldron bubbling over with excitement and positive energy. Things went a little off-course, but if *someone* here reports what happened to the *human authorities*, there will be no escaping the bad press." He smirked at Nimue. "At least the witch authorities understand the need to keep it all under wraps."

"I won't tell anyone, I swear!" Mia said. "I just thought..." Her face looked green. "I've been feeling guilty is all. But of course I wouldn't want to ruin the convention!" Her eyes widened. "Please, you have to believe me!"

"Okay, dear. We're just talking." Pound's eyes shone dimly, then he waved his wand at Mia. "Befuddle Charm!"

"Hey, wait—" said Nimue.

But Mia shook as the magic hit her. Then her eyes went cloudy, her body straight, but her expression blank.

"What did you do that for?" Nimue asked.

"Would you have preferred I hurt her?" Pound proposed. He trained his wand on Nimue. "I could do the same to you. All I ask is that you let this convention go on. No harm, no foul."

"Of course I'll let the con continue!" Nimue said. "You know I need to keep this town safe. Like you said, we've been discreet for a reason." She frowned. "You want the cauldron's energy, don't you? But it doesn't work like that. It's never bubbled over with positive energy."

"But it has with negative energy. Once. Long before you were born," Esmerelda said. She shook her head. "Bernadette only just managed to avoid a catastrophe."

"I know." It was a cautionary tale her grandmother had told her before. "But the opposite has never happened. Too much good energy hasn't resulted in a burst of energy one could seize for themselves. And if it did, it'd be impossible for one witch to harness."

Pound grinned. "But maybe not two." He stared at Esmerelda. "Right, darling? Didn't I forgive you for what you did?"

Nimue's voice raised in pitch. "*You* killed Glinda, Esmerelda?" There'd been the hissing sound on the show-room floor. Of course. Why hadn't she realized that meant she'd been *there* during the murder? "But what about Kovac?"

"He wouldn't make a move like that without his boss's permission." Esmerelda pinched Pound's chin like he was a little baby. "The bodyguard and I both had

Invisible Charm perma-charms, so I accompanied him to find the pin the other dolt had dropped, but when I saw Glinda had found it, well… I couldn't let her alert anyone to the fact that Vanedestine was about to make a visit. Kovac had that little dinky weapon on him and he was too chicken to do anything with it. I took it from him and used it."

"That's why the toy sword popped briefly into existence in the air in the History Charm! It was passing from one to the other, and it took a moment for Esmerelda's Invisible Charm to make it invisible again."

Nimue grimaced. How was Soren going to handle this? He hadn't even handled the rumor about his parentage that well.

Pound blinked, his saccharine smile too fake. "You could have taken her out," he said. "Befuddled her. Put her to sleep, like we did everyone else."

We? So he'd been the invisible warlock who'd put Prue to sleep after Esmerelda had Sleep Charmed Bernadette. That made sense, now that she knew how closely the two worked together.

"Yes, well, I panicked… You understand." She patted his knee under the table. "Didn't help that I saw her face and I remembered how she was the end of our little group and now she was about to be the end of the vision you and I have, of a convention so successful, the cauldron boils over with positive energy. I knew she'd tattle *right* to Zelena or Soren or Nimue." Her voice lowered. "Didn't help that she swung by the hotel practically *every morning* to share coffee and pastries with *my* husband, either. It was, like, get over him already." She huffed. "A wife can only take so much, even if she's not that into her husband."

"The other coffee! And the cruller!" Gowdie said to Nimue.

That was right. They'd spotted Clarke with coffee and a cruller yesterday morning. Glinda had lied and said they'd been for Humphrey because… she hadn't wanted to draw attention to the fact that she was close to Clarke?

"You were the end of our group," Pound said through clinched teeth.

"I never would have cheated on you with Clarke if not for *her*. She needed to be taught a lesson. She said I was a bad influence on you!" Esmerelda scoffed. "If anything, *you* were the bad influence on me."

"That was kid stuff."

"We were over fifty at that point." Esmerelda laughed, the sound shrill. "'Kid' stuff like researching how to harness the energy of the cauldron for one's own gain? Of course, I always thought you were just talking big until you *finally* came back with an idea for harnessing it!" She turned to Nimue. "Apparently, it just has to *overflow* a bit. Bubble with too much good energy. Though I don't know how his wretched human son's presence was supposed to help much with that. All these years, all these successful conventions? And his *son* would make all the difference?"

"I guess we'll never know since *someone murdered my sister* and fed negative energy into the cauldron!" Spittle flew from Pound's mouth.

"Oh, sure, blame me. One little burst of negativity just brought the whole plan crashing down." Esmerelda's eyes seemed to be growing red.

"And I don't suppose you'll tell me where you took my sister's body now?" Pound snapped.

"She's fine! Better than fine! I made her all nice and pretty for her funeral. I'm not a monster!" Esmerelda was breathing hard now, her hair falling in waves over her face, her voice growing shrill. "I just had to make sure you'd play nice! You will, won't you?" Her voice grew softer. "You'll still play nice with me?"

Pound stood from the booth, shoving the table forward into Nimue and Mia to make room to stand. "Hurt Charm!" He waved his wand at Esmerelda as O'Leary pulsated on his shoulder.

Esmerelda shrieked, her familiar's grating hiss even louder, and curled to the floor.

Nimue got to her feet, but not before Pound turned to her. He didn't even need to wave his wand to shout an order at Mia. "Attack her! Attack Nimue!" He stepped out from the booth and over Esmerelda's convulsing body.

Mia shoved the table back to make room, something clattering to the ground, and turned toward Nimue, her arms outstretched toward her neck.

Gowdie took to the air and breathed fire.

"Wait!" Nimue shouted at her familiar. He nodded and dive-bombed to the floor instead.

She launched herself at Mia and pressed the Undo Charm perma-charm crystal in her palm against the woman's forehead, just as the woman's hands wrapped around Nimue's neck.

Nimue focused, channeling the perma-charm crystal's energy. "Undo Befuddle Charm," she whispered.

Mia's eyes grew clearer, her hands lowered. She opened her mouth to speak, clearly dazed, but Nimue turned around, launching herself at Pound's back, just as Gowdie dive-bombed to the ground and flew back up, the Invisible Charm perma-charm crystal between his hands.

O'Leary hissed and sprung outward, straight at Gowdie. But Nimue couldn't focus on him.

Pound struggled to point his wand in Nimue's direction, but she used the leverage of wrapping her arm around him from behind to keep his wand arm pinned down. He just managed to graze the wand with the tips of his other hand's fingers, each twitch of his muscle loosening his torso from Nimue's fleeting grip. She couldn't let go of the crystal, so she had to take Pound down—and fast.

"Go for the legs!" shouted Gowdie, using the spin-kick he'd practiced once on a popcorn kernel to send O'Leary the snake flying.

Before Pound's familiar could warn him—assuming she was still conscious after her own familiar's super kick—Nimue let the criminal go, causing him to stumble, and she crouched and spun. Her leg slammed into his ankle and she put all her force into the kick, feeling like a superheroine in a flashy Stellar Comics Extended Universe movie.

It worked. Pound tumbled to the floor and Nimue didn't hesitate, crawling forward to put the crystal against Esmerelda's body and willing the Hurt Charm on her to undo. "Undo Hurt Charm." It must have worked because Esmerelda stopped twitching, stopped shrieking, just breathing heavily.

"Hurt—" Pound said again, rolling to get back up, but Gowdie roared, breathing a little plume of fire and dive-bombing straight at the wand in Pound's hand. The wand fell, and Gowdie touched it with the Invisible Charm perma-charm crystal he'd picked up from the floor, him, the crystal, and the wand all vanishing from sight before anything hit the linoleum.

"No!" shouted Pound, getting back up to his knees and reaching out, searching for the wand. He looked at his snake, who shook her head as if to clear it from beside him on the ground. "Sense that lizard, already! Find him!"

O'Leary hissed.

"I'm a dragon, dimwit," Gowdie said, somewhere nearby but unseen. *"Have you ever seen a lizard fly?"*

Nimue searched for the source of her familiar's voice and hugged him, even though she couldn't see him. Footfalls echoed out from the lobby, dozens and dozens of onlookers, probably, coming to see what the fuss was about.

"Give it to me!" Pound shrieked, launching himself at Nimue barehanded.

Nimue shielded her invisible, though tangible, familiar.

"Don't move!" shouted Zelena.

Zelena!

Nimue looked up to find almost the entire security team with their wands outstretched in Pound's direction.

At the front, Ren stood tall, his own wand in hand, Nimue's grandmothers beside him.

He'd gotten her message.

Nimue smiled up at him as Pound reluctantly put both of his hands up and let Zelena approach.

While she and Cary grabbed his hands and pulled them behind his back, Charity and a few others helped Esmerelda to her feet—keeping her hands behind her back as well.

"I found something that belongs to you." Ren came over and handed Nimue her wand.

Nimue grinned and with a clatter of the Invisible Charm crystal hitting the ground, Gowdie materialized into view.

Balfour skipped over and rubbed her head against Gowdie—a first, as far as Nimue remembered. Gowdie's cheeks turned a navy blue.

"Thank you," Nimue said, a little breathless. Her cherrywood wand felt so good in her hand. "I see you got my message and assembled the cavalry."

"Of course." Ren grinned, and the smile lit up the grumpy warlock's features. "We make a good team." He held a hand out to her and she grabbed it, allowing him to pull her up.

CHAPTER TWENTY-SEVEN

"And then we met Superstellar-Man," Sophia, one of Tituba's nieces, continued in her long assessment of her family's day at Comic Hero Con so far, "and he said, 'I shall triumph!' for me when I posed like this." She let go of the table at which Tituba and Nimue were sitting and posed with one arm straight out to her side and the other on her hip, her heels clicking carefully together. She was wearing a white version of Megastellar-Woman's costume, complete with fluttery cape. Her curly, brown hair was in two pigtails atop her head, a bright-white, toothy smile complementing her ashen-brown complexion.

"Wow," said Tituba after swallowing her latest bite of her dinner. She'd grabbed some gluten-free pizza for all of us from one of the food service stands on the show-room floor. Her brother and his wife and other kids had already finished eating and returned to the showroom floor, but Sophia had been particularly antsy for some auntie-time and had stayed behind, ostensibly to "finish her meal." She'd only taken another bite since.

"Your pizza is going to get cold," Tituba reminded her. She took her wand out of her holster at her hip and waved it over Sophia's plate. "It probably already *is* cold. Warm Charm."

Sophia sat down at quickly bopped Graves, Tituba's frog familiar, on the nose, followed by a rapid set of pats to Gowdie down his long, scaly back before picking up her pizza. "He signed my book *and* my hand." Her pizza still in the air, she held up her other hand and showed off Maverick's scribble in marker on the back of it.

Graves ribbited.

Tituba smiled as she finished off her own pizza. "Graves says he's got Maverick's signature, too. Gowdie got it for him."

"You met Maverick, too?" Sophia asked Gowdie. Gowdie let out a little grumbly roar that Nimue knew to be, *"Oh, that's quite a story, kid."* But she didn't translate for him. The less the public knew, the better.

They hadn't made Glinda's death public, and they decided they wouldn't. It was entirely a Cauldron Cove matter, and both Vanedestine Redferne and Esmerelda Southern had been handed off to the Witches and Warlocks of the Pacific Coast and the Witches and Warlocks of the Greater Midwest respectively for punishment for their various crimes. Pound's arrest was already being reported by human news sources because of his position as top of the warlock special effects company used in some of the most popular superhero movies of all time, but there was no mention of a murder, or his time spent at Comic Hero Con. The closest it got was mentioning that he was on the Board of the Comic Enthusiast Society. His secret son—or sons, Nimue supposed—weren't a part of the story at all.

Sophia scarfed down the rest of her pizza and then scooped Graves into her hands. "Auntie! Can we go now? Please? Daddy got a reservation for the Book Scene Booth—"

"It's called the Comic Scene Booth this convention," Tituba corrected her.

"And I want do issue 138 of *Superstellar-Man*! Oh, please come with me!" She whirled on Nimue. "You, too, Auntie Nim?"

"Afraid not, kiddo," Nimue said, winking. "I'm still working. But as your aunt's boss, I'll let her take a break."

"Yay!" Sophia got to her feet, then frowned, passing Graves back over to her aunt. "I have to go to the bathroom first!" Then she took off, skirting around the tables full of people enjoying the free snacks and beverages in the Con Suite or bringing their paid items in where there was room to eat sitting down.

"Sophia! Hold up!" Tituba shouted, placing Graves on her shoulder and her wand back in its holster. She put a hand on Nimue's shoulder. "You still doing fine?"

"Totally," Nimue promised. It was the truth.

Tituba scoffed. "I still can't believe you went through all of that without telling me."

"I told you!"

"*After* it was all over." She shook her head.

"You were busy with the con. We all were."

"Not busy enough to not help track down a…" She

lowered her voice. "You know. Glinda was *my* co-worker, too. Glad she'll get some justice."

Nimue nodded. "Although I've just about had it with Cauldron Cove residents proving to be…" She left the rest unsaid.

Tituba patted her shoulder a couple of times. "Next time, you let me know. Any time of day, I don't care." She jutted her chin toward the exit. "Make sure he's holding up all right. Now I need to track down that niece of mine before she gets so excited, she takes off to the showroom floor without me."

Nimue turned to watch her go, searching for whomever her best friend had indicated needed "taking care of."

Soren stood in the doorway leading to the hallway, talking with Clarke as well as Mia Estrada in her Megastellar-Woman costume. Their faces were grim—an expression Nimue wasn't used to seeing on the wavy-haired Soren, even if it was almost permanently affixed to that face whenever Ren was in charge of it.

After performing a Hover Charm to move their waste to the nearby garbage bin, Nimue stood up and Gowdie took to the air, letting out a little playful spurt of fire whenever he caught con-goers whispering and pointing at him. A group of them clapped as dragon and witch approached the hallway, Gowdie doing a quick loop-de-loop before landing on Nimue's shoulder.

That got Soren's attention, too.

Balfour trotted out from around Soren's ankles and meowed.

Gowdie preened, his back straightening. *"That's right. I'm a showoff. If you've got it, flaunt it, I say."*

She grumbled and stuck her nose up in the air, but then she wove around Nimue's ankles, greeting her.

"Hi," Nimue said awkwardly to the cat who'd never much seemed to like her before recently.

Clarke smiled. In the crook of his elbow he carried Frone, his blue red panda familiar. She lifted her head and cocked it, letting out a small chitter-like grumble.

"Hi," Nimue said again, this time to the two warlocks in front of her. "Is anything wrong? That is, I mean—"

"More wrong than it already has been?" Clarke chuckled darkly, but he sighed, stroking his beard. "No. I know I should be at the hotel, but Soren thought it'd do me some good to get out, take a tour of the latest convention. We ran into Ms. Estrada on the way." He looked around at the long hallway, though there wasn't much to see beyond the Comic Hero Con banners hung overhead. "Impressive. It's been so long since I've actually attended a con that I've forgotten how fun it can be. Just to… get out among more people. The hotel is great for that, too, but that's more where con-goers go to seek privacy and unwind, you know? Here's where the real action's at." He fingered the badge that hung from a lanyard over his neck, a special VIP badge his son must have gotten for him. Not that he would have needed it, apparently, if the hotel's master keycards would give him access. No wonder Esmerelda hadn't had any issues getting around the Bessa.

"I'm glad you're enjoying it," Nimue said. "And you,

Ms. Estrada? Would you say you're happy with how it all turned out?"

The other woman grimaced, her sad expression a bit at odds with the superheroine she was cosplaying as. "I am," she said quietly. "Even the rest of the board is… Well, or maybe it's more they can't stop focusing on what Van was up to." So that was the name Vanedestine Redferne went by outside of Cauldron Cove? Nimue supposed having Maverick's last name as a given name would have raised a few eyebrows, considering they both worked on the same movies.

Mia took a deep breath, shook her shoulders, and then smiled. "You know what? I'm *glad* he's out of the picture. Now I don't have to worry about how I 'owe' anyone for my position. If the rest of the board doesn't like what I do as leader of the CES, too bad. They can vote me out next election." She turned, dramatically whipping her cape around her with one arm. "*I* would love a chance to just going back to enjoying conventions as a fan. Speaking of…" She winked at Nimue. "You were right. The Comic Scene Booth is better with the illustrations."

Nimue smirked. "That actually *was* your idea."

"Yes, well, I would have talked myself out of it if not for you." She nodded at Nimue and Soren. "Thanks again! I hope we wind up working together next year. I have another election to get through before then, but *I shall triumph*! And if I don't, well… Their loss! No Comic Hero Con will ever beat this one." She trotted off down the hallway, back toward the showroom.

Almost as if to verify the truth of Mia's statement, deep beneath their feet, the cauldron hummed with positive energy. There hadn't been any signs of it "bubbling over" with good energy yet. Nimue wondered if Pound and Esmerelda had even been right about thinking it could do that. She'd only ever known it to "bubble" over with negative energy, so she wasn't used to thinking about the cauldron shaking the ground as anything but bad.

Balfour meowed and Gowdie laughed. *"If we work with Mia next year, we just hope she's mellowed out by then."*

She should, Nimue thought back to him. *As long as Pound is out of the picture.*

Soren laughed, too, and Clarke seemed suddenly out of place, a trace of sadness still weighing him down.

Nimue didn't know Clarke well, but she put a hand on his upper arm anyway. "If there's anything I can do to help…"

"You're sweet," he said, his voice cracking. "Bernadette and Prue have been more than gracious, helping me the past few days at the hotel and at… at home." He swallowed. "Soren too, of course, even though he's so busy with the convention."

"I'm never too busy for you, Dad," Soren said, his eyes shining. A tear escaped just one. "I mean, sometimes I'm not even in my body, but when I *am*, you can always count on me."

"Hey," Clarke said. "We've been over this. You're my son. And your mother… Whatever she did, that had nothing to do with us." He bit his lower lip. "I never apologized to Glinda. We slowly became friends again over the years, and I looked forward to seeing her almost every morning at the hotel… But I was too embarrassed to tell her I was sorry. Too much time had passed, and I thought it was too late. Now it really *is* too late." Clarke looked between Soren and Nimue, a mischievous twinkle in his eye lighting up his sullen face. "Don't make my mistake, kids. Don't wait until time passes you by. Don't delay saying you're sorry." He winked. "I'll let you two get back to work."

"Oh, no, I don't mean to interrupt time between the two of you—" started Nimue.

"But, Dad…" added Soren.

"I'll take the con in by myself. Just observe everything, you know?" Clarke said before wandering down the hallway. He waved over his shoulder. "You two enjoy your time together. It goes fast. Even for us witches and warlocks with extra of it."

Nimue stood awkwardly looking at Soren for a moment, holding her hands together in front of her. "Should we check in with Cassie?" she asked after a moment.

Soren nodded, and they walked side by side toward the nearest teleportation pad, this one inside the Con Suite.

It was nice for Nimue to notice her witch network crystal not lit up with dozens of urgent messages. It was the last day of the con, and things were going smoothly.

"So how have you been?" Nimue asked quietly once they'd both stepped through to the employees-only floor. It was empty up here, but her voice still carried.

"All right." Soren held his arms out for Balfour to jump into them. "Considering."

Before they could get to the end of the hall and their

shared office, Nimue grabbed his elbow and tugged him aside. They got a good view of the showroom floor below from here. Swarms of people moved through the various booths, at the back of which was the autograph and photograph area.

Maverick Vanedestine was there, with the longest line. He was currently posing for photos with fans, tossing out dramatic Superstellar-Man poses beside adults and kids of all ages, and laughing, his handsome face never more rosy than it was when interacting with these fans. To the side, Davies stood stoically, looking back and forth, his hands clasped on the briefcase in front of him. His looka-like, Kovac, had been easily taken out by Ren, even with a borrowed wand, and then taken into custody by the Witches and Warlocks of the Greater Midwest. They'd yet decide if they wanted to pursue charges against the body-guard through human authorities, considering the man was a human, but he'd used perma-charms illicitly during his work for the warlock criminal, so the punish-ment may have rested with them in the end.

Jaxson and Esther were on the other side of Maver-ick's photo shoot, sharing a cup of coffee each and laughing at something one of them had said. Every few moments, Jaxson glanced over at his boss, but he seemed less likely than Davies to jump anyone who so much as looked at Maverick wrong. Nimue hoped Maverick fired Davies, eventually, but she knew that was probably just because she didn't much like the guy. Now he wouldn't need someone to do his father's dirty work for him, though. Maybe Jaxson could help him hire nicer body-guards like him.

Nimue leaned on the bannister and looked back at Soren. "I think Pound being arrested by a council of witches has perked Maverick up. Now he doesn't have to deal with his rotten father."

Soren winced. "He's-He's not actually my dad, you know."

That was news to Nimue. Unless he meant… "Clarke raised you."

"He did, but… Bernadette performed the Origin Charm on me at my request." He smiled broadly. "Vanedestine Redferne had nothing to do with my creation. Who knows if my mom *wanted* the rumor to be true or was just using it to get to Pound. Maybe she started it herself. I don't know. I don't feel like visiting her in council custody anytime soon."

Gowdie grumbled. *"I thought at least that would mean he was half-brothers with a superhero."*

Balfour meowed.

"Okay, a man who plays a superhero."

"That's great," said Nimue, her heart thudding. She nudged Soren with her elbow. "But if that hadn't been the case, it wouldn't have changed anything."

"I know." Soren leaned beside her, looking down at the convention in progress below. "I just… needed some time to deal with that."

"It's probably a good thing Ren dealt with their arrest, considering how the rumor upset you," Nimue said. "And that he was the one to take on Kovac to save Clarke and Maverick."

"Which he did without help because he didn't want to wait for the cavalry," Soren said. Balfour hissed.

"Other than Balfour's, of course." He kissed his cat's head. "His only hesitation, apparently, was that he worried you'd need help. But he decided, so says Balfour, that he trusted you to handle yourself. To buy him time so he could do what he needed to do and get back to you."

Nimue felt herself blushing and Gowdie giggled, rubbing her face with his cheek. *"I told you it's your second bloom."*

"All right, all right." Nimue rubbed Gowdie's head. She looked at Soren. "Seems he trusts you, too. I've hardly seen him since then."

"He also has a few things… he needs to think about," Soren said. He smiled broadly. "I've already made up my mind."

"About what?"

Balfour meowed and Gowdie let out a little *"Hmm."*

"Well, we're moving, for starters," Soren said. "You were right that we've spent too long in that basement. We're looking for a townhouse."

"Oh! There's one next door to me for sale." Nimue stopped herself and blinked. Was that a weird thing to suggest?

"That might be nice." Soren clamped his lips together before adding, "I'll ask Ren if he could handle it."

"Handle… the move?"

Gowdie giggled. *"Handle living so close to you, of course! Balfour said they've decided to be more open to people. Soren and Ren."*

More open…? She thought back. She studied Soren, but he was staring down at the showroom floor.

"Oh, don't we have Home Adornment Expo next month?" he asked.

He'd changed the subject. Nimue felt a little let down. "Just in time for Thanksgiving," she said. "Willow's visiting her father over break and stopping by for the con."

"It'll be nice to see her again," Soren said. "I can't believe she's in college already."

"Yeah…"

Clarke was right. Time flew.

"Maybe you can help me walk the showroom floor at the expo next month? Get some redecorating ideas for my next home?" Soren shrugged casually, as if he didn't mind if she said *no*. But his ears were reddening.

"I'd like that," Nimue said. Her stomach fluttered.

"Gentlefolk, thank you again for your attendance at Comic Hero Con." The voice overhead was Cassie's projecting out over everywhere in the Bessa at that moment.

Nimue stiffened. "Is it time already?"

Soren brought up his witch network projection screen. "Yes. Almost forgot about that."

"Forgot about what?" Gowdie asked.

Nimue ruffled his scalp. "A surprise. Mia got a call just this morning, and she asked us to make an announcement shortly before con's end. Cassie set it up. Guess you were too busy talking to Graves when I got the message."

"The Comic Enthusiast Society is happy to announce… Stellar Comics Studios is making a Megastellar-Woman film! And all of you with Comic Hero Con badges will have the opportunity to be extras in it next summer!"

The crowd below let out a roar, the shriek unlike anything Nimue had ever heard. She put her hands over her ears as even Gowdie got excited, taking off into the air above.

"*An extra!*" Gowdie said.

Nimue laughed. She wasn't sure dragon familiars could be included, or if she would have time to take him to a set, but she'd see what she could do. Maybe Willow would like to go along.

"What's that?" Soren asked, and before Nimue could ask him to elaborate, she felt it, too.

The ground shook beneath them and they both stumbled, clutching the bannister.

The cauldron beneath their feet was happy—and it had just bubbled over with positive energy.

JOIN WITCHY EXPO SERVICES IN:
HOME IS MY ZAPPING PLACE

Witchy Expo Services. We host your convention, expo, or trade show—with a dash of magic!

Nimue Toothaker is excited for the upcoming holidays because it means her daughter is coming home from human college for a visit—just in time for one of Witchy Expo Services's biggest trade shows of the year: Home Adornment Expo. Unfortunately, due to a slight miscommunication, her daughter is bringing her dad and step-mom along as well, and Nimue's parents decide to finally head home for a visit. Nimue may be operating a trade show for home décor, but her crowded townhouse couldn't possibly spare another inch of space.

Hosting family for the holidays is made more complicated by Nimue exploring a potential romance with her co-Head Witch General Manager of Witchy ExS, especially when her family would expect him to be the *last* warlock Nimue ever thought of dating. The two are busy practically around-the-clock with the expo, but Nimue is determined that her new love interest won't spend the holidays without her—even if they have to keep their own celebrations secret so her family doesn't find out yet.

What neither expects is for the giant cauldron beneath the convention center to pose the biggest threat they've ever faced. Harnessing overflowing positive energy proves as potentially dangerous as dealing with an overflow of negative energy—and adding a shocking murder in a vendor booth to this volatile mixture is the last thing Witchy ExS needs. Nimue needs to discover the truth behind the disturbing act, as well as its connection to the cauldron itself, before she loses her home sweet home to go back to.

Dahlia Poplar is a genuine witch, an unofficial gofer, and Luna Lane's only cursed resident.

With a werewolf best friend, a vampire ex-boyfriend, and a ghost for a hanger-on, Dahlia is far from the most unusual dweller of her sleepy small town, but she's the only one unable to leave. Dahlia has to perform at least one good deed per day—or she's one step closer to turning to stone.

Fortunately, the residents of Luna Lane have plenty of tasks for Dahlia to complete to avert the curse until Cable Woodward, fetching professor and nephew of her elderly neighbor, stops by for the semester on sabbatical. Attempting to help Cable's uncle work through the trauma of losing his wife, Dahlia uncovers the man's collection of board games, which leads to him reminiscing about the long-forgotten Luna Lane Games Club.

Dahlia reestablishes Games Club, only to find evidence of a number of horrible demises connected to the original group. While trying to uncover the truth about the deaths, Dahlia has to fight off her curse, protect her elderly neighbor from becoming the next victim, and most vexing of all, keep Cable from figuring out Luna Lane's supernatural secrets. Only with eerie board games like these, there may not be a loser —or even a winner— who survives.

Luna Lane's witches, werewolves, and vampires welcome you to the Spooky Games Club—in which even the winners could find themselves six feet under.

ABOUT THE AUTHOR

Amy McNulty is an editor and author of books that run the gamut from YA speculative fiction to contemporary romance. A lifelong fiction fanatic, she fangirls over books, anime, manga, comics, movies, games, and TV shows from her home state of Wisconsin. When not editing her clients' novels, she's busy fulfilling her dream by crafting fantastical worlds of her own.

Sign up for Amy's newsletter to receive news and exclusive information about her current and upcoming projects. Get a free YA romantic sci-fi novelette when you do!

Find her at amymcnulty.com and follow her on social media:

amazon.com/author/amymcnulty

bookbub.com/authors/amy-mcnulty

facebook.com/AmyMcNultyAuthor

x.com/mcnultyamy

instagram.com/mcnulty.amy

pinterest.com/authoramymc

In this case, fashion is death…

Bianca's determined to live a normal life in Edenville with her family, and she has no intention of getting involved in another case. While attending a fashion show, a model, also a childhood friend of her sister, collapses off the runway. Dead. Not the show Bianca planned on attending.

Detective Sims shows up to solve the case, but Bianca can't keep silent. Too many clues are surfacing, and with a month-long fashion event in town, the suspects remain in Edenville. There's no harm in Bianca investigating one more time, though Detective Sims wants her to stay away.

Can she discover the motive behind this unexpected death? Bianca's life at risk with another killer isn't wise. Not to mention the lives of her loved ones.

Laney isn't looking for love. She's perfectly happy with the life she's built for herself in the little town of Foreston, Washington. She's a successful businesswoman, the owner of an alterations shop with a clientele across the northwest. She's the chair of the local Victorian house museum's annual fashion show. And she has a reputation for a magic touch: the rumor around town is that anyone who wears one of the period costumes she designs in her spare time will be blessed with good luck.

That's what they say, anyway. Laney knows the truth is a bit more complicated—anything she wills while sewing has a tendency of coming to pass. It's a supernatural gift from the fae who are said to inhabit the woods surrounding the Paine Estate, and it's taught her to keep a guard on her notorious redheaded temper. But keeping her temper becomes difficult when journalist Paul Nelson comes to town to do a feature about the museum. With his stunning good looks and swoon-worthy English accent, Paul is charming, irresistible… and just so happens to be Laney's ex.

Laney wants nothing more than to keep Paul at arm's length, but when she stumbles across a series of break-ins at the museum, she may have no choice but to trust the dashing reporter who once broke her heart to help her catch the culprit. And when a nearby forest fire threatens the safety of the town—and of the woods—will Laney be able to put her old feelings aside in order to protect the magic of Foreston? Or will that same magic lead to an unexpected happy ending?

www.ingramcontent.com/pod-product-compliance
Lightning Source LLC
Chambersburg PA
CBHW061056190726
48286CB00006B/1767